Amplified

TARA KELLY

HENRY HOLT AND COMPANY ♪ NEW YORK

Henry Holt and Company, LLC
Publishers since 1866
175 Fifth Avenue
New York, New York 10010
macteenbooks.com

Henry Holt® is a registered trademark of Henry Holt and Company, LLC.
Copyright © 2011 by Tara Kelly
Library of Congress Cataloging-in-Publication Data
Kelly, Tara.
Amplified / Tara Kelly. — 1st ed.
p.   cm.
Summary: When privileged seventeen-year-old Jasmine Kiss gets kicked out of her
house by her father, she takes what is left of her meager savings and flees to Santa
Cruz, California, to pursue her dream of becoming a rock musician.
ISBN 978-0-8050-9296-7 (hc)
[1. Rock music—Fiction.   2. Rock groups—Fiction.   3. Interpersonal relations—Fiction.
4. Santa Cruz (Calif.)—Fiction.]   I. Title.
PZ7.K2984Am 2011   [Fic]—dc22   2011005790

First Edition—2011 / Designed by April Ward

Printed in the United States of America

3 5 7 9 10 8 6 4 2

For Maestro

Amplified

Chapter 1

I said no to my dad this morning. The five-foot-seven soup can of a man nobody denies. It's got to be his arctic blue eyes; they're like the edge of a knife. And still, I told him I wasn't going to Stanford or *any* college next year.

Now I was stranded on Ocean Street with a few hours to find some rat hole to rent. So much for a graduation present.

Smoke billowed from the hood as I got out of my Jetta, the melted rubber stench burning my nostrils. At least it was white smoke, which had something to do with coolant and not a fire—or so my limited knowledge of engines told me.

"Woo! Holla, baby," a tanned boy yelled out the window of a silver car. Summertime in Santa Cruz was all about the strip mall of tourists inching their way down Ocean to the Boardwalk.

I sat on the curb to call a tow when an old blue Camaro pulled within inches of my bumper. Tinted windows, a bass line that made the ground vibrate—this should be good.

A guy hopped out of the driver's side and slammed the door shut. His footsteps were heavy and purposeful, the sound of combat boots. I got a better look at him as he walked around the rear of his car. His head-to-toe black clothing matched his scowl. The last thing I needed was some guy with a chip on his shoulder yelling at me.

"Already calling a tow!" I wiggled my cell at him.

He pointed behind me. "Your car is in front of an auto shop."

Sure enough, there was a big sign that said PETE'S AUTO. "Great, thanks." I waved my hand to dismiss him.

"You're blocking the entrance, genius."

I stood up, telling him to buzz off with my eyes. He was a lot taller than he looked from the ground, but I was used to that. Crappy views at concerts and being the first person relegated to laps in a crowded car were also perks of being five foot two.

He glanced at my car and smirked. His eyes were an odd shade of green—bright like he was wearing contacts. "I'll be right back."

Camaro Boy headed for the auto shop and yanked the door open, nearly hitting a homeless guy leaning against the outside wall. The long-bearded man didn't seem bothered, though. He pointed at my car and let out a phlegm-filled cackle.

"Yeah, hilarious," I muttered.

Smoke trickled out of the engine now. I could at least *pretend* to know what was wrong. Dad, one of the best cardiologists in San Mateo County, taught me that trick. Seem confident— no matter how unsure of a situation I was.

I popped the hood and squeezed my eyes shut before attempting to pry it open. Burned fingertips and guitar playing didn't exactly mesh. Dad bought this junker off his colleague's son, seventy thousand miles and all. *New cars don't teach values*, he'd said.

"I wouldn't attempt that just yet, little lady." I jumped at the sound of the gravelly voice behind me, expecting to see the homeless guy. Instead, a clean-shaven man with thinning blond hair held his hand out. "I'm Pete, the owner."

"Jasmine," I replied, shaking his grimy hand.

Most mechanics didn't have a trustworthy smile. This guy did. "She's got a bit of heatstroke, huh?" He motioned to my Jetta and winked.

I nodded and plastered a friendly grin on my face. Maybe he'd be willing to help me move it at least.

Camaro Boy emerged from the shop dressed in a blue shirt with the sleeves rolled up. His dark chestnut hair stuck up in places, like he'd wrestled with his clothes. Despite the barbell through his eyebrow and the glare, his face was sweet—what I would call boyishly cute. Too bad he had the charm of a housefly.

"Let's get this moved out of the street," Pete told him.

"What do you need me to do?" I asked.

Camaro Boy rolled his eyes. "Get in and put it in neutral—it's the letter *N*."

"Yeah, I got it."

Pete muttered something to him as I got in the car, his tone disapproving.

After we got my green clunker in front of the garage and Camaro Boy parked, Pete disappeared inside the shop and Camaro Boy poked his head in the window. "If you want us to look at your car, I need you to come inside and fill out some paperwork."

My dad would've told me to shop around, but I needed every cent I had. Towing a car wasn't cheap.

I climbed out and slammed the door. The frame groaned in response. Too bad cars couldn't feel pain, because this one deserved it. "Where's Pete?"

Camaro Boy held open the shop door for me. "Lunch."

I grabbed the door and waved him in first. He raised his eyebrows but didn't protest.

The waiting area consisted of a blue table surrounded by folding chairs. Old license plates, tires, and pictures of classic cars littered the walls.

Camaro Boy walked behind the white service desk and shoved a clipboard toward me. "We can speed everything up if you'd fill that out."

I scanned the paperwork. An address—great. I was still seventeen, technically a runaway. Not that Dad would report me.

"Do you have a name?" I asked.

"Yes." He stared back at me, blinking.

"What is it?"

"Clover." He looked away and typed something into the computer. His mouth kept twitching, like he was trying to hold in laughter.

"Seriously?"

He pushed his sleeve up, giving me a view of a blue clover tattooed on his forearm. "I'm half Irish."

And half shithead.

I took the paperwork, plopped in one of the hard chairs, and started to fill it out. Every now and then, I'd glance up and catch him watching me. But he wasn't checking me out. His eyes were missing that playful spark guys get when they like what they see. Not that I was on the receiving end of that much.

Mousy brown eyes, stringy hair, and a generous bust and backside didn't fly with the guys at Peninsula Hills Prep. Or Ken and Barbie Prep, as my best friend, Jason, called it. I'd finally gotten the nerve to talk to my crush at graduation and got this response: *You're that chick who plays guitar. What's your name again?*

A tinny version of Placebo's "Meds" sent me fumbling through my backpack.

Clover, or whatever his name was, nodded in approval. "Good song."

4

I flipped my phone open, forgetting to check the caller ID. "Hello?"

"Where are you?" Dad asked.

"Nowhere special." I gathered my stuff and walked out of the shop, not wanting Clover to be privy to my personal life. "You wanted me gone. I'm gone."

"That's not what I wanted. You made that decision."

I squeezed my eyes shut, my stomach tightening. It was always my fault. "You said I had fifteen minutes to pack my things and get out."

"You're blowing off college!"

I had the power to make him stop. Just hang up. But my hand seemed melded to the phone. Despite everything, he was the only family I had. "I'm not. I'm deferring my enrollment. There *is* a difference."

"So, what's the plan? You can't hide out in your chubby friend's garage forever."

"His name is Jason, okay? *Jason*." I didn't have a plan—Dad knew that. All I wanted was time for me, for my music. A break from pleasing him, the big, dark cloud looming over my head. Trying to *fix* everything about me.

"And is Jason going to let you live with him?" Dad asked.

"He'll be in Maui until the end of August."

"When school starts."

"They're upping my hours at the café. I'll find a place," I lied.

Like I'd stick around Woodside. A town run by rich people with a penchant for the Wild West didn't exactly have a music scene.

"Serving coffee won't pay rent around here."

"I'll figure something out."

Dad let out his sarcastic chuckle. "There's a great answer."

"I just need a break—a year at most. It's not a big deal."

"A break from what?" His question cut into my ear. I had no reason to be unhappy. My childhood wasn't like his.

"Why don't you ever listen to me?"

"Say something worth hearing, and I will. Give me a valid reason."

A pressure grew in my throat, and my breath shook. I moved the phone away from my mouth. No reason would be acceptable. According to him, I had only one thing going for me: my brains. And I couldn't contribute to society without a degree.

"You can't, can you?" he continued. "Because you haven't really thought about what you're doing."

"It shouldn't be like this."

"How did you expect me to react? 'Oh, you don't feel like going to college? That's okay, honey—just lounge around the house. I'll keep paying your bills.'"

I kicked a rock across the parking lot. It felt good, but not good enough. "No, I knew you'd throw me out." He loved his ultimatums and deadlines, and I'd always ended up doing what he wanted. Too afraid he'd actually let me go. Not this time.

"You think it's easy for me to show you the door? Because, believe me, you're going to be sorry you chose that route. You don't have a fucking clue what you're up against out there."

"Guess I'll find out."

"Go right ahead, Jasmine." He sounded empty, maybe even disgusted. "But you'll be doing it on your dime. So you'd better make it count."

"I've done everything you wanted me to." I gritted my teeth. *"Everything*—even if the result wasn't what you wanted. All you could say to me at graduation was, too bad I didn't quite make salutatorian. Oh, and you wished I'd worn nicer shoes."

"I'm not the bad guy you think I am."

"I never said you were!"

"You don't have to."

My fingers tightened around the phone. "I need this time off to focus on music. To breathe without worrying about homework and classes. I've never been able to do that."

Click.

"Dad?"

Silence.

I snapped the phone shut and stared at the display, my knees shaking. The salty air reeked of freedom, but I felt like I was going to vomit.

Clover flung open the door to the shop. "You done with that paperwork?"

"Uh . . . yeah." I handed him the clipboard.

He glanced at the first page and gave it back to me. "Addresses come in handy."

I followed him into the shop and tossed the clipboard onto the desk. "I don't see why you need my address. Just call me when it's ready."

He leaned against the wall and folded his arms across his chest. "You're right. If you decide to rip us off, I'll ask around for the blond girl who drives a Jetta. That'll be real easy to narrow down."

"I'll wait here until you fix it, then."

He shook his head. "Some things take longer than a day to fix. And this isn't the Embassy Suites."

"Fine." I clenched my teeth and scribbled my dad's address on the form, making it as illegible as possible. "Happy?"

He studied the paper, occasionally glancing at me. Something was amusing to him, because a slow smile crept across his face.

"Woodside, huh?" He cocked his head and put a finger on his chin. "You know, I never would've guessed *that*."

I rolled my eyes. "I need to get my stuff out of the car."

My stomach did flip-flops when I gazed down at the boutique amp head and 1x12 speaker cabinet in my trunk. Carrying an amp around town *wasn't* an option. I'd had to roll it out on my computer chair just to get it in the car. The entire setup cost me most of the birthday and Christmas checks I'd saved since birth. The remainder of my savings was sitting in my backpack, plus what I'd earned from a few months at the café. It added up to sixteen hundred bucks, which seemed like a lot. But the starting rent for a room around here was about five to six hundred.

"Is that a Diezel Herbert?" Clover asked from behind me, a hint of surprise in his voice.

I slammed the trunk shut and faced him. "Yes."

"Whose is it?"

"Mine, obviously."

"You can't leave it in your trunk like that. Our garage is full. Your car is going to be parked outside tonight."

"I can't take it with me right now."

He shifted his weight, looking almost shy. "I've got storage space in the shop I can lock it up in."

"And how much would that cost?"

He shook his head and chuckled. "How does a hundred bucks an hour sound?"

"Leave it in the trunk and keep the car locked." I opened the back door to grab my Taylor acoustic and PRS electric—these babies sang like nothing else I'd played. And they were irreplaceable.

I hadn't realized he was right behind me until I backed into him and tripped over his foot. The weight of the guitars about sent me right on my ass, but he managed to grab my arm and hold me steady. "Mom and Dad will get you a new one anyway, right?"

I ripped my arm out of his grasp and backed away. "I've got a spare key. I'll be back to pick it up later." *If I find a place and a way to get it there.*

"We close at five thirty. Make it before then. I'll have your estimate ready." He took the clipboard off my roof and grinned. "Jasmine Kiss? Is that seriously your last name?"

"It's Hungarian." I grabbed my guitars and walked away without another word.

Sweat formed at my temples as I hobbled down Ocean Street, a maze of decrepit buildings and sagging palm trees. Music from the passing cars became a wash of distortion, and grunts of frustration could be heard at every red light.

Santa Cruz had always called to me. The ocean, the grit, and the people who didn't fit in anywhere else. People like me. I could dye my hair blue or do something crazier—like get my nipples pierced. But most of all, I wanted to join a real band and rock out every night. All I had to do was find a decent room and a cool job, like at a music shop. Everything would work out. I'd make sure of it.

Maybe I was being naive. Even stupid. I mean, who would trade Stanford for being homeless? I'd be lying to myself if I pretended I wasn't scared shitless.

But I had to know if I was meant to be a musician. Otherwise, I'd spend the rest of my life regretting it. Asking myself . . . what if? And it's not like my dad really knew me—he didn't even know my favorite color or song. On my last birthday, I had to remind him I was turning seventeen, not sixteen. How could he possibly know what was best for me?

The handles of my guitar cases were making my hands raw. I set them down, reached into the small pocket of my backpack, and pulled out a folded piece of paper. It contained the tiny list of rentals that I had some chance of affording.

SC Room $650/mo Share w/clean family. NO PETS. Drop by Sat&Sun 1–4pm

This looked convenient enough; it gave an address on Washburn Avenue—just off Ocean Street. I threw my hair into a loose ponytail, not wanting to look like I'd been electrocuted.

By 5:20 p.m. I was working on my second double-shot mocha and watching tourists, freaks, and homeless people parade down Pacific Avenue. There was a hair color to match every crayon I used as a kid. A woman in a frumpy blue dress stood in front of the café passing out flyers. Half a cigarette hung from her lips and a cross dangled from her neck. A skinny guy with chains for suspenders took one from her and ripped it in half, shaking his head.

The rental situation down here was far more dismal than I'd expected. If I could sum up a few of the listings I'd seen in one sentence each, they would look like this:

SC Room $650/mo Share w/clean family. NO PETS. Drop by Sat&Sun 1–4pm

Very NOT clean family wanting to rent out their laundry room. Literally.

SC Lg room in great house, nr metro, priv bath, $700/mo incl util.

Yuppie couple wanted a live-in babysitter in exchange for a "sweet" deal on rent.

*SC Sm guest house w/kitchen, $675/mo+util, nr
downtown, great view*

Guest house was an old trailer with moss growing on the windows and a view of the neighbor's swimming pool.

*SC Room, $700/mo+util, 2 blks frm beach, cat OK,
female pref.*

Owner was a guy in a red robe who tried to get me to use his self-built sauna.

*SC Room in cute house, live w/artists, nr Pacific,
$650/mo*

They turned me away at the door when I told them I wasn't vegan.

*SC Studio in historic house, nr UC, clean female
prfrd, NO PETS, 700/mo+util*

Creepy as hell Victorian house that smelled like old sheets.

*SC Share condo w/grad student, 1 blk from UC, no
pets, quiet person pref., $700/mo*

Promising until the grad student launched into a twenty-minute tirade about his former roommate.

Two listings remained; those I'd planned on seeing if all else failed.

*SC Big room, share w/4 females, nr boardwalk,
$600/mo, boys not allowed*

*SC Seeking roommate to share apartment. Must
love kids! $550/mo.*

I pulled out my laptop and clicked on my bookmark for Craigslist in Santa Cruz to see if there were any new listings in my price range. Nothing. Unless I knew how to make my own compost or practiced a polyamorous lifestyle.

I sighed and clicked on MUSICIANS. Maybe I'd have better luck with bands. Someone always needed a guitarist.

Lots of bands seeking drummers, which wasn't surprising. Good drummers were a rare breed—always in high demand.

Looking for funk guitar player.

Not me.

WANTED: Rhythm guitarist for punk rawk band!

It's rock, people.

Can you shred like MAB?

Definitely not.

Looking for a live-in lead guitarist (industrial rock)

Promising!

My guitar playing could be described as eccentric and atmospheric. I loved complicated and layered effects—making my guitar sound like an entirely different instrument. Most mainstream rock bands weren't into that. But industrial and electronic rock were genres I loved because the guitar playing was more about experimenting than straight up shredding or doing solos. I never had to fit a neat little formula.

I clicked on the link and began scanning the ad.

C-Side (c-side.com) is looking for a fierce lead guitarist TODAY. Must love industrial rock and be *comfortable onstage. We need someone who can move in and share the rent with us ($650/month + utilities). Studio/practice space on-site. Guys strongly preferred. We're holding tryouts all day at the below address. Come before 7pm!*

The address was on West Cliff, a curvaceous street with houses on one side and cliffs overlooking the Pacific Ocean on the other. Jason and I loved hiking around the cliffs and finding a great ledge to picnic on. We'd watch the sun morph into kaleidoscopic bands over the water and fantasize about the guys we wanted to kiss. The thought of having that magic at my fingertips every night was pretty intoxicating.

But I was not a guy or comfortable onstage. I'd never performed in my life.

"Meds" hissed out of my jeans pocket. I fished out my cell, hoping it wasn't Dad, but Jason's number flashed across the screen.

"Hey, sexy," I answered. Just picturing his round cheeks and contagious grin eased my worry.

"I just got your message! I'm so sorry, Jazzy."

"Well, I'm homeless, but at least I'm finally free, right?"

Jason slurped something—more than likely a piña colada. "I wish I was there to help you. Have you found a place yet?"

I cupped my hand over my forehead to block the sun from my eyes. "The Jetta freaked out as soon as I got off 17. So I'm looking for a place on foot."

"Do you want me to get a flight back? I will, seriously."

As much as I could have used the help, I couldn't ask Jason to leave Maui. His boyfriend's parents were letting the guys spend the summer at their vacation house as a graduation present. "Don't worry about me. Just enjoy yourself."

He took another slurp. "I know you need me right now."

"I'll figure something out. I always do."

"It's not too late to go to Berkeley with me. We could get a cute little apartment, paint the walls yellow, and laugh at all the freaks on University. You know you wanna."

"You should go to UCSC instead. It has a cooler view."

The phone beeped, telling me someone else was calling. A local area code. Oh God. My amp. "Hey, I have to go—they're calling about my car." We said good-bye and I clicked over to the other call. "Hello?" I squinted in anticipation of a sarcastic comment.

"Jasmine?" Clover's voice almost sounded sweet on the phone.

"Yes."

"This is . . . from Pete's . . . I've . . . estimate . . . on . . ." A green-haired Bob Dylan had just set up shop on the bench near me, making it impossible to hear much.

I pressed the phone into my ear. "Can you repeat that?"

"Your . . . gasket . . . leak . . . thousand dollars but . . ." Coffee oozed up my esophagus with the mention of that much money. No way could I swing that anytime soon.

"I'm sorry—can't hear you. Call me tomorrow, thanks." Under regular circumstances I'd feel bad about hanging up on someone, but I wanted a roof over my head before dealing with Clover again. So I gathered my things, ignored my throbbing shoulders, and began the mile trek to West Cliff. *Guys preferred* my ass; they just hadn't met *me* yet. At least that's what I wanted them to think. Otherwise, I was screwed.

Chapter 2

My heart thudded when I reached the West Cliff address—a swampy green castle. The house was two stories with a white balcony running across the front. I figured those rooms were taken for sure, but it didn't matter. I could open a window and listen to the ocean every night—maybe even the sea lions. Classy, white-framed windows lined the house, but the front door was painted a dark purple.

I rang the doorbell and took a deep breath, appreciating the hiss of waves behind me.

The door swung open to reveal a girl with cherry-colored braids and a stoic expression. Her kohl-lined eyes scanned me from head to toe, and her full lips broke into a smile. "You don't look like a Dave."

"No . . . I'm Jasmine." I put one guitar down and held my hand out, but she just stared at it. "I hope I have the right address. I'm here about the listing for a—"

"Did you miss the part that said guys strongly preferred?" she interrupted.

Keep smiling. "I'm just asking for a chance."

She eyed me up and down again, crinkling her brow. "Did you catch what kind of music we play?"

"Well, of course, but—you're in the band?" I tried to hold her gaze, but her eyes were so intense, like she was trying to forklift information from my head.

"I'm the singer."

"So you guys are like, what—Celldweller, the Birthday Massacre maybe?"

"We're like nothing you've heard before."

"Is that Dave?" a guy's voice sounded behind her.

"No, it's an adorable metalhead chick," she said over her shoulder.

I looked down at the ground, trying to conceal a blush. I had no idea where she got metalhead from—maybe my messy ponytail and ripped jeans?

"Har, har." A guy with black dreads pushed past her. His eyes widened when he saw me. "Oh—what's up?" He reached for my hand and shook it with a tight grip. "I'm Bryn."

"Jasmine." I tried not to stare at him too long. Blue eyes against dark skin and a white T-shirt that hugged the right places. The guy was hot—not that it mattered. I didn't come here to meet boys.

Bryn glanced at my guitar cases, chewing on his lip ring. "No offense, but we're looking for a guy to move in." He met my gaze with a squint. "Less weird that way, you know?"

"The ad said guys preferred, not mandatory."

The cherry-braided girl laughed softly behind him. "She's got balls, or maybe it's desperation. Hard to tell."

"You've already got one girl in the band—why not two?" I raised my eyebrows at both of them, like I couldn't believe they hadn't thought of that. Maybe it came off as cocky, but anything was better than seeming desperate.

"Veta doesn't actually live here." Bryn nudged her. "She just thinks she does."

"Bite me," she said.

Bryn eyed Veta's long legs and the frayed denim skirt that barely covered them. A slow grin spread across his face.

She pinched his lips together. "Keep dreaming, pretty boy."

Okay, then. I focused on the ground.

"Let her in. She can't be any more girlie than me," another male voice called from somewhere in the background.

Bryn opened the door a little wider and waved me in. "Nah, man. You can wear all the poofy skirts you want. It don't change the dangly parts underneath."

The owner of the third voice sat on a murky yellow couch in the living room. "Hey, I'm Felix." He waved before gobbling down a spoonful of whatever was in his red mixing bowl. Felix had a Q-tip of blue hair and more eye makeup than Robert Smith in his prime.

The downstairs looked spacious despite the turquoise shag carpeting and dark furniture. Band posters, paintings, photographs, and sketches covered every inch of the walls.

"How old are you?" Veta asked. "You look thirteen."

I set the guitars down and shook my hands to get blood back into my fingers. "I'm almost eighteen." So maybe October didn't count as "almost," but close enough.

The three of them exchanged a look I couldn't quite interpret. But I could've sworn Bryn mouthed "jailbait."

"Why—how old are you guys?"

"We're nineteen." Bryn nodded at Felix. "He's twenty."

Felix grinned at me. "Don't worry. Our bassist—the Brain—is, like, fifteen."

"He's seventeen." Veta laughed.

"Cool." I allowed myself to exhale. "Why's he the Brain?"

"He just finished his first year at UCSC. He skipped ten grades or something," Bryn said.

"*One* grade, technically." Veta rolled her eyes.

"Yeah, I—never mind." I wanted to say I knew how that went, being younger than most of my graduating class. But the age subject wasn't going to win me any points, and I definitely wanted to avoid any talk of college. "You're renting a room, right? Can I see it?"

"This one doesn't waste any time," Veta said.

"Follow me," Bryn said.

"Don't get your hopes up, Goldilocks," Veta called behind me as I followed Bryn upstairs.

Part of me wanted her words to be true. If the room was awful, I wouldn't be tempted to join a band right away and humiliate myself. I'd never played in front of anyone but Jason. Still, these were the kind of people I'd always wanted to hang out with. They seemed artistic and free. Nothing like the douches back home—all bred to be carbon copies of their parents.

The staircase led to a loft area that separated four rooms. I had to keep my mouth from dropping open when I saw a black leather couch and a matching pool table—even the *cloth* was black. Shelves filled with thousands of CDs sat against the walls.

Bryn stopped and grinned at me. "Sweet pool table, huh? It's my uncle's—he owns this place."

"Oh, is that why the room is so cheap?" Rooms on the ocean didn't come cheap in this town. Usually they were closer to a grand.

"Yeah, he's giving me a deal. But it also means that everyone wants to live here—so you better rip on that guitar."

No pressure or anything.

I held my breath when he pushed open the white door to the vacant room—the Pacific Ocean glittered just outside those windows. The room formed a decent-sized rectangle, and it included white walls and the same blinding turquoise carpet. But it could've been a Porta-Potty for all I cared. I was already dreaming about playing my acoustic on the balcony and watching the fog roll in over the water.

"Nice, huh?" Veta's husky voice in my ear made me jump. Felix stood behind her, still munching on what looked like Cocoa Puffs.

"Why isn't this room already taken by one of you?" I asked.

Bryn looked down at the carpet, playing with his lip ring again. "Well, our bassist had it, but he moved back there when Teddy moved out." He nodded to one of the rooms on the other side of the loft. "He said it was quieter or something."

"Does he have a problem with the sound of the ocean?"

Felix snorted, and Veta elbowed him in the ribs. "Sometimes West Cliff gets a lot of traffic," she said.

"Yeah, but it's not *that* bad. Sean is just weird," Bryn said.

"Mmm-hmm." Veta squinted at him. "And you'd be right next door to Bryn, which is a real pleasure."

"Where do you live?" I nodded at her.

"In the fourth dimension." Felix wiggled his fingers in her face, and she slapped them away.

"I live with my mom. It's free."

"And convenient," Felix said. "Veta and her mom run this psychic shop across the street from the Boardwalk. They live right above it."

"Yeah, they read the auras of tourists all day," Bryn said with a half smile.

Veta yanked one of his dreads. "Don't knock it until you've tried it."

"Nah, I've got more productive things to spend my money on." Bryn jutted his chin at me. "Have you played live before?"

Live? Sure, every night with an audience of one. "Yeah—of course."

"Good," Bryn said. "A couple of guys dropped by who've never played in front of anyone outside of—I don't know, their mom? We've got a gig coming up next month opening for Luna's Temptation. Not the best time to find out you can't handle the stage."

Luna's Temptation was one of the biggest industrial bands to come out in the last few years, and they had a huge fan base. Especially in the Bay Area. That show would be packed. "Yeah, no—that would be bad." It wasn't too late. I could politely excuse myself. Not that I had anywhere to go.

"Then there was that one schmuck who lied about playing guitar in the first place. What, like, he didn't think we'd notice?" Veta laughed.

I inched toward the staircase. "Well, I love the room, and I've been playing the guitar since—forever. So, if you're willing to consider a girl, I'm definitely interested."

The only sound heard was the clinking of Felix's spoon as the three of them exchanged a glance.

"You gotta try out before we'll consider *anything*, babe," Veta said.

My fingers tore at the threads framing a hole in my jeans. "Right, obviously. When would be a good time?"

Bryn studied me, zeroing in on my hands. "Now?"

I smiled wide even though my face had probably lost all color. "Sure, let's jam."

Bryn motioned for me to follow him downstairs, where I grabbed my guitars. Then they led me into the backyard toward a matching guesthouse—just when I *thought* I'd seen everything. Green vines with red edges crawled up the walls, and there was a blue graffitied elf on the front door. My heart picked up with each step; once I got over the initial awkwardness of playing for strangers, my fingers would stop feeling like jelly—I hoped.

After Bryn let us in, I took in the well-endowed music studio. Soundproofed walls, mics and more mics, a shiny green drum kit, an eighty-eight-key MIDI keyboard, and a Mac Pro with a thirty-inch flat screen. An SG Goddess guitar the color of a faded blueberry lit up the back wall.

"What's your band's name again?" I shoved my shaking hands into my pockets.

"C–Side," Bryn answered, booting up the computer. "We should leave a note for Dave on the front door. Tell him to come back here."

"I'll do it," Felix said, shuffling outside.

I assumed Dave was also trying out. Maybe I'd get lucky and he'd have car trouble too. "Is there a story behind the name?"

"Me and my brother—the bassist—came up with it in high school," Veta said. "Our mom's shop is called Seaside Psychic, and we grew up here, so . . . it just fit."

"Where the hell is Sean, anyway?" Bryn asked. "I thought he was just going in for a couple of hours."

Veta snatched the blue SG guitar from the rack. "Yeah, well, we don't all have Uncle Moneybags to pay for our shit."

"Whatever, I work," he answered.

"Yeah." She rolled her eyes at me. "He works twenty grueling hours a week for his *uncle*."

"And I still make more than you do." Bryn chuckled, grabbing a pair of drumsticks off the computer desk.

She flipped him off and nodded at me. "You going to get set up or what?"

The door swung open, highlighting Felix's 'fro and large shape. "Nobody's here yet."

Good—the last thing I needed was more of an audience. My competition, no less. I opened my electric guitar case and ran my fingers along the smooth body of my purple sparkled beauty.

"Is that a PRS?" Veta asked. "I've never seen one that color before."

"Yeah, it's a '95 CE Holoflake. Only about six of them were made, but I got this one cheap." I pointed to a chip at the bottom—just another reason to love it.

Veta shrugged. "Gives it more character." Her eyes ran along the fret board. "It really is gorgeous."

"It's very you," Felix said as he hooked up a laptop to the MIDI keyboard. There was something sweet about a guy the size of a football player in a blue taffeta skirt. "Do you have an amp?"

"I've got a Diezel Herbert, but I don't have it with me." And it would suck to play through anything else.

Bryn let out a low whistle. "Nice. We got one you can use, but it's no Diezel." He nodded at a combo amp in the corner. "And there's an effects processor over there." He pointed to a little silver box with a couple dozen buttons on the floor, a blessing for lead guitarists who liked their effected guitar sounds and textures.

"Cool, thanks." I played entirely by ear and went wherever a song took me. Once in the zone, I lost all control over my fingertips and needed a variety of sounds at my disposal.

"What's that?" Felix asked as I pulled a mini staplerlike contraption from my backpack.

"It's an EBow—you hold it on the strings and it sustains the note you play. Almost sounds like a tripped-out flute."

He grinned and went back to fiddling with the laptop. I created my own patch on their processor, adding the effects I used the most—except for wah. I snagged a dusty wah pedal sitting next to the amp. Hopefully it wouldn't sound as neglected as it looked.

After everyone got set up—Bryn behind the drums, Felix armed with the keyboard and laptop, and Veta behind the mic—Bryn said they'd play the song once through first. Felix would play a prerecorded bass line so I wouldn't miss anything.

Bryn counted off and slammed the kick drum, Veta backed him up with grinding power chords, and Felix ran a melodic arpeggio over everything. They sounded kind of like the band Garbage on steroids—Bryn wasn't shy about the tempo and Veta's distortion was pretty raunchy. Her vocals surprised me the most; they were sugary and fluid—not rough like her speaking voice.

It was the kind of song that I'd dance like a fool to in my bedroom. It hypnotized me, sent tingles up my spine, and took me somewhere completely different.

These guys were really good. Maybe too good. But I had no time for doubts, because they were starting again.

My fingers were slick against the strings, and I couldn't tell the difference between Bryn's chaotic beat and my heart. Air escaped my lips, reminding me to breathe. This was it. A chance to be part of a band that completely rocked. And I couldn't even move.

I closed my eyes and allowed myself to feel the music for a few seconds, pretending it was just me and Jason in his stuffy garage. I yearned for the cinnamon incense he always burned to cover the stench of rusty tools and old engine oil. It made me feel safe. Hidden from the world, from my dad. The one place I could be myself.

The band around me became just another track Jason and I would jam to. We used to imagine ourselves as the guitarists, playing for thousands of people. And I always told myself—one day it would be real.

I heard a gentle delay texture bouncing over the top of the verse— just subtle enough to complement Veta's riff but not disrupt her vocals. I played a mere three notes and let the delay effect fill in the gaps. My concern was making the song better, not how fast I could shred.

A break in the song featuring Felix's atmospheric synths and an electronic drum loop gave me a perfect opportunity. I let the overall mood interpret the strings—which turned into almost a bluesy escapade with the wah pedal. When the live drums and Veta's rhythm started up, I ran the EBow over the strings, taking advantage of the lack of vocals. Each humming note took its time to build until the passionate scream of my guitar filled the room.

When they launched into another verse, I backed off, but Veta didn't return to the vocals. I opened my eyes, and she leaned into me, chugging another chord progression on her blue guitar. This time I let my fingers fly, following every change with a visceral melody. When I hit on something, she backed me up, almost harmonizing. Neither of us had to guess where the other was going— we just knew.

A flicker of light caught my eye, and I turned in time to see two guys walking through the studio door. The taller guy scanned the room, pausing on me. Every blazing nerve on my skin wilted when I met Clover's gaze.

My hands fell away from the guitar, causing the strap to detach, and my purple beauty crashed to the floor. The sound of wood hitting thinly carpeted concrete seemed to echo forever.

"Ever hear of strap locks?" Clover asked.

The blond guy who came in with him snickered and whispered something in Clover's ear.

Veta rushed over and stroked my guitar like it was a wounded animal. "Oh my God. Your baby."

"It's cool. She knows how to take a beating." I held my breath as I picked her up. There was another knick at the bottom, but the damage appeared to be minimal.

"What are you doing here?" Clover asked. He still had his blue mechanic's shirt on and oil stains on his hands.

"Stalking you, apparently." I glared at him, hugging the guitar to my chest.

Veta glanced from me to him. "Did I miss something?"

"We met earlier. My car broke down," I told her.

"Thanks for dropping by to *stalk* me. But chicks need not apply."

"Since when, dear brother?" Veta asked, mouth agape in mock surprise.

Clover rolled his eyes when the rest of the band laughed. "To live here."

Dear brother. Just my luck. I busied myself with opening the guitar case. Time to pack up and get out of here.

"Where you running off to, Goldilocks?" Veta asked. "Don't let Sean scare you off."

"You mean Clover?"

Veta let out an exaggerated sigh, shaking her head. "You're such a dork, Sean."

"Maybe I should've gone with something more creative. Like Jasmine *Kiss.*"

"It's my real name. Get over it."

"Awesome!" Bryn said.

"Are you trying to break into the porn business?" the guy who came in with Sean/Clover asked. With raccoon eyes, fishnet sleeves, and possibly his little sister's jeans, he looked like every other goth/emo/whatever boy who frequented the mall.

"Like I haven't heard that before." With burning cheeks and panicking to find a comeback, I felt like I was back in seventh grade and getting cornered in the cafeteria.

"Now, now, children." Veta shook her head. "You need to hear her play, Sean. She nailed the first song."

Felix, who had until now busied himself with his laptop, grinned at me. "Definitely."

"You're pretty good." Bryn flipped a drumstick in the air and caught it. "Don't know about the wah pedal tangent in the middle, though. We're not an Eric Clapton tribute band."

"Don't mind Bryn," Veta said. "He just doesn't want us to stand out from every other band with synthesizers and guitars."

"It didn't go with our sound at all," he continued. "It was totally random. No offense."

There wasn't much I could say. I went with what I thought the song called for, not necessarily something that fit neatly into a genre.

"Are you Dave?" Bryn nodded at the guy with raccoon eyes.

"Yep."

"Sorry, man." Bryn motioned to me. "We're doing one more song and then you're up."

Dave shrugged. "No rush."

My stomach twisted at Bryn's words. Obviously I hadn't convinced him yet.

"What happened to your rule, Bryn?" Sean asked. He unbuttoned his work shirt, revealing the black Skinny Puppy tee I first saw him in.

Bryn held up his hand. "We'll talk about it later, man."

"Whatever." Sean grabbed a green bass off the wall rack. A Warwick bass no less—thick sound, gorgeous body, no frills. At least he had good taste in instruments.

The band debated which song to play next, "Encryption" or "Acceleration."

Dave walked closer to me, his dark eyes combing my every move. "Do you always hold your guitar like that?"

I dropped my pick. "Do you always shop at Hot Topic?"

The chatter of the band stopped.

Dave bent down, snatched my pick, and handed it to me. "Good luck." He grinned and backed away.

I made the mistake of looking over at Sean. He shook his head at me as if he'd been listening to every word. "Try not to drop anything this time," he mumbled.

I pressed my fingers into the strings again, my throat raw, my legs weak.

C-Side launched into the next song with a pulsating bass line from Sean. Felix cranked up a swirling pad, his head bobbing to the kick-heavy beat. Veta rolled her hips into her guitar, every part of her lithe body shedding a confidence I couldn't even fathom.

She grabbed the mic when Bryn's beat softened. "Lost in pictures. Writhing with conviction. You walk among the phantoms you breed."

The contrasting melodies in the song blurred into nothing but noise in my head. I killed the delay effect and plucked a couple of notes. Somehow my fingers landed on the eleventh fret instead of the twelfth. I muted the strings before the sound could carry too much.

Dave leaned against the back wall. He made a get-on-with-it gesture with his hand.

I squeezed my eyes shut, but Jason's garage didn't greet me this time. Instead, Veta's strawberry-scented perfume took up each breath, and I pictured Dave snickering. I could even imagine Sean's thoughts. *This girl isn't just a clumsy idiot. She's a clumsy idiot who can't play guitar. Or read auto shop signs.*

The lump in my throat might as well have been Texas.

Something brushed my shoulder and warm breath hit my ear. "Don't let that jackass psych you out." Veta nodded toward Dave before twirling back around and grabbing the mic. "You rise above it all. Press my back against the wall. And I can't hear a thing but your sweet encryption."

Dave cupped one hand behind his ear now, straining to hear my nonexistent notes. Screw it. I'd rather be another crappy guitar player than the one who chickened out.

I started slow, letting a couple of high notes ring out as an added texture. But the sound felt too crisp for the bottom-heavy song. It needed to get a little muddy. Something an added chorus effect could provide. It certainly worked for the Cure, and they'd been around for the last hundred years.

I played a bit faster, picking up a rhythm. The notes were right, but my playing was sloppy. My fingers felt stiff and numb. Still, I carried on, hoping nobody noticed that my hands were the only part of my body that moved.

Veta howled "encryption" into the microphone, and the song ended, just like a light switch. Flick, and it was over. My chance. My dignity.

All eyes fell on me as if they were waiting for something. Probably an end to the feedback screeching out of my amp. I fumbled with the volume knob until the only sound left was a low hum. Nobody said a word, not even Dave.

I glanced around the room. "So, uh, yeah."

Brilliant last words.

Chapter 3

Waiting outside C-Side's studio was senseless, pathetic even. Especially when I had nowhere to sleep that night. But Veta had told me to hang out until Dave finished his set. Who knew why. The guys'd had nothing to say—not even Bryn.

Dave's guitar was black and pointy, like the invisible horns on his head. His melodies squealed through the walls at predictable times. Fast, technically perfect, and a total KMFDM rip-off. Their later stuff too, which just didn't compare. He'd yet to change up the sound or try anything that wasn't completely safe.

The music stopped, and a couple of hoots echoed inside. Who was I kidding? Dave didn't screw up once. He had it in the bag.

I grabbed my guitars and walked toward the long driveway. The ocean whispered across the street and glittering waves melted into the horizon.

The door crashed open behind me, revealing a chorus of voices and laughter. I picked up the pace, my shoulders inching toward my ears.

"Hey, Goldilocks!" Veta called.

What now? Turn around and wave, maybe. Tell her I really needed to pee.

Footsteps approached me from behind, and I spun around to face Veta. She had a notebook in one hand and a lit cigarette dangling from the other. Bryn led Dave toward the main house, going on about his *tight* guitar playing. Sean, aka Clover, watched us for a second before following the rest of the guys inside.

"Where're you sneaking off to?" Veta blew a trail of smoke over her shoulder.

"Just needed some air."

"Right."

"So why'd you ask me to stay?"

"Why not?"

I squeezed the handles of my guitar cases. "I don't know."

"I need a better reason than that to persuade Bryn to break his rule."

"Why didn't the ad just say guys only?"

"Bryn thought it would sound sexist."

"Um, it is."

She gave me a half smile. "Nobody expected a doe-eyed girl from Kansas to show up."

"That's Dorothy, not Goldilocks."

"Same difference." She flicked her cigarette to the ground. "Are you still interested in the gig? Because that second performance isn't gonna help your cause."

"I'm interested." Was I insane? Her brother hated me. "But I don't think your brother is. In me. I mean, the band—with me."

"Don't worry. Sean doesn't discriminate. He hates everyone equally."

"And Bryn is antigirl, apparently."

She laughed this time. "Oh, quite the contrary. Can you hang out awhile?"

"Well, I—"

"Got somewhere better to be?"

"Look, I don't have a . . ." I paused, hearing the advice my dad told me over and over. *Nobody respects a person who dumps their problems on everyone else. You're inviting people to take advantage of you.* "I need to g—"

"Okay, that Dave guy? Sounds like a replica of Teddy—our old guitarist. And Bryn is the only person who wants another Teddy. The rest of us want more ingenuity, less show pony."

"What happened to Teddy?"

Veta glanced back at the house. "He hooked up with my brother's girlfriend. Sean's been aggro since the breakup. Don't take it personally."

I felt a pang of what could've been sympathy for Sean. But his attitude toward me sure *seemed* personal. "I'm still in the running, then?"

She nodded. "You've got tricks I haven't heard yet. And you knew when to scale back and let me shine. That gets you everywhere with me. You're a little sloppy, which Bryn hates."

"I'm not sloppy. It's just—"

"The defensive thing isn't going to help you either."

"I'm not—"

"Exactly." She grinned. "I'm heading inside. You're welcome to join me. Or not." With that, she turned around.

I had every reason to take off, but all I could think about was how well the two of us connected musically, like we'd jammed together for years. C-Side wasn't some lame garage band. They were going places. Places I had no business going without experience.

I followed her anyway.

The scent of dirty socks and grease hit my nostrils as soon as we entered the house. I followed Veta into the kitchen, which wasn't nearly as kept up as the rest of the house. Pans, grocery bags, and overripe fruit decorated the marble countertops, and a tower of dishes sat in the sink.

Felix was cooking something on the stove, and Bryn leaned against the cabinets, watching him.

"Want more bread with that butter?" Bryn asked, wrinkling his nose at Felix's frying pan.

Veta laughed and hoisted herself up on the island. I glanced at the contents of the pan, a half inch of butter surrounding a grilled-cheese sandwich.

"He actually butters the bread before he puts it in, too," Bryn said.

"I hope you don't eat like that in twenty years," I said, feeling queasy.

"Hey." Felix turned and pointed a black spatula at us. "I'm six foot five. I need more than you munchkins."

Bryn patted the bit of belly peeking over Felix's skirt. "You were saying?"

"Oh, screw you." Felix waved him away. "Just because I don't spend nine hours a day banging barbells around . . ."

"But that's how he scores all the hot surfer chicks," Veta said.

"No, that's because I rock the board," Bryn said.

Sean walked into the kitchen. Without Dave, thankfully. "Sorry, man. Felix owns you out there." His smile faded when his eyes landed on me.

Felix thrust his spatula into the air and made a mock cheering sound.

Veta jumped down and wrapped her arms around Felix's torso. She nestled her head against his wide back. "You still need to teach me to surf."

"And I can't do it on the sand." Felix glanced over his shoulder at me. "She's scared of the water."

"I am not. I just don't like swimming in it—it stings my eyes and stuff."

"She's afraid that the *boogie mermaid* is going to get her," Bryn said.

When Felix laughed, she pulled away from him. "I never said anything about a mermaid. But she *is* real."

"No," Sean said, leaning against the refrigerator. "It's your over-active imagination that's real."

Felix cupped a hand over his mouth and whispered to me, "She sees dead people."

Great, I thought.

He got an elbow in the side from Veta. "Sometimes I see things," she said, ignoring Felix's laughter. "And sometimes it's just a feeling. But a couple of years ago, I was swimming at Pleasure Point with Sean, Bryn, and some other people, and—"

"We'd just dropped some acid," Bryn interrupted.

Veta decked Bryn in the shoulder hard enough to make him wince. "We were sober," she continued, moving closer to me. "I felt this force pulling me under. Like a compulsion. And I saw this woman's face. Her eyes were so . . ." She wrapped her arms around herself. "They were like black holes."

"Wow." That's all I could say. I didn't want to give her crap like the guys. But I'd never been one to believe in ghosts—my guess was, she'd lost consciousness and hallucinated without being aware of it.

"Veta," Sean's soft voice broke in. "You were knocked under by a wave."

"It doesn't change what I felt and what I saw."

He held up his hands in surrender while Felix kept his eyes glued to the frying pan and Bryn picked at a scab on his arm. The hiss of bubbling butter seemed deafening.

Sean walked over to the sink and opened the dishwasher. His shoulders sagged.

"I was going to empty it tonight," Felix said.

"Find a new line, Felix. You're like a broken record." Sean shook his head and grabbed a handful of silverware.

"Sean's our housewife," Bryn said, exchanging a grin with Felix.

Sean flipped him off and shoved a couple of glasses into the cabinet. He and his sister shared the quick-middle-finger gene, it seemed.

"How long have you guys known each other?" I asked.

Felix plopped his sandwich onto a plate and tore a corner off. "I transferred to UCSC last year, and I'd see Bryn around at different surfing spots." He licked greasy crumbs off his thumb. "But they've known each other longer."

"I met the Ramirez twins"—Bryn motioned to Veta and Sean—"my first day at Santa Cruz High."

"Quit calling us twins. It confuses people," Veta said.

Bryn rolled his eyes. "Whatever. They were in the same grade, so that's what everyone called them. Anyway, when I first met Veta, she was beating some poor schmuck over the head with her skateboard. She claimed she was defending Sean."

"I was!"

"Sean was the epitome of skinny geek," Bryn continued. "What were you, like, a hundred pounds?"

Sean turned and folded his arms, the muscles in his forearms tensing. He wasn't ripped like Bryn, but "skinny geek" certainly didn't fit him anymore. "At least I didn't have a mullet."

"Whatever. It wasn't a mullet."

"Yes, it was!" Veta giggled, her eyes shifting to me. "Where are you from?"

"Over the hill. Near Redwood City."

"Woodside, to be more specific," Sean added, giving Veta a significant look.

"Right, but not many people have heard of it. I guess Sean is special."

"I've never heard of it," Felix said.

"Our heinous aunt and spoiled brat cousin live there." Veta wrinkled her nose. "Are your parents taking care of your rent? That's good news for Bryn. Teddy could never keep a job."

"I—"

"How anyone pays rent isn't my business. As long as they pay," Bryn said.

I smiled and nodded, hoping my eyes weren't showing the shitstorm occurring in my brain. I ached to tell them I wasn't some spoiled brat, but the more money they thought I had, the better.

"Is Dave still here?" Veta asked. When Bryn shook his head, she continued. "Good. Raise your hand if you think he blew monkey balls." Her hand shot up, along with Felix's. I decided to follow suit.

Sean brushed past me and put away a colander. "I thought you were worse."

I wanted to shove a moldy spoon in his mouth. Or something equally disgusting. Maybe Felix's sandwich.

"How about we not discuss this in front of Jasmine?" Bryn asked.

I checked the time on my cell. 7:31. At least motels were open late. "It's fine. I can leave."

"No, you're welcome to hang out," Bryn said. "But we're not making our decision tonight, despite whatever Veta told you."

Veta wrapped her arm around me, making my entire body stiffen. "Come on, guys. You can't say no to these eyes. She's like a stray kitten."

I pulled away from her, my face on fire.

"So take her back to Mom's and give her tuna like you do the rest of them," Sean said.

Veta's mouth fell open. "No way. I've been feeding them that spinach lasagna crap you made for Mom's birthday."

I let a grin slip, taking a little too much pleasure in the wide-eyed look Sean gave his sister.

"Check that out," Veta said. "She smiled."

I stood a bit taller and shrugged. "It's been known to happen."

"She's always like this," Bryn said, nodding at Veta. "Don't let it scare you too much."

"I'm fine."

"Okay, I'm out." Felix crammed the rest of his grilled cheese into his mouth. Before even swallowing, he threw his arms around me in a bear hug. "It was really cool meeting you."

My arms froze in place. In the nearly eighteen years with my dad, I could think of one time he hugged me: the day after Mom left. And Jason and I weren't exactly the huggy types. "Thanks. You too." I backed out of his embrace.

"Pop a mint before you get there, Felix. You don't want Samantha smelling your cheese breath," Veta said.

The tips of Felix's ears turned red as he left the kitchen. "Like I even have to worry about that."

"Just make your move already," Bryn called after him. "You'll still be a virgin at thirty if you don't step it up."

"Thanks for announcing that!" Felix said before shutting the front door behind him.

Sean chucked a Gatorade lid at Bryn's head. "You're such an ass."

"Yeah, really. What *are* you compensating for?" Veta asked.

"Guess you'll never know." Bryn tossed the lid at her.

She caught it before impact and clenched her fist. "Thank God for that." Her eyes softened when they fell on me. "I'm hungry. We should give Jasmine a C-Side initiation."

"And if we pick Jasmine, we will," Bryn said.

Veta's lips barely held back a smile. "It'll give us a better idea of who we're dealing with."

Bryn chuckled. "Fine, whatever."

"I'm sorry—are you guys a band or a cult?"

"It's just a little bonding thing we do every week." Veta winked. "Don't worry. You'll love it."

I wasn't so sure.

Chapter 4

The sound of grinding chains and heartfelt screams warned me against taking another step. Seventy-five feet in the air and nothing but rickety beams of wood to keep me alive? Veta failed to tell me that the C-Side initiation was a death mission.

"I think she's scared," Bryn said. "We might have to carry her on."

"What's with the wide eyes, Goldilocks? It's only one of the shortest roller coasters on the planet," Veta said, tugging my arm.

I tore my arm from her grasp and bumped right into Sean. His hands gripped my shoulders as the heels of my boots probably mangled his toes.

"Sorry."

He pushed a lock of hair out of his eyes, and the setting sun ignited the yellow in his irises. "I'm getting used to it."

I backed away from him, nearly colliding with a woman pushing a baby stroller this time. The Boardwalk was a smorgasbord of boldly colored shirts and cheesy visors; crowds always made me dizzy.

"I'll sit this one out. That pizza didn't agree with me." I clutched my stomach and tried to look queasy, which wasn't difficult with the scent of cotton candy and waffle fries dominating the air.

Veta peered at me under a fan of mascara-caked eyelashes. "I smell bullshit."

I looked up at the red train of contorted faces zipping around the track. The wooden beams shivered with every twist and turn. "Isn't this thing, like, a hundred years old?"

"Pretty much," Sean said. "And sometimes you can hear the wood crack just as you're about to take that first plunge."

Before I could respond, Bryn scooped me up in his arms and threw me over his shoulder like a rag doll. I sucked in my breath and tried to squirm out of his grip, but he just held on tighter. We headed down a long, narrow hall toward the boarding area. The spicy tomato sauce from our dinner crept up my throat.

"I think I'm going to puke," I said.

He lowered me to the ground as soon as we reached a line of people. "Don't do it on me."

I sighed. Jason had tried to get me on a roller coaster numerous times, but I'd always bolt as soon as we came close to that cold, metal turnstile. I hated the way it counted people. Spin. *Click.* Spin. *Click.* That *click* seemed so final.

As we reached the front of the line, Veta waved to a blond ride operator. "Bianca! Save the front car for me."

Bianca grinned and motioned for her to come over. Veta grabbed my hand, but I hung back, shaking my head. I didn't want to be the first to take that plunge.

"I'll go," Bryn said, taking Veta's hand.

I glanced back at Sean, regretting my decision to stay behind. Sure, the front would be freaky, but being alone with him was downright awkward.

"You're holding the line up." Sean's breath tickled my ear.

I picked the first empty row I came to, figuring he'd ride in a separate car. But the heat of his skin stayed behind me. He smelled really good, like cedarwood and motor oil. Then again, I also loved the stench of gasoline. My olfactory system couldn't be trusted.

The next train pulled up, all squealing brakes and cranking metal. I balled my hands into fists and took a deep breath. "So, you're going to ride with me?"

A flushed-face couple exited the coaster car in front of us.

"Sure," he said, nudging me forward. "I figured you'd want to know what's up with your car, since you hung up on me."

My car. Money. Shit.

"Right." I climbed into the hard seat but didn't touch the thick metal bar that would pin me inside.

"Has your car overheated before?" He slid in next to me.

"Um . . ." I sucked in my breath when he yanked the bar over our laps. It clanked into place just before skimming my thighs. "I don't know." I was trapped. Stuck. Nothing else mattered.

His green eyes combed my face, a smile playing at his lips. "First time?"

My heart fluttered an extra beat. "None of your business." Open mouth, insert foot.

He ran a finger over his lips, as if it would somehow disguise his smirk. "Anyway, your head gasket blew and coolant got into the cylinder. Which really sucks, because . . ." His words suddenly blended together like background music—we were moving. And a really dark tunnel loomed ahead.

But so what? This wasn't a big deal. It couldn't be much different from a car ride. Over a cliff.

Screams and hoots pierced my ears as soon as the train entered the darkness. My head grew light with the jerking and bobbing, and I found myself grabbing at anything that proved I was still conscious.

Warm hands pinned mine against the bar. The pizza had

become a blizzard in my stomach. Just when I thought I couldn't take any more, the dimming sky appeared above me.

But I couldn't breathe just yet—we were starting the climb up the track, and it looked like a hell of a lot more than seventy-five feet.

"You almost took my eye out back there," Sean said, his hands still on mine.

"I don't know what you're talking about."

"Right." He released his hold.

I gripped the bar hard enough to make my fingers ache. *Clang clang clang.* Going up this track sounded like the slow, painful winding of a clock.

"I'll order your gasket Monday, and we'll get it in a day or two," he continued. "Your car should be ready soon after."

We were halfway up the ramp now—maybe twenty more seconds until impact. "Uh-huh."

"Usually that costs at least a grand." He sighed. "But my sister likes you. So, I'll knock it down to eight hundred plus tax. Cool?"

Ten more seconds. "Doesn't sound like much of a deal to me." I shivered as a blast of freezing air hit my cheeks. It was so quiet that high; even the squeals seemed muffled.

"Do you have any idea what replacing a gasket entails? Look it up online if you don't believe me."

"Is there some kind of payment plan?" I squeaked out just as the first car reached the top.

Sean squinted at me. "You don't have the money."

"I—I—" I couldn't finish my sentence because my stomach was in my throat, and we were careering toward the ground.

When the ride ended, I wished they had posted an additional warning with the height minimum: *A sports bra is suggested for those larger than a B cup.*

Sean grabbed my arm when we reached the exit hallway, but I pulled away and kept walking. He blocked my path instead.

"I've broken a nose before, pal," I said.

His serious expression turned into a laugh. "Really?"

"Yes." This technically wasn't a lie. It happened during a softball game in fourth grade. The catcher's face caught the back end of my practice swing. "Now, please move."

"Oh, good. You said 'please.' I'd hate to be assaulted by someone without manners."

"What would you know about manners?"

He held his hands up. "We can talk about this in front of Bryn and Veta if you want."

I exhaled and leaned against the wall behind me. "Generally, payments are made after the car is fixed. You haven't even ordered the parts yet."

"I need you to approve the estimate first."

"Fine, it's approved."

His eyes narrowed. "Do you have a job down here?"

"I'm looking." Or I would be, first thing in the morning.

"You moved to Santa Cruz without a job lined up?" He chuckled, shaking his head. "Do yourself a favor, princess. Work it out with Mom and Dad."

"You know *nothing* about me or my situation."

He leaned closer. "I'll take a guess. Your parents wanted you to be someone you aren't, so you've come here to express yourself and get that butterfly tattoo you've always wanted."

"Wrong."

His eyes didn't move from mine. "Am I?"

"Completely." I shoved past him. "I hate butterflies."

"We'll need full payment when you pick your car up," he called after me. "And it'll be ready by the end of the week at the latest!"

I slowed down when I saw Veta and Bryn waiting outside the exit. This would never work, not with Detective Dracula back there, sniffing around my business. Ducking and running was an option. But that would probably piss Veta off and make Sean happy. And why would I want that?

Veta cocked her head and studied my face as I approached. "Was your picture really that bad?"

"What picture?"

Sean appeared next to me, avoiding my glare.

"Didn't you show her the photos?" Veta nodded behind us.

I glanced back at the ride exit, where people were giggling at images on several TV monitors. Now *that* was just cruel.

"She nearly took my eye out on the ride," he said. "I can't imagine what she'd do if she saw that picture."

"Can it, Sean." Veta grabbed my arm and led me away before I could respond. "I'm sure she looked adorable."

My cheeks burned when I heard him snickering behind me. Assault charges were not out of the question for me tonight.

I spun around and faced him. "Just spit it out. What was so funny about it?"

"You mean besides this?" He bugged out his eyes and opened his mouth as wide as it would go. Veta and Bryn stifled their laughs.

"At least I was in it."

He crinkled his brow. "Meaning?"

"I don't know. Do vampires photograph better these days?"

He tilted his head back, his grin widening. "Oh, here we go. What's next? You going to tell me it's not Halloween?"

"Enough already!" Veta said, pulling me with her again. "You're like a couple of six-year-olds. Who's up for the Double Shot?" She motioned to a tower where a mass of screaming people plunged to the ground.

"I'm down." Bryn's dimpled smile reminded me of a kid on Christmas morning.

The chilly night air brought me back to reality. "You guys go ahead. I need to make a call."

Veta opened her mouth to respond, but Bryn was already dragging her away. I'd have to thank him for that later.

Sean hung back, watching them until they reached the long line.

"Aren't you going with them?" I asked.

He shrugged and eyed the ground.

"Scared?"

That got him to look up. "Didn't you say you had a call to make?"

I rolled my eyes and walked away, searching for a quieter place. Somewhere away from *him*.

An orange bench next to an empty kiddie ride called my name. I sat down and closed my eyes, listening to the breath of the waves behind me. Everything would be okay. It had to be.

I dialed 411 and scanned the area where Sean had been standing. A black hoodie covered in band patches wasn't hard to miss. Maybe he'd joined the others.

An annoyed operator began to rattle off the number to every hotel or motel within walking distance. Only, I'd left my stuff at Veta's shop across the street. Always thinking ahead, I was. I ended up writing on my jeans with the lucky green marker Jason had given me. He'd gotten the digits of many boys with that thing. At least it wasn't permanent.

I dialed the first number, and a tired-sounding voice greeted me. "East Cliff Inn."

"Yeah, hi. I need a room for tonight."

The girl sighed. "We're completely booked for the weekend. You really need reservations this time of year."

That lump returned to my throat. "Do you know of any other places that might have a vacancy?"

"For tonight?" She let out a sharp laugh. "No."

"Great. Thanks for *all* your help." I stabbed the END CALL button.

The next few places also had reactions of the not-another-idiot-tourist variety. But the last number led me to the magic word: yes.

"You got lucky. We just had a cancellation tonight," the man said. "It's a king bed. Nonsmoking."

"Book me. I mean—I'd like to reserve it, please."

"Okay, I'll need your name, address, and a credit card to hold the room."

I swallowed. "Can I come down there and pay cash? How much is it?"

"It'll be $565 plus tax. And we require a major credit card to reserve the room."

My blood ran cold. Of course. What did I expect from a hotel with a fancy French name? It sounded like a place my dad would stay. "Um, never mind. Thanks."

The sound of screaming patrons, creaking metal, and tinny music swirled around me, making it hard to think or breathe. What if I had to sleep out here tonight? I didn't even have a jacket. Or a blanket. Where would I pee?

"Are you okay?" a guy asked.

I looked up to see Sean carrying two slushy red drinks. "What— are you stalking *me* now?"

His mouth fell open, and something between a laugh and a grunt came out. "No, I—"

Veta tackled him from behind. "Hey!" Her eyes widened at the drinks. "Is that for me? Aw, dear brother, you shouldn't have." She snatched one from him and took a sip.

Sean sent me a look I couldn't quite read. A mix of curiosity and annoyance, maybe. "You got through the line fast," he said to Veta.

She grinned. "Crystal is one of the operators tonight."

"I thought she hated him." Sean nodded toward Bryn. He stood about twenty feet away, chatting it up with two girls in bikini tops. Weren't they cold?

"Not anymore, apparently."

"I'm gonna take off," Sean said. "Got work early tomorrow."

"Okay, see ya later." She raised her cup, a playful grin on her face. "And thanks."

"No problem." He rolled his eyes and walked toward the arcade.

"I need to get going too," I said, standing up.

"Let's cut through the beach. It's prettier." Veta shook her head at Bryn. One of the girls was playing with his dreads. "I think he'll be busy for the rest of the night."

A group of guys passed us. They eyed Veta up and down, but I didn't even get a glance. Not that I would next to her. Hot, long-legged girl in a miniskirt or a short one in an old Taylor guitar tee and jeans? Tough call.

"Does that piss you off?" I asked.

"Getting eyed like a juicy steak? I'm used to it."

I followed her down the steps to the beach. "I meant Bryn. Flirting with those girls."

She raised an eyebrow. "Are you kidding?"

I looked away. "Well, it seems like you guys have a thing."

"Ha!" She nudged me. "We fight over chicks at shows, hon. He usually wins. Stupid groupies."

"Oh." I let out a laugh, feeling rather stupid. "You aren't into guys, then?"

"Nope. I hooked up with a few in high school. None of them

ever did anything for me." She looked out at the water. "Then I met Sophie."

"Are you still with her?"

"She dumped me when she moved to New York." Veta pulled a pack of cigarettes from her sweatshirt and used her teeth to yank one out. The flame from the lighter created shadows under her eyes.

"I'm sorry."

She exhaled a stream of smoke and shrugged. "I'm over it."

Despite my racing thoughts, there was something peaceful about the sea on a clear night. I loved how the moonlight tangoed between the ripples of water. The only other people around were couples sucking face and bums rummaging through the trash cans.

God, that would be me soon. Hungry, cold, filthy.

"So what's your story?" Veta asked. "Are you going to school here?"

"No, I'm kind of . . . exploring my options?"

"I'll buy that." She passed her drink to me. "Want the rest? It's great after a crappy day. Me and Sean call them bad-day slushies."

My dry mouth cried for it. "But you haven't had much."

"I just wanted a couple of sips."

"Thanks." Ice never felt so good slipping down my throat. The cherry syrup made it addictive.

"You never really answered me before. Are the 'rents footing the bill for this little exploration of yours?"

I'd hoped she hadn't noticed. "Well, I have some money saved. Enough, you know. And I'm job hunting tomorrow."

A knowing smile spread across her face. "Right. Good luck with that."

"Jobs are tight here. I know. I'm prepared."

"Of course. You're a tough chica." She punched me hard enough to send an ache up my arm.

I bit my tongue, hoping the pain didn't show on my face. "I manage."

"We're looking for a cashier at the shop, if you're interested. The pay is crap, but it's entertaining."

"Like, ten bucks an hour?"

"Closer to minimum wage."

"Ouch."

"For sure. I've got two jobs, and I don't even have rent."

"You give psychic readings and what else?"

"Web design. I've got mad coding skills." She wiggled her long fingers. "It's not steady. But dough is dough."

Maybe Veta actually believed she could read minds and predict futures. But she didn't seem naive. Anyone who knew anything about psychology could do a little mind reading. The rest was luck.

Even so, I wanted to like her. She'd been so kind to me. I just couldn't figure out why. My dad had beat into my head that people usually want something in return. Nothing came for free. Not that I could blame him—my mom really did a number on him. On both of us.

We walked across the street and Veta unlocked the faded red door of her mom's shop. She peeked inside before shutting the door softly. "My mom's doing a session," she whispered. "I'll grab your stuff."

I waited outside the building, an aged, off-white structure with SEASIDE PSYCHIC and CHRISTINA RAMIREZ, PHD printed in black letters across the window. Maybe her mom was doing a séance. It was the only thing I could think of this late.

Veta tiptoed out with my guitars and backpack a minute later. She studied me for a few seconds before speaking. "Do you need a place to crash?"

Yes. God, yes. But staying with her meant more questions. I wasn't exactly the best liar. Sooner or later she'd figure out I was homeless and desperate. "No, I'm covered. Thanks."

"What about a ride?"

"I'm staying a couple of blocks down. The East Cliff Inn."

She nodded, that knowing grin still present. "Okay, then. See you tomorrow morning at nine?"

"What—why?"

"My mom likes to do interviews before the shop opens."

Had I agreed to this? "Sure, I guess I could drop by."

"You guess or you will? Because Mom hates no-shows almost as much as showing up late."

"Shouldn't it be the other way around?"

"If you're late, she's gotta listen to your lame excuse."

"Got it. But I mean—you're already doing so much, trying to get me in the band." It's not like I had anything to give in return. And I hated feeling dependent on someone. In my world, that meant failure.

"It's just an interview, hon."

"Okay, well . . ." I glanced over my shoulder, not wanting her to see the uncertainty on my face. "I'm gonna go. But hey, thanks for everything. I mean it."

"Sure," she said. "Be careful, Goldilocks. Don't talk to strangers."

I tried to smile. "That's Little Red Riding Hood."

"See you tomorrow. Don't be late." She winked and went inside.

Working at a psychic shop? My dad would never let me live that down. Just one more thing to prove that he was right and I was wrong. But screw him. This wasn't about him . . . or his approval.

I looked back at the ocean, an icy breeze hitting my cheeks. Some guy hooted in the distance and glass broke across the street. A car slowed as it passed me, but I couldn't see inside. I wrapped my icy fingers around my cell in my pocket.

He'd make me beg to come home, and then he'd add even more conditions. No. This was the decision I'd made. I needed to suck it up.

Twenty minutes later, I stood in the parking lot of Pete's Auto, hands numb and feet throbbing. I'd never been so glad to see that green Jetta, sitting so innocently in a space next to the garage.

Maybe it was the guy who'd jammed his headphones over my ears, making me listen to Michael Jackson's "Thriller." Or the SUV full of drunk creeps following me for a block and a half. But the thought of curling up on my back seat didn't seem so bad. Spare keys really did come in handy.

My plan was simple. Pete's Auto didn't open until 8:30. I'd set my cell alarm to go off at 7:30 and have plenty of time to get changed and cleaned up at the diner across the street. Nobody would ever know.

I shoved my guitars across the front seats and crawled into the back. Thankfully, the apple-scented tree hanging from my mirror covered most of the smoky engine stench. My big gray hoodie sat in a heap behind the passenger seat, begging me to use it as a blanket. The graduation teddy bear Jason gave me would work as a pillow.

Jason. I needed to hear his voice.

The aching in my feet moved up my legs, and my eyelids felt like they weighed five pounds each. I snuggled up with my hoodie and speed-dialed Jason.

"Jazzy!"

I pulled the phone back from my ear slightly. "You sound wasted."

He gave me his guilty chuckle. "Did you find a place?"

"Not yet." I started blabbering about my day. Veta and the band. The roller coaster. Everything but where I'd ended up for the night. My throat ached by the time I finished.

He was silent for a few seconds. I could picture his dark eyes gazing up at the ceiling as he thought of something to say. "I can't believe you went on your first roller coaster without me."

"I was forced against my will. I'm sorry!"

"I know." The smile was back in his voice. "Are you staying in a hotel?"

"Yeah. Found a nice, cozy little place." With wheels and a sunroof. What a deal.

"Awesome—better than a park bench, right?"

"Yeah, actually." I hated lying to Jason, but nobody could know about this. Ever. I felt like such an idiot.

"Are you sure you're okay? Because if you need me, I'm—"

"Stop! I'm fine. I've got your lucky green marker and my guitars. I'm covered. Now, tell me about Maui." I closed my eyes.

He talked about drinks called Lava Flows and making out with Anthony in the sand. I wanted him to crawl through my window so he could tell me all about it over cookie-dough ice cream and John Cusack movies. But I'd never be able to do that again, at least not in the bedroom I'd known for the last seventeen years.

Chapter 5

A thudding beat and a rumble grew louder until it seemed to be right outside my door. I draped my arm over my face.

What was Carmen doing here at ass o'clock in the morning? Maybe Dad didn't want his beauty sleep this weekend. She'd better not start the vacuum.

I rolled over, punching whatever happened to be nearest. Since when did she listen to Skinny Puppy?

A car door slammed. My eyes flew open. Rays of light shot through the sunroof above me, and teddy bear eyeballs pressed into my cheek.

I squinted at my cell. 8:31 a.m. My breath quickened. No bell symbol showed on the screen, indicating that the alarm hadn't been set. I couldn't even remember saying good-bye to Jason. Had I?

Sean's blue Camaro sat a couple of spaces away, and he appeared to be getting something out of the back. If only he'd fall in and get lost for a few minutes.

I leaned over the front seat to grab the handle of my electric guitar. Lifting upward from that angle was a little tricky, and I nearly knocked out the driver's side window. Sean glanced over his shoulder. I shoved the case to the floor, ducked, and waited.

The car door slammed. Footsteps.

Then nothing.

I lifted my head high enough to get a glimpse outside. No Sean, but the shop door was swinging shut. Perfect.

I threw myself over the seat and snagged my acoustic, preparing to make a run for it. But the sound of Sean's voice made me freeze.

He walked toward my car, a phone pressed to his ear. "You wanted a call back. I'm calling you back."

I pulled my hoodie over my head, not that he wouldn't notice a body-sized lump and two guitars in the back seat.

He unlocked and opened the driver's door. "Too bad. I don't have time later."

The car shook with his body weight. I pulled the hoodie off and smoothed my hair back, wincing as my fingers got caught in tangles. Sean had one leg in and one leg out, but he hadn't seen me yet.

Maybe he wouldn't stay long.

He moved his cell a few inches away from his ear. A girl's muffled voice rambled on for what seemed like eternity.

I inhaled slowly through my nose, hoping my heart wasn't as loud as it sounded. He was close enough for me to smell his shampoo. Something kind of fruity, like blueberries. I felt like an assassin in a movie, preparing to pounce on the driver from behind.

Sean jammed my keys into the ignition. "Because I don't have anything to say, Amy."

Amy. Possibly the infamous, cheating ex? Or maybe he was just this pleasant with everyone. Hard to tell.

"You done yet?" he asked. "I've got work to do."

The voice on the other end told him not to *be like this*. Or something similar.

My ankle throbbed under the weight of the acoustic case.

"Whatever. I gotta go." He tossed the phone onto the seat and rested his forehead against the steering wheel, muttering, "Fuck."

My palms were wet from the growing heat in the car. If I didn't take a full breath soon, I'd probably pass out.

"Uh, hi." The words escaped my lips before I could stop myself.

Sean reeled around. "What the hell are you doing?"

My mouth fell open. "I . . ."

"You *what?*"

"Well, Amy sent me to kill you. But I forgot my black gloves. See?" I waved my hands at him, all smiles.

His glare didn't falter. "What are you doing here, Jasmine?"

I looked down at my hands. "I forgot something."

"Something you just had to have at eight thirty in the morning?"

"A toothbrush. The motel didn't have any of those midget ones."

He squinted at me. "Where're you staying?"

"The, um, East Cliff."

"What was wrong with the Walgreens across the street?"

"I like my toothbrush, okay? It's electric. And I wanted to check . . . my amp." Yet another thing I'd forgotten to do last night.

I opened the door and pushed my acoustic case forward. Sean climbed out and grabbed the other end, setting it on the pavement.

"How's your amp doing?" he asked as I climbed out with the electric.

"It's . . . fine."

His lips did that twitchy thing again, like he was going to bust out laughing any second. "That's interesting."

I folded my arms across my chest. "Why?"

"Because I put it in storage yesterday when you didn't show."

Heat crept into my cheeks. "I told you to leave it in the trunk. I—I'm the customer. You get paid to listen to me."

"I'm a mechanic, not a therapist."

"That came out completely wrong." I raked my hands through my hair, not sure if I wanted to kick him or myself. "Don't you have other customers? I've got a job interview to get to." That made *no* sense.

"There are a couple of cars in the garage, but I doubt I'll find the owners in them. What are you interviewing for?"

"Does it matter?"

"Just wondering why you need the guitars."

Great. More questions. "Is there a bathroom I can use?"

"I hope so."

"God, I don't have time for this!" I exhaled, wishing I'd quit letting this guy get to me.

Scan closed the distance between us and studied me for way too long. Even his silence made me squirm. The jerk.

"It's inside. To the left." He reached out and touched my hair.

I backed away, tucking the lock behind my ear. "What are you doing?"

He opened his hand, revealing a crumpled gum wrapper in his palm. "You might want to do something with your hair. It's a mess."

Every inch of my skin burned. I motioned to the tufts of chestnut hair standing up on his head. "Yeah, well, I guess we won't be doing each other's hair anytime soon."

Without waiting for a response, I hoisted my backpack over my shoulder and ran inside the shop.

The clock on the wall read 8:42. It took fifteen minutes to walk to Seaside Psychic, which gave me no time to look interview-ready. Scrubbing my face and sticking my hair in a ponytail would just have to cut it. Thank God, I wasn't a girlie girl.

Running with two guitars was quite the feat, especially since I couldn't remember the last time I'd exercised. My lungs tickled and sweat peppered my back as I cut across the Boardwalk parking lot. Fine strands of hair escaped from my tight ponytail, proving that no amount of scalp pain would keep them at bay.

I reached the faded red door of Seaside Psychic just as Veta opened it. She stood in the doorway, holding a white cat with a gray spot on its head.

"This is Sprite, our psychic kitty." The cat hopped out of her arms and ran back inside. "What's with the guitars?"

"Oh." I paused to catch my breath. "I don't trust leaving them in the hotel room."

She raised her eyebrows. "I used to be a hotel housekeeper. We didn't make a habit of stealing from rooms, especially since we're the first people who get blamed."

"I didn't mean—"

"You should get in here." She stepped back, holding the door open for me. "Before you're officially late."

I walked inside, trying not to let my mouth hang open. Somehow I'd expected small round tables with crystal balls and tarot cards—maybe some beaded curtains. But with bare walls, a shiny hardwood floor, Japanese-style room dividers, and racks of arty clothing, the shop looked like a cross between a yoga room and a trendy clothing store.

Then there was the Clash's "London Calling" blasting in the background—not exactly New Age material.

Veta shook her head. "We get the same reaction from every tourist that comes in here. We like to keep this space as neutral and uncluttered as possible. And me and Mom make some of the clothes ourselves."

"Wow." My throat ached for water.

"Guess you really like Taylor guitars." She motioned to my rumpled black tee.

"I, uh, kinda overslept."

"No kidding. Anyway, Mom doesn't like us to wear black while we're working. Too many people associate it with negativity." She grinned and slipped off her black sweatshirt. A belly-button ring and golden skin peeked between the waistline of her patchwork skirt and white tank top.

The music was turned down to a more reasonable level. "Is that your friend, *mija*?" A shorter, darker version of Veta came out from behind one of the dividers.

"Mom, this is Jasmine."

Her mother gave me a warm smile, holding out her dainty hand. "I'm Christina Ramirez, but call me Tina." She had a strong grip for a tiny woman. "Sorry about the loud music. I go back to my punk days when I'm in cleaning mode."

Veta leaned toward my ear. "Or when there's a new guy in her life."

Tina shot her daughter a dirty look before focusing on me. She had the same eyes as Veta: hazel and curved up a bit at the corners. Gorgeous but intense. "Your energy is very scattered."

I focused on Sprite and the toy bee he pawed around the floor. "Oh, sorry."

"Why, honey?"

"I'm guessing that's not a good thing?"

"That depends." She grinned and waved at a white couch to the left of us. "Have a seat."

Veta plopped onto one end and I took the other, setting my guitars in front of me.

Tina sat in a wooden rocking chair across from us. "Are you going to serenade us?"

"Oh no, I—"

"She doesn't trust housekeeping," Veta broke in.

"That's not true. I was raised by maids." Oh God.

"Do your parents run a housekeeping business?" Tina asked.

I licked my dry lips. "Nannies. I meant nannies. They took care of the house too."

"She's from Woodside," Veta said, as if that alone explained *everything* about me.

"You'll have to forgive my daughter." Tina settled back into the chair and crossed her legs. "She doesn't have an off button. We love her anyway."

Veta replied by sticking out her tongue. I imagined my dad's reaction if I did that to him. It was hard to keep a straight face.

"So, Jasmine," Tina continued, "what are your thoughts on alternative medicine?"

Well, there was the time Jason and I bought a psychic healing book and gave the grounding cord a sexual connotation. "My dad never said anything positive about it, but he's a cardiologist and a pretty conventional guy."

"Yet you want to work here?"

I glanced over at Veta. She flipped through a guitar magazine. "Veta said you were looking for a cashier. And I'm not really picky. Psychic readings sound kind of fun."

Tina cocked her head, a smile tugging at her lips. "Would you like one?"

"No." I folded my arms. "I'm sure they'd be cool to watch, though."

Veta snickered. "Chicken."

"I'm not afraid."

"Then what's the problem?" She looked up from her magazine.

"There isn't one, I guess." Besides it being completely uncomfortable.

Tina nodded and squinted at me. "Your fourth chakra is out of balance."

"My what?"

Veta elbowed me. "It means you need to get laid."

I leaned forward, inching my hands toward my guitar cases. What was wrong with her? Her *mother* was sitting right across from us.

Tina rolled her eyes. "It can mean a lot of things. That's your heart chakra. Your love center."

"Mom's got a PhD in psychology, so she's, like, the psychic Dr. Love of Santa Cruz."

"Great." Maybe she could explain why I'd never had a real boyfriend. Just a couple of really bad make-out sessions.

Tina sighed. "Here's the deal, Jasmine. I need someone who can count money *accurately*, be pleasant to the customers who deserve it, throw out the kleptos and drunks, and not rip us off at the end of the day. Can you handle that?"

This was by far the most bizarre interview I'd ever had. "Do the kleptos and drunks come in a lot?"

"We're across the street from the Boardwalk, babe," Veta said. "We get our share of junkies and garden-variety crazies too. But don't worry, we've only been held up once."

"Uh, how exactly would I throw them out?"

"Tell them to leave or you're calling the cops. If that's not enough, you gotta get all Matrix on their asses." Veta studied my face and laughed.

Her mom put her hand over mine. "She's only kidding. Raul and Jeff at the café next door have helped us." She gave Veta a weary glance. "And don't let those skinny arms fool you. Veta can usually hold her own."

That café back in Woodside was looking awfully nice. After all, rich women going apeshit over lowfat milk in their nonfat lattes weren't exactly life threatening.

"What do you think, Goldilocks? Interested?" Veta asked.

I looked at my green backpack. It contained all I had time to grab yesterday: a few T-shirts, a couple of pairs of jeans, and some bras and underwear. My entire life. "Sure, yeah."

"You don't sound very enthusiastic," Tina said.

I sat up straighter. "Oh, I am. I like the atmosphere and stuff. It's very, um, modern."

"I pay nine an hour. And it's thirty hours a week." Tina's smile widened. "Still like the atmosphere?"

"Definitely." I gave her my best ex-barista grin. "Thanks for considering me." My mind raced for something else to say. "Do you want me to fill out an application or give references?" Nice work. Quitting my only job without notice. No address. That would look great on paper.

Tina squeezed my hand. "Relax. You're a breath of fresh air, honey. Can you stick around? Veta can start training you today."

I pulled my hand away. "Wait, I'm hired? Don't you have to interview other people?"

"We have," Veta said. "And if you saw them, you'd understand our enthusiasm over you."

"Thanks, I think."

"One thing, though, Jasmine," Tina said, studying my shirt. "We try to avoid wearing black and—"

"I don't usually look like such a slob. Honest." Technically, not a lie. Just in case Tina could sniff me out with her psychic nostrils.

Tina grinned. "No worries. I've got one kid with bright red hair, one whose entire wardrobe is black, and my youngest likes to draw on her clothes. Kind of like you." She motioned to my jeans.

My cheeks burned as I remembered the marker. If only the phone numbers had smeared more. They could've passed for grass stains.

"Mom had blue hair at our age. Must be genetic," Veta said, reaching for my arm. "Come on, you can borrow some clothes off the racks."

"Not so fast." Tina kept her eyes on mine. "She hasn't accepted the offer yet."

"I'd love to work here." I looked down at my hands. "But I can't start right now."

"We're heading into the busy season. We really need someone now."

It would be dumb to pass up this opportunity. It wasn't like employers were dying to hire a seventeen-year-old runaway who walked out on her last job. "I need a couple of days to find a room to rent. Hotels get expensive, you know?"

"You've already found a great room," Veta said. "Unless you're not interested anymore?"

A phone rang from the second floor, and Tina excused herself. I waited until her heels finished clacking up the stairs.

"What if you guys don't pick me? I need a backup plan."

Her eyebrows inched closer together. "How about waiting for us to decide first? Me and the guys are meeting up at lunch, and I'd planned on fighting for you."

"And I appreciate that. But—"

"I won't bother if you don't want me to." She leaned back against the couch, watching a man push a cart outside.

"Wait, I don't—"

"I'm not going to bat for some chick who's already given up."

"I haven't! I just don't have much time." If only telling her the truth didn't mean killing any chance I had to get into this band.

Veta met my gaze with a sneer. "The world doesn't revolve around your schedule, Woodside."

I stood up. "Enough with the Woodside crap already."

"Look, I'm sorry." She rested her elbows on her knees, eyes downcast. "But I really need to know—are you actually interested in joining C-Side, or are you just looking for a nice room?"

"You're the psychic. You tell me."

She studied me, letting a few seconds pass before answering. "I know you think what me and my mom do is a joke. But we don't read people without their permission."

"I—I don't think it's a joke. It's just not something I'm used to. But you *do* try to read people—you've been doing it to me ever since we met. And your mom said my chuk-uh was all out of whack."

She snorted a laugh. "*Chakra.* And it was obvious to her. She'd have to dig to tell you why, though."

"Do you believe in what you do here?"

"Yes—even though a lot of people I care about don't, including my little brother and sister."

The frustration in her voice caused a familiar, tight sensation in my stomach. I looked down at my scuffed-up Docs. "I know the feeling."

"What's it gonna be? Are you sticking around or not?"

I shifted my weight, part of me wanting to stay and the other itching to run. My fingertips still buzzed from the tryout, craving another song. Another chance. Veta's fierce lyrics and vocals lingered in my mind. She inspired me. But the thought of being onstage, playing for an actual audience, made me want to duck and cover. Which would be effective only if there were an earthquake.

Chapter 6

The first customer who walked into Seaside Psychic didn't give me comfort in my decision to stay. A woman wearing tennis shoes under a green dress looked anxiously around the shop. Between her pale cheeks and blazing eyes, she looked to be a couple of gasps away from a heart attack.

"Where's your mother?" she asked, her blue eyes narrowing at Veta.

Veta slouched forward, resting her elbows on the countertop. "She's doing a phone session right now."

The woman made a huffing noise, letting her pink beach bag slip from her shoulder. "This is an emergency. He wants to meet me for coffee at three o'clock, *today*!"

The corners of Veta's mouth twitched upward, as if she was trying to smother a laugh. "I can give you a fifteen."

Crazy Lady nodded at me. "Who's she?"

Veta placed a hand on my shoulder. "This is Jasmine, our new cashier. Is it cool if she sits in with us?"

"Fine. Let's just hurry."

As Veta led us away from the register, she introduced the woman as Regina Price and mouthed "pain in the ass" when Regina's back was turned. We walked behind one of the dividers, where there was a cheap black folding table and matching chairs. I expected something a little more elegant.

"Simple and cost effective," Veta whispered to me as we sat around the table. Two white candles and a digital recorder made the centerpiece. "Didn't you and Tina do a telephone session yesterday?" she asked Regina.

"We did, but that was about the man I'm meeting tomorrow. This other fellow e-mailed me ten minutes ago."

"She's trying the online dating thing," Veta said to me.

I nodded and gave Regina a quick smile. Decent guys were hard to come by—online or anywhere—and her neurotic appearance probably didn't do her any favors.

"His name is Richard," Regina said. "I've been writing to him since last week. But you know I prefer to write for at least a month before I—"

"Did you print out a picture?" Veta interrupted. As Regina dug through her massive pink bag, Veta leaned toward my ear. "It really helps me to have a picture of the person or an item they own—takes less energy to pick up on things."

"I've got it. Right here." Regina tapped her finger against a crumpled piece of paper.

Veta sighed and picked up the picture. A man with slicked-back hair and very white teeth sat with a golden retriever. Neon grass melted into a crisp blue sky behind them. He belonged on the front page of a dating Web site. The kind of friendly, airbrushed face people paid $19.95 to meet—but never did.

"This is fake." She shoved the paper back to Regina. "Consider this a freebie unless you have any other questions."

I bit my tongue to hold in the laughter building in my chest.

Regina ran her hands through her salt-and-pepper hair. "How can you tell?"

"Easy! How old did he say he was?"

"Forty-eight."

"Then you're dealing with a real Photoshop pro here. Because this guy doesn't look a day over thirty-five." Veta pointed at the hand petting the dog. "Looks like he forgot to stamp out his wedding ring."

Regina squinted at the picture. "S-some people look younger. It's possible."

Veta shook her head and grinned. "Hey, look at those pecs. I don't blame you for hoping."

Pink washed over Regina's cheeks. "Don't be ridiculous. He wrote me very nice things."

"I'm sure he's a regular Cyrano," Veta said.

The bell on the door jingled, and hissing voices mixed with giggles echoed around the shop.

"Sounds like tourists." Veta nudged me. "Go out there and tell them we do fifteen-minute readings for twenty bucks. They usually aren't interested in more than that."

I nodded and made my way to the front door, almost bummed to miss the rest of the conversation. Two girls and two guys stood just inside, gazing around the shop.

"Are you sure they give readings here?" one of the guys whispered.

"Hi, can I help you?" I asked.

"Do you guys do palm readings or whatever?" the brunette girl asked. She sported an orange bikini top a size too small.

"Were you looking for palm reading specifically?"

The four of them looked at each other and giggled. "It doesn't matter," the other girl said. "How much does it cost?" She wore a denim skirt that barely covered her crotch.

"We, I mean, *they* can do a fifteen-minute reading for twenty dollars."

They huddled together, daring one another to be the first to go and eyeing me with amusement. I kept smiling because my old boss always told me never to let the customer see me frown. Any lapse meant I was letting them get to me, and many people tried to get free coffee out of that.

"Where's your turban?" the girl in the orange bikini asked.

The blond girl in the denim skirt shoved her. "You're so mean," she whispered with a grin.

"It's not rocket science, kids." Tina came up behind me. "You either want a reading or you don't."

I figured they'd turn around and leave, but their eyes widened at her, like she'd turn them into toads if they didn't comply. How such a tiny and demure-looking woman could be so intimidating was beyond me.

Tina took them behind one of the dividers just as a middle-aged couple wandered in. He wore golf shorts and a gold watch. She had a soccer-mom haircut and several bags from boutique shops. Maybe they were looking for directions to Starbucks.

The guy caught my eye and walked toward me. His wife stayed behind, looking constipated with her elbows pressed into her sides.

"Hi, how are you?" His mouth quirked up in almost a shy grin.

I responded with the autopilot niceties I'd used at the café. "Are you here for a reading?"

"Actually, no." He lowered his voice, putting his hand on my forearm. "Do you sell nipple clamps?"

I backed away. "I'm sorry, what?"

"We don't." Veta appeared next to me. "But there's a great sex shop on Pacific. Ask for Kat. She'll hook you up."

"Great, thanks!" He waved at us. His wife rolled her eyes and mumbled something to him on their way out.

"Some think psychic equals kinky," Veta said.

"That guy could've been one of my dad's friends," I blurted, my mouth hanging open.

Veta punched my arm. "You'll get used to it, Goldilocks."

Would I?

By noon, my stomach was aching for a sandwich, crackers, or maybe some human fingers. Really, anything crunchy sounded good. Tina wasn't kidding about it being busy. Sometimes there was up to an hour's wait for readings. Veta and Tina answered everything from whether a lover was cheating to *Should I talk to the fairies in my backyard?* And of course the ever popular, *When will I die?* They didn't even attempt to answer that one.

Luckily, learning the cash register was the easiest part of the job. Making custom massage oils and lotions? Not so simple. Too many brown bottles with weird names. Veta made me a chart I had to memorize, detailing the purpose of each essential oil.

"Let's say a customer comes in with a headache," she explained. "I'd suggest lavender or chamomile. Rub a little on the temples."

"Aspirin usually works for me."

"It can also eat your stomach lining."

"Only if you take it, like, excessively."

"That's true," a young voice said. It came from a blond girl reading on the couch. Her book was at least a thousand pages long—like one of those mammoth fantasy titles. She'd been there for the last hour but gave me a rather snotty "no" every time I asked if she needed help.

Veta threw her head back. "It's so time for lunch. Lock up, Wikipedia."

The girl put her book down with a dramatic sigh. She couldn't have been more than twelve. Definitely too young to work here. At least, I hoped.

"Who's that?" I asked.

"My little sister, Zoe. She's got the whole apartment to herself, but she insists on reading down here." Veta lowered her voice. "I think she secretly likes us."

"It's hot up there." Zoe plopped back on the couch and resumed reading. She was petite like her mom, but round faced and pale. Like a doll.

"You don't look alike."

"She's got a different dad from me and Sean. Pete—you might've met him at the garage."

I remembered his warm smile. "Very briefly. He seemed nice."

Veta leaned against the counter, folding her arms. "Pete's awesome. He's like a dad to me and Sean too."

"What about your biological dad?" I shook my head when she frowned. "Sorry, that's none of my business." I hated it when people asked about my mom. It was easier to pretend I never knew her than to tell them the truth.

"All Mom's told us is, he's tall, rich, and Irish. Oh, and Sean looks like him. But it took years to get that out of her. She used to just call him the *pendejo*." Veta grinned.

"Hence your issue with rich people."

She twirled the end of her braid around her finger. "Like you?"

I motioned to my old jeans and the white Seaside Psychic T-shirt I'd borrowed. "Uh, look at me."

"There's a difference between being poor and having no fashion sense. Your refusal of the sundress points to the latter."

"I don't wear dresses. Ever."

"Me neither," Zoe said without taking her eyes off the page. "But I don't have boobs yet. What's your excuse?"

Veta covered her mouth, laughing.

I folded my arms across my chest. "Boobs are overrated."

"Okay, I gotta go meet the boys." Veta slipped her velvet purse over her shoulder. "Wish yourself luck."

Forty-five minutes later, I was sitting in Raul's Café, staring at my laptop and making a small dent in my bean-and-cheese burrito. Veta said the café next door had the best burritos in town. And maybe they did. I'd have to try one when my stomach wasn't in my throat.

There were two new listings for rooms in my price range. One down the street—the *worst* part of town. Then again, I'd spent last night in my car.

I called the other place, another room in some family's house. Taken.

"Please tell me a nasty stomach virus is preventing you from eating that." Veta stood over me, her thin eyebrows raised.

"Oh, hi." I pressed my laptop shut. "It's great. I got distracted."

She slid in across from me and tore off the back end of my burrito.

"Didn't you just eat?" I asked.

"Yeah, but these things are like crack."

"So what's the verdict?"

"Can I have another bite?"

I glared.

A wide, feline smile took over her face. "Well, there's good news and bad news." She drummed her fingertips against the plastic table. "I bet you're the type who wants the bad news first."

I exhaled, stuffing my hands in my lap. "Just tell me."

"The bad news is, Bryn thinks you've got talent, but he's not sold on your confidence and stage presence. And Sean . . ." She shook her head. "What the hell happened between you two?"

"Nothing! I mean, his first words to me were, 'Your car is in front of an auto shop, genius.' He treats me like I'm the biggest ditz on the planet." Not that it was entirely undeserved.

"He thinks you're full of shit."

He must've told them about finding me in my car. "I was getting my toothbrush. It wasn't what he thought."

Veta wrinkled her nose. "Huh?"

"This morning in my car . . ." I trailed off when her confused expression didn't change.

"I'm dying to hear the rest of this." She tore off another chunk of my burrito and relaxed back in the chair.

I gave her the same story I told Sean. "Then he started interrogating me. Like he didn't buy it."

"Usually hotels have those little—"

"I know, but mine's electric. I'm attached."

Veta's smile faded, her eyes narrowing at me. She knew. I squeezed my hands into fists and prepared for her to call me out.

"Sean's always been a skeptic," she said. "Or a judgmental prick, depending on who you ask."

I let a smile slip despite myself.

"But this thing with his ex and Teddy . . ." She paused as if wondering how much to tell me. "Teddy was his best friend. And Amy *was* one of mine. We grew up together." She looked out the window, still drumming her fingers against the table. "First loves can fuck you up."

"I wouldn't know."

"There's a shocker."

I tried not to read too much into her words, but they still stung.

Like the time Dad told me being average looking was a blessing. It would be easier to succeed without boys chasing me.

"Sean knows he has to get over it," Veta continued. "He hasn't liked anyone who's tried out. And we need a new guitarist, like, yesterday. But it's a small scene and a lot of people are pissed at us right now."

"What do you mean?"

She scrunched her nose. "Let's just say Teddy is a well-liked guy around here. He always gives a lively performance—crowd surfing in a raft, wearing nothing but a Speedo and tiara. You name it, he's probably done it." She laughed. "Don't look so freaked, babe. We don't expect you to do that stuff. But I won't lie—you'd have some big shoes to fill."

"Okay . . ."

"Anyway, certain people—mostly Teddy's friends—don't think it's fair that he got booted over some chick. But Sean couldn't work with him and, quite frankly, neither could I."

"Makes sense."

"Which brings me to this," she said. "Bryn brought up the fact that you're a higher risk for dramarama."

"Why—because I'm a girl? Give me a break."

Veta leaned forward, the hint of a smirk on her lips. "Jailbait girl living with three guys. Two of them over eighteen. Get the picture, Goldilocks?"

A blush crept up my neck. "Well, it's not like I would, I mean, Sean's cute, but—"

"You think my brother's cute?" Her playful tone made me cringe. Why did Sean's name have to come flying out of my mouth?

"Um, sure." I folded my napkin into minuscule squares. "But he's not my type at all. That's what I was trying to say . . ."

"Good—as long as the attraction stays superficial."

"There's no attraction!" I exhaled a laugh. "God."

Her eyes did that squinty thing again. I crumpled the napkin in my palm.

"You aren't his type either. Or anyone's in the band. I pointed that out to them."

A sinking feeling settled inside, which annoyed me. I didn't want to be one of those girls who needed validation to feel worthy.

"Get that look off your face. That's good news."

"I don't have a *look*."

"I know this is awkward," she said. "But we gotta deal with any potential elephants in the room now. We don't have time to make the wrong decision."

People exaggerated on their résumés all the time. This wasn't any different. I had the skills and, most certainly, the motivation. They'd never have to know.

Unless I lost it onstage.

"Okay, here's the good news," she continued. "We've narrowed it down to you and Dave. Hope you don't have any plans tonight."

"Why?"

"Because you two are going to battle it out after work. Winner gets to move in tonight."

My throat tightened. "Battle . . . how?"

"We're giving you guys boxing gloves and locking you in the studio."

"Uh . . ."

"A guitar face-off, doofus. We're going to have Zoe tape it and everything. I can't wait."

"T-tape it?"

She grabbed the last fourth of my burrito. "Uh-hmm. So we can review it and see who brought it the most. It's hard to watch you while we're playing."

My palms went clammy. "Great. Who's going to play Tyra?"

"Probably Felix. He watches that show religiously." She licked her fingers, her eyes widening. "You guys should do a catwalk with your guitars."

"Whose idea was this?"

"Mine. And you're welcome." She stood up, pulling her purse over her shoulder. "Time to get back to work."

I gaped at her, but she turned around and walked out the door, the sun igniting her hair like a red bulb.

Cameras hated me, especially video cameras. But that was the least of my problems. What if I looked at the strings too much? Or didn't move around enough? I hope they didn't expect me to dance. Jason told me I danced like a cat with Scotch tape on its paws.

Chapter 7

The band told Dave and me to wait outside while they set up. They either wanted to make us sweat or kill each other. Probably both.

Dave sported glitter around black-lined eyes and meticulously spiked hair. Chiseled abs and biceps showed through his mesh shirt and he kept his chin high, telling the world he was an alpha male, sparkles and all.

I folded my arms and avoided eye contact. My official buzz-off pose.

"Nervous?" he asked.

"Do you care?"

"If you choke up like you did yesterday, I've got this."

"And if you—" The door squeaked open, interrupting my comeback.

Bryn poked his head out, his dreads hanging in his face. "We're ready."

I waved Dave past me. "Ladies first."

He paused, scanning my body. "I'd probably look better in a skirt."

"Too bad your legs won't get you the gig."

Dave grabbed his gear and walked inside. I took a deep breath as I followed. If his plan was to psych me out, he certainly knew the right place to start. There was a reason Jason and I hid out in his garage. At least there we could focus on what really mattered: the music.

"Dave, you can set up over there by Sean," Veta said. "You're on my side, Jasmine."

I let out a soft sigh of relief. The farther away I was from Dave and Sean, the better.

The band had already taken their positions, each member fiddling with his or her instrument. Zoe circled the room, sticking a mini DV camera in their faces. She wasn't having much luck with Sean.

"Quit it!" she yelled at him. "Your skeevy palm is going to ruin the lens."

"That's the point."

At least we agreed on something.

I plugged my guitar into their combo amp, gazing enviously at Dave. He had his own equipment here, which gave him a huge advantage.

"Smile!" Zoe thrust her camera at me.

I waved. "Don't shove that thing in my face while I'm playing, okay?"

"You can film me." Dave grinned at her. "I won't yell at you."

Oh, please. Could this guy get any more phony? Zoe didn't seem particularly interested in him, though. She moved on to capture Felix muttering profanities at his laptop. He looked especially cute today with his blue hair in pigtails.

"Everyone ready? I got a friend coming over at nine," Bryn said.

"Which *friend*?" Sean asked, pushing his hair out of his face. "The blonde who crashed Daddy's Mercedes or the one who thought Hemingway was a designer?"

Bryn's lips spread into a wide smile. "The one whose friend wants your number."

Sean rolled his eyes, like he wasn't even flattered. "Give her Teddy's."

I bet a lot of girls wanted his number. Until he opened his mouth.

"I've seen a couple of your shows," Dave said, nodding at Bryn. "The chicks love you."

"Is that why you're here, Dave?" Veta asked. "Hoping to get a little action?"

Dave tuned his pointy guitar, narrowing his eyes at her. "I have a girlfriend."

"Okay, enough dicking around. Here's the deal," Bryn said, using his drumstick as a gavel. "We're going to play the song three times. You'll just listen the first time. Then we'll give you each a go at it. Whoever kills it more gets to stay. Clear enough?" When we both nodded, he continued, keeping his gaze on me. "And don't just stand there. Pretend you're onstage doing a show with us."

I scanned the room, hugging my guitar closer to my body. *Don't just stand there.* Great. Any movement more than a couple of feet in any direction and I'd be bumping into someone or something. What did they expect me to do—twirl in place? Do a headstand?

Dave announced that he'd go first, which was fine with me. More time to prepare.

The song began with a kick drum loop. Felix added in a bouncy synth after a couple of measures, but the intro needed more punch. I could hear a fast, almost James Bond–like riff cutting in, or maybe even starting from the beginning.

The loop Felix was playing stuttered, and Veta busted in with a steely combo of power chords. Sean backed her up with a simple but effective bass line. They made me want to mosh, and I hated mosh pits.

The song was solid; it reminded me of Rob Zombie—only with sultry female vocals instead of his growl. This wasn't a bad thing—I dug Zombie. But C-Side's music needed that extra nudge, something to really set them apart.

The band went right from the end of the song to the beginning again. Dave simply bobbed his head to the intro, missing a huge opportunity. Once the song gained momentum, he dove in with a fast and dirty lick, relying on pinch harmonics to dress it up. Making a guitar squeal for added emphasis sounded cool, but some guitarists didn't understand the concept of moderation. Still, it was a difficult technique to master. And Dave kicked my ass in the shredding department. He'd probably spent as much time practicing scales as he had jacking off.

Zoe followed Dave's movements with the camera. He jutted his hips out and tapped the heel of his boot like some rock star in a bad '80s flick. Hooded eyes, pursed lips. He looked proud of himself.

Veta switched from the sultry vocals of the verse to the balls-out chorus. "Back-seat love affair. Give me that leather stare. Hardened ecstasy. You'll never come down." Even with hair in her face and tank top straps falling down her shoulders, the girl defined stage presence. She kept her eyes forward, glaring at some invisible force, while keeping a tight and unbreakable rhythm.

I spread my feet farther apart, mimicking her stance, and moved my shoulders to Bryn's beat. Maybe I'd capture a little of the magic. Then I caught Sean's eye, and that plan went to hell. He'd been watching me observe his sister, a smile playing at his lips.

I quickly focused on Felix. A grin lit up his face as the sound of his chirping pad filled the room. What must it be like to feel that at ease?

Bryn was a machine of sweat and muscle, every motion controlled as he drove the rest of the band forward. He seemed incapable of error.

But he was only human. All of them were—I needed to remember that.

Dave saved his slickest moves for last. He'd come close to stealing the song while Veta was singing, but he really let loose during the vocal break. His fingers flew up and down the guitar's neck as he rocked back and forth. Bryn intensified the beat, nodding his head in approval. Was he deaf?

Dave hit every note, but he had nothing to say. No passion. A solo without a story was like a singer with perfect pitch but a dead voice. Technique got a musician only so far.

I peeked over at Sean, but he appeared to be in another universe. Eyes shut, fingers steady, and not much else. That gave me hope.

The song came to a steamy end, and Dave gobbled up the last drops of time with a blast of feedback. He flashed me a shit-eating grin.

To my surprise, Bryn kept the beat going and called out, "You ready, Jasmine?"

Hell no. "Uh . . ." I shifted my guitar strap higher on my shoulder and fumbled my hands into position. "I guess."

"If you aren't, don't waste our time," Sean said.

The doubt in his eyes made me burn inside. He'd love to be right about me. Someone needed to give him the memo about not judging a book by its cover.

"Go ahead," I said.

A string of thoughts clashed in my head, most of them highlighting the many ways I could mess this up again. Dad always said if I really wanted something, giving myself permission to screw up wasn't an option. Neither was falling down and crying. According to him, if my grandmother had emigrated from Hungary with that attitude, she would've starved to death.

I closed my eyes, replaying the song in my head and using Bryn's beat as momentum. That James Bond–like riff came back to me, and I let my fingers do the talking. Felix's synth joined in, matching my rhythm perfectly. It gave a taste of what was ahead, a massive explosion of sound.

When Veta's riff kicked in, my focus shifted to her vocal melody. Songs always put images in my head, kind of like watching a music video. Something to care about and be inspired by—if only for a few moments.

The chorus made me feel reckless, like I was kissing some guy I barely knew. Back of his car. 2 a.m. Cold leather seat against my skin. The kind of scene that called for a glass slide. Although a beer bottle would've been cooler.

I put the slide over my pinkie and went from one note to the next, keeping the lick sparse and mindful of Veta's vocals. It added a nice bluesy edge and gave the song more personality.

Then I remembered that I was supposed to be moving around. Crap. I swayed gently to the beat and opened my eyes, meeting the lens of Zoe's camera. She watched me through the mini screen, looking bored out of her mind. That couldn't be good.

Veta leaned closer to her mic and delivered the next verse in a harsh whisper. I backed her up with a dreamy arpeggio, coloring in a flange effect. The notes sounded like they were drowning in a mythical ocean, the kind with mermaids and cerulean waves. It fit Veta, her softer side at least.

I'd done a great job of avoiding Dave until the end of the second chorus, just before the bridge. Movement in my peripheral vision caught my attention. Huge mistake.

Dave rocked from side to side and pretended to play along, his entire body stiff. He shut his eyes and furrowed his brow for added effect. God, he looked like he was doing the potty dance. He *wished* that was an accurate imitation.

I turned away, my fingers digging into the strings. My hands began to sweat and an itch probed the back of my neck. *Just get through this bridge. It's almost over.*

I let the first note of my solo ring out after Veta finished her last vocal line. At least, I *thought* she'd finished. She shot me a confused look and kept singing. My face felt like an oven.

Veta backed away from the mic, giving me an encouraging smile. *Last chance, Jasmine. Keep going.*

My fingers swept the fret board, leaving my mind in the dust. Bryn's beat pushed me forward and Veta's riff encouraged me to be relentless, unforgiving. I bent the hell out of certain notes, letting them really sing, and barely let others breathe. A pause here, a little vibrato there. Growing in complexity by the second. The melody told them the story I couldn't. My story—in all its raw and unrehearsed glory.

I just hoped they bought it.

Dave and I were relegated to the living room of the main house. He got comfy in a black leather recliner and channel-surfed their plasma TV. I paced back and forth, hands clenched at my sides.

C-Side had been in the studio for twenty minutes now. Watching Zoe's video. Debating. Possibly laughing at my lack of dance moves.

"So I'm curious," Dave began.

"Good for you."

"Why do you want to play for C-Side?"

I stopped pacing and folded my arms. "Why not?"

He raised his pale eyebrows. "Are you even into their music?"

"I wouldn't be here if I wasn't."

"I think you're in the wrong place."

"Why—because I forgot my tanker boots and eye glitter?"

"Because you come off like a band geek doing her first talent show." He motioned toward the studio. "Their words, not mine."

I moved in front of the TV, blocking his view. "You mean Sean's words?"

"That's the bassist, right? He wasn't the one who said it."

My back stiffened. "I know what you're trying to do, and it's not working."

"Have you ever played a live show? Honestly?"

My heart pounded a little harder. Was my lack of stage experience that obvious?

A smile tugged at his lips when I didn't answer. "Because I've played at Slim's and the DNA Lounge in San Francisco. The Catalyst here. They need someone who knows how to work an audience."

Movement caught the corner of my eye, and I turned to see Sean standing in the kitchen entranceway. "Dave," he said. "They want to talk to you in the studio."

Dave turned the TV off and hopped out of the recliner. "You get to do the dirty work, huh?"

Sean shrugged, his expression unreadable. "Guess you'll find out."

Dave rolled his eyes and made his way out of the room. I waited for the door to shut behind him before meeting Sean's gaze. Couldn't Veta have broken the bad news to me? Sending her brother was messed up.

Sean plopped onto their mustard-yellow couch and motioned to the space next to him. "You want to sit?"

"I'm fine where I am, thanks."

He sat forward, studying my face. "I'm not going to bite."

"Just say what you came here to say." I closed my eyes. "Please."

"*Have* you played live before?"

I looked down at the turquoise carpet. "Eavesdropping is creepy."

He exhaled a soft laugh. "I was standing there in plain view."

"Look, I don't have a lot of time, so I need to know . . ."

"Right." He checked his watch. "The dinner rush is almost over. Prime time for Dumpster diving."

I ran my hands through my unwashed hair, wondering if it looked as bad as it felt.

"You were like a deer in headlights in the video," he continued. "That's not going to fly at a show."

"Video cameras weird me out."

"As opposed to hundreds of people watching you?"

My mind grasped for an answer. Any answer. "I can handle it."

"Let's hope so. Because Veta and Felix think you can pull it off. And, lucky for you, Dave's a tool. So you're in."

I sucked in my breath. "*In the band* in?"

He squinted at me like I was the biggest dope. "Uh, yeah."

Happy chills swept across my skin. I wanted to jump up and down and scream like some fan girl. But I managed to contain myself, sort of. "Thank you! I mean, not you—*them*. I know this wasn't your choice—"

"You can save the acceptance speech." He stood up, shoving his hands into the pockets of his cargo pants. "Look, you played well tonight. You've got a distinctive style—I can see why my sister is all amped up over you."

"But?"

"You better be ready to 'handle it,' as you say. Now is a real good time to come clean if you have any doubts."

I hugged myself tighter, aching to admit the truth. That I was terrified, but I was determined to make this work. At least then I'd be free of this knot in my stomach.

"Music is my life," I said. "Walking away isn't an option."

"Wanting to make music and being able to hack it in a band are two different things."

I hated the all-knowing glint in his eyes. Showing weakness would never earn me respect. Not from him. "Can I go back to the studio now?"

"Go ahead."

I walked past him, keeping my eyes forward. Sean could discourage me all he wanted. He wasn't getting rid of me that easily.

Veta stood outside, smoking a cigarette and talking to Felix. Dave carried his amp out of the studio, his eyes meeting mine for a brief second. Wow, he practically snarled. Where was a camera when I needed one?

"There's our new guitarist." Felix gave my shoulder a squeeze.

"Hey, girl!" Veta snatched me up in a hug, burying my face in her strawberry-scented hair. "Sean told you, right?"

I pulled back, squirming out of her embrace. "Yeah, but I would rather have heard it from you."

"And miss out on bursting Dave's bubble? No way." She glanced back at the house. "Besides, I want you and Sean to get to know each other better. He played nice, didn't he?"

"If condescending is nice for him, sure."

She sighed, giving Felix a knowing look. "I'll talk to him."

"No—don't," I said. "I'm fine. Like you said—he's having a tough time." Sitting on an ice cube sounded cozier than another forced one-on-one with Sean.

"Thanks for coming out, man." Bryn stood in the studio doorway, handing Dave his guitar cord. The last of his equipment, I hoped.

Dave draped the cord over his shoulder. "Sure." He shot me another dirty look and turned back to Bryn. "Hope that works out for you."

That? I was a *that* now?

"Better luck next time," I said as he walked away.

Dave flipped me off before fading into the darkness of the driveway.

"Loser!" a girl's voice called behind me.

I turned to see Zoe sitting on the lawn, sneering in Dave's direction. A flashlight and a gigantic book sat on her lap. If I were into hugs, I totally would've hugged her at that moment.

Felix put his hand on my arm. "That guy needs anger-management lessons."

"I know," Veta said. "And I wasn't even harsh when I broke it to him. I was just, like, sorry, but we think Jasmine is a better fit, yada yada—"

"He turned bright red!" Felix jumped in.

Bryn approached us, quirking an eyebrow. "When you *ladies* are done, I need to talk to Jasmine inside." He gave me a light slap on the back. "Good job tonight."

"I'm not in trouble already, am I?" I asked after Bryn went inside.

"No." Felix laughed. "Unless you don't have the rent."

God, I hope he didn't want a huge deposit. Trying to hold Sean off with the car was going to be hard enough.

"So, anyway," Veta continued, "Dave basically told us we were idiots and then he was, like—"

"*I've got another offer anyway.*" Felix deepened his voice and flared his nostrils to mock Dave.

Veta yanked on one of his pigtails. "Let *me* finish the story."

"Why?" Felix poked her. "You rarely let anyone finish a sentence."

She waved her fist at him in response. "You wanna go? I'll take you down like the teddy bear you are."

I laughed and shook my head. These two made it easy to forget my problems. "So *then* what happened?"

"Bryn asked what band offered him a spot," Veta continued. "And Dave said Newton's Whore, Amy Castellano's band—which we didn't even know existed."

"Sean's ex, Amy?" I asked. "I didn't know she was a musician."

Veta nodded. "She plays bass and thinks she can sing. But really, all she can do is screech and look pissed off."

Felix made a claw with his hand. "*Mrowr.*"

"Well, it's true," she responded.

"Newton's *Whore*—isn't that a little degrading?" I asked.

Veta shrugged. "That's Amy. She's a physics major and has this twisted obsession with Isaac Newton. I'm sure she thinks it's cute. But get this—Teddy is going to be her drummer."

"I thought he was your last guitarist," I said.

"He plays drums too," she said.

I jammed my hands into my pockets. "Are you going to tell Sean?"

Felix and Veta exchanged a glance. "Yeah, we need to. Dave mentioned they were trying to get a gig at the Roach," Veta said.

"I'll do it," Zoe said, a persnickety grin on her face.

Veta narrowed her eyes at her little sister. "Better not." She shifted her gaze to me. "Zoe isn't into icky love stuff yet. She doesn't get heartbreak."

"Dating is stupid," Zoe said. "All people do is kiss and fight."

Veta smirked. "I bet you wouldn't feel that way if Nick Slater asked you out."

"Gross." Zoe lifted her book closer to her face.

"Who's that?" I whispered.

"Bryn's little brother," Felix answered. "Zoe has a huge crush on him."

"Do not."

"I should get her home," Veta said, ruffling my hair. "I'll see you tomorrow. Nine o'clock sharp."

"I'll be there." Long, hot shower and change of clothes, here I come. After I talked to Bryn of course. Fun.

After what felt like the best shower of my life, I went out on my balcony and took in the salty breeze. Sea lions argued against the white noise of the ocean, and muffled music could be heard from the cars parked along the cliffs. Pure heaven, minus a bed and $845.

Bryn wasn't too keen on letting me wait until July 1 to give him July's rent. Nope. He wanted the rest of June and next month's rent up front. That left me $45 short of what I owed for my car and no money for food or bills. In other words, I was screwed. At least he'd been generous enough to scrounge up a sleeping bag and pillow.

I pulled my hoodie tighter and focused on the moon sliver hovering over the water. It seemed so placid and sure of itself, even with shadows hiding most of its glory. The moon always made me a little hungry too, but I had my dad to thank for that. He'd told me it was made out of Swiss cheese when I was five. *Best cheese in the universe*, he'd said. I'd actually believed him. Just like I bought everything he said the year after Mom left.

Tears won't bring her back. They'll only slow you down.

I hadn't been able to cry since. Even after I'd made Jason pinch my arm until it bled in the second grade. I'd convinced myself that I couldn't cry like other kids because I was immune to pain. I wasn't.

I pulled my cell from my pocket, checking for missed calls. None. Dad used to bombard my phone if I stayed at Jason's past eleven. Now that I was gone, I could be lying in a ditch somewhere, for all he knew. Did he even care where I was? Part of me wanted to know, *had* to know. The other part knew I'd just be disappointed.

I highlighted Dad's name and hit SEND anyway.

"Hello?" he answered on the second ring, sounding gravelly. Tired. "Jasmine?"

"Dad." The word came out in barely a whisper.

"How are you?"

"How do you think?"

"Hang on. Which way?" A woman spoke in the background, telling him to take a left. It sounded like Tammy, his latest girlfriend. Or maybe "dinner date" would be the more accurate term.

"I guess you're driving," I said.

"We're on our way back from . . ." His voice broke up, muffling his explanation. ". . . on 84 right now. The reception isn't good. Can I call . . . tomorrow?"

"Sure." I mumbled bye and flipped my phone shut, letting out a shaky breath. What did I expect? He was Dad, the man with the winning poker face.

I'd just set the alarm on my cell and nuzzled into the red sleeping bag when I heard the noise. At first I thought it was the naughty channel on someone's TV—*prayed* it was someone's TV. But the vibrating wall told me otherwise. And then there was the giggling and the occasional grunt. A female voice calling out Bryn's name completely sealed the deal for me.

Disgusted and wondering what the hell I'd gotten myself into, I got up and planned to watch TV downstairs until the escapade ended.

When I opened my door, my eyes met Sean's. He was coming out of the bathroom, looking annoyingly cute with disheveled hair and blue-plaid pajama bottoms. I looked away when I realized the ensemble didn't include a shirt.

"I didn't know you were still up," he said, sounding almost apologetic.

"Well, I can't really sleep, because, um . . ." I nodded at Bryn's bedroom.

He chuckled. "Get used to it."

I figured we were done until he started walking toward me. *Don't stare, don't stare*, my mind screamed. But my eyes didn't listen. They focused on the tattoo encircling his left arm. Quarter notes and barbed wire.

He reached into his pocket and handed me something rectangular. "I'm assuming you don't have one, or you'd be using it."

My fingers brushed his as I took the iPod from him. I'd had an iPod, but it broke right before graduation. "You're loaning this to me?"

"You need it more than I do." Sean ran his fingers through his hair, and I tried not to let my eyes wander below his neck. "I don't know what kind of music you like, but I've got a ton on there."

"Thanks. Um . . ." Maybe he'd taken his happy meds. "Do you want me to slip it under your door in the morning?"

"That works."

We stared at each other for a few seconds. His eyes seemed more intense in the dim lighting of the loft. My mouth opened, but no words came out.

Just say something. Don't let him think his naked torso has left you speechless.

He shifted his weight. "Okay, well . . . good night?"

" 'Night. And, you know, thanks." I fumbled for my doorknob. "Again."

He nodded and walked away, but I could've sworn I saw the flicker of a smile.

Real smooth, Jasmine.

As I drifted off to one of Sean's playlists, I made an interesting discovery: We had almost identical music collections.

Chapter 8

Veta shot me a dirty look when I pushed open the door of Seaside Psychic at 9:10 a.m. "Sorry," I said, panting, "Felix was t—"

"Taking an hour-long shower—I know. You're still late, and it's only a ten-minute walk." She resumed counting a drawer full of cash.

"I really am sorry, Veta. I ran all the way here." Things were bad when a cheap sleeping bag felt like silk on my skin. *Just five more minutes*, I'd kept telling myself.

A giggle erupted from the white couch. Zoe sat there clutching another book, studying me. Sprite, their *psychic kitty*, was curled up on her lap.

"Sleep well?" Veta wore a knowing smile.

"Yeah, thanks for the warning." I glanced at Zoe again. "Bryn has a real . . . exercise addiction."

"I'm almost thirteen, not five," Zoe said. "It's not like I can't figure out what you're talking about."

"Oh." I looked at Veta for help, but she just shook her head and laughed.

"You don't like our brother much, huh?" Zoe asked.

"Well, I don't really know him."

She smirked. "He's only a jerk to the girls he likes."

"Good to know." I tried to make my laugh casual, but it sounded more like something was stuck in my throat. "Where's Tina?"

Veta rolled her eyes. "She's on the phone with Regina Price—that woman never shuts up." She tied her long hair into a ponytail, allowing a few bright red locks to escape. "Lucky for you, though. She probably doesn't know you were late."

"She won't fire me, will she?"

"Not the first time," Zoe said. "But if it happens again . . ." She grinned and made a slicing motion across her throat.

"It was only a few minutes," I mumbled.

"More like *ten*. And don't get too comfy." Veta walked toward me, narrowing her eyes. "I'm not going to cover your butt next time."

I held up my hands in surrender. "What should I be doing right now?"

"Make sure the shop looks presentable before we open. Wipe down the front counter, the display case, and reading tables and straighten the clothes and waiting area." She jabbed her thumb over her shoulder. "Cleaning stuff is in the closet."

I nodded and headed for the back, reminding myself that I was lucky just to have this job. Cleaning wasn't exactly my specialty. I'd never really done it, outside of tidying up during my after-school shift at the café. When business was slow, I'd make a beeline for the broom. I mean, really, who could screw up sweeping? My coworkers didn't like me much.

The shelves in the closet were lined with several natural cleaners. All purpose seemed like a safe bet, so I grabbed the bottle and attacked the front counter first. Spray and wipe. How hard could it be?

Veta sat on the couch, flipping through a magazine. "Do you believe in ghosts?" she asked.

"Take a wild guess."

"I'll go with no." She grinned, shaking her head. "How can you play like you do and have such a closed mind?"

Zoe snorted and muttered something like "Here we go."

"Hey, show me concrete proof and my mind will open right up," I said.

"Maybe I can."

I stopped wiping and faced her. "Please don't tell me you talk to ghosts."

"Not like I'm talking to you. It's mostly intuition. Sometimes images will pop in my head or I'll get strong feelings."

"That's called daydreaming."

"What makes you so sure?"

"I'm pretty sure I control the thoughts in my head," I said.

"Pretty sure isn't sure." Veta got up and walked behind the counter, running her finger along the top. "It's amazing how much plain water can help with cleaning." She reached underneath and tossed me a spray bottle. It slammed right into my chest. "And one more thing?"

"Yes?"

"Use the glass cleaner for the glass next time." She winked and began rearranging the oils on the shelves.

The shop was either chaotic or dead for the bulk of the morning. I preferred the quiet to the sheer insanity that walked through the door. "Garden-variety crazies" didn't begin to describe some of these people.

Crazy #1: A guy dressed like the grim reaper, scythe and all, came in to ask directions to Denny's. When Veta told him, he curtsied and said, "Good day, milady."

92

Crazies #2 and 3: A couple groped each other on the couch while they waited for a reading. Customers complained. Veta asked them to take it outside. They apologized. All was well until they got into a yelling match. The gist was, she thought he had checked out Brittany at Pizza Hut. Cuss words and crying followed. Customers complained again. Tina eighty-sixed them but offered to see them again—separately.

Crazy #4: A woman approached the counter and stared at me for a good minute before speaking. She looked pretty harmless—jeans, T-shirt, graying shoulder-length hair. "Your eyes are so striking," she said. "What sign are you?" When I told her, she backed away, informing me she "didn't do business with Scorpios."

Crazy #5: The UPS guy asked me what time I got off work. This might've been flattering if he wasn't old enough to be my grandfather.

The shop emptied around 11:30. I hung out behind the counter while Veta and Tina traded stories about wacky regulars. As if they expected people who frequently came in for psychic love readings to be sane.

"Jasmine is giving us that skeptical look again," Veta said, raising her eyebrows at me.

"It's just . . . never mind." I busied myself with wiping the array of fingerprints off the glass counter (with glass cleaner).

"Jasmine," Tina said. "I'm going upstairs to make some tea. Why don't you join me?"

"Um, alone?"

Tina cracked a smile. "Well, I think Zoe is in her room drawing, if that makes you feel better."

I glanced at Veta, who crinkled her brow like I was the silliest person on the planet. "It's not that—I'm—am I in trouble?"

"No, honey. We just haven't had much time to talk since you started," Tina said.

This couldn't be good. "Sure. Okay."

I followed her up narrow wooden stairs that creaked under my feet. She opened a white door with a deadbolt and waved me inside.

Their apartment was small but charming. Hardwood floors, sunny yellow walls, and the musky smell of incense were the first things I noticed. The entryway led to a tiny kitchen with older appliances, a blue refrigerator, and a white-tiled table surrounded by four chairs.

"Have a seat." Tina grabbed a red teakettle and filled it with water. "I usually have chamomile after a busy morning. Helps calm the nerves. Would you like some?"

I sat on one of the chairs, folding my arms in my lap. "That's okay. Thanks."

She settled across from me. "Sure I can't twist your arm? It's great for relaxation."

I gave her the most sincere smile I could manage. "Okay, I'll try a little."

Tina's hazel eyes combed my face, more than likely trying to see inside my mind. I focused on the blue and white vase in the middle of the table. The kaleidoscopic patterns looked like a swarm of tiny butterflies itching to come to life.

"Beautiful vase," I said.

A soft smile spread across her lips. "*Mi abuelita*—my grandmother—made it right after I was born."

My right leg jiggled. "I love your apartment. It's . . . cozy."

"Thanks. The rent kills me, and three kids sharing one room was never a picnic. But it means a lot to us being so close to the water."

I couldn't imagine sharing my room with anyone, much less two people. Having my own space kept me sane. "Where did they all sleep?" I covered my mouth. "Sorry . . ."

Tina chuckled. "No, it's a very reasonable question, actually. Once Zoe decided she wanted her *own* bed, she stole Sean's. He slept on the couch."

"Oh—that was nice of him."

"I think he preferred it, and I can't say I blamed him. My sister and I shared a room growing up. Our fights were brutal." She looked at my clasped hands. "Anyway, I wanted to tell you not to be afraid to ask any questions about what we do. We learn to develop a thick skin in this business."

I exhaled, trying to think of the best way to word my thoughts. "I know you believe in what you do—and I respect that. But I don't understand how it's possible to see inside someone else's head, much less predict their future."

"Fair enough. Let me ask you this—do you know why we dream?"

"Well, there are, like, a million theories on that . . ."

She nodded. "What's *your* theory?"

"I once heard that dreams are conscious and subconscious thoughts from our day all jumbled up. And, I don't know—that makes the most sense to me."

"Have you considered that perhaps none of us knows the answer yet—at least not in its entirety?"

"Well, yeah. There's never been a consensus."

The kettle whistled through the kitchen, and Tina got up. "My belief is that dreams are messages from ourselves, from those around us—and even from the spirit world. And if you're open to them, they're gifts. They can give you new insight." She got out two yellow mugs. *"Mija?"* she called toward the hallway. "You want some tea?"

"No." Zoe's voice sounded behind a closed door.

Tina dropped bags into the mugs and poured the hot water. "Watch—she'll change her mind in about five minutes."

I felt like I was back at Jason's house. His mom knew everything he'd do before he did it. I always wondered what it would be like to have a parent understand me so well. Or even one who cared enough to try.

"Have you ever dreamed of a specific event right before it happened?" Tina plopped a mug in front of me and sat back down.

"Thanks," I said, breathing in the earthy steam. "I had a dream about a pop quiz in English once—should've listened to that one. And . . . that's about it." But it wasn't. Two days before my mom left, I dreamed of watching her pack. I kept tugging on her and screaming her name, but she couldn't hear me. Her face was so docile, almost like a statue's.

"How do you explain something like that?" Tina asked.

I leaned back and shrugged. "Coincidence, I guess."

"It's possible. But I used to have psychic dreams all the time—enough that I couldn't chalk them up to coincidence. I had to learn how to control them. Now I choose what I want to see—most of the time."

I took a small sip of the tea, hoping the mug would hide the doubt probably on my face. The perfumelike taste made me crinkle my nose.

She grabbed a bottle of honey from a cabinet and pushed it in front of me. "Try that."

"So you believe that you can actually control your dreams?"

"It's no easy feat, but it's something anyone can learn to do. I'm not special." She took a sip and closed her eyes, like it was a scrumptious brownie. "There is so much science can't explain. We don't even fully understand our own brains. But I've found truth in what I do. I've helped people improve their lives, and I've improved my own. That's what matters to me."

I squirted a healthy amount of honey into my mug. "It must be a good feeling—to be so sure."

Zoe's door swung open and she appeared in the kitchen with charcoal smudges on her cheeks. She gave her mom a timid smile. "Did you save any water?"

Tina rolled her eyes at me and smirked. "What'd I tell you? It's on the stove." After Zoe retreated downstairs with her tea and a book, Tina continued. "I know how crazy I sound to a scientific mind—Sean and Zoe remind me all the time. But I thought it would make you feel more comfortable to understand where Veta and I are coming from. And, if you're up for it, I'd like to give you a reading. A small one—nothing heavy."

I gulped down a glob of honey. What was I so afraid of? That Tina could close her eyes and know my every thought? See my life like a movie? That would be impossible. But I had to admit, she made me a little curious. Maybe a lot curious. "Okay. When?" I asked.

"Well, Veta hasn't hollered for us to get our butts down there yet. How about now?"

I sat up a little straighter. "What do I need to do?"

"Think of a question—anything. Just make sure it's something you're comfortable with me answering. Otherwise, I'll be dealing with some major firewalls."

"Do you need to hold my hands or anything?"

She cocked her head, her lips twitching the same way Sean's did. "Do you *want* me to hold your hands?"

"Not really. No."

She laughed. "Okay, then. All I need you to do is focus on relaxing. If you need to close your eyes and picture yourself on a beach, go for it. If a rock concert is more your speed, imagine that. Whatever makes you feel at home."

I took a few minutes to think of a question. It had to be vague enough to make inferring anything from it difficult. "Did I make the right choice?"

Tina's eyebrows rose. "Ooh, that's one I get every day." She closed her eyes, her chest rising. Then she exhaled slowly, like a blood pressure cuff deflating. "Now is a good time to go to your happy place."

I shut my eyes and imagined myself in Jason's garage. That was the closest place to home for me.

"I'm going to describe a variety of images I'm seeing, and then I'll interpret them," Tina said. "If you've got any questions or need clarification, let me know."

"Okay." I bit my tongue to avoid laughing, mostly because I felt silly.

"I see you running down a highway, but you keep looking back. Which tells me you made your decision in haste and you're not entirely sure of yourself."

"That's true . . ." Basic psychology said I wasn't certain of my decision. Why else would I ask?

"Bear with me, Jasmine. I'm just dipping my feet in the pool, so to speak." Several seconds passed. With the constant hum of the refrigerator, the pause felt like ten years. "There's a strong male energy around you. It's almost stifling—a lot of guilt. Your father?"

I opened my eyes. "What exactly are you seeing?"

Her brow crinkled. "Not much. You're shutting me out."

My heart started pounding. "I am?"

"Well, I got a big wall in my face at the mention of your father. But we don't have to talk about him, okay?"

I allowed myself to exhale. "I'd appreciate that."

"We can stop this at any time. Just let me know."

"I'm good. Go on."

She was quiet for another few moments, her eyelashes fluttering. Sweat began to pepper my back.

"I'm not seeing your mom," she began. "Is she—"

"Can we not talk about my parents—please?"

Tina's eyes opened and her lips parted.

"Sorry," I said. "I don't mean to be rude. It's just—I'd rather not . . ."

Her face softened. "Your parents have a lot to do with your question. That's why they came up."

"I don't see how."

"I'd say ninety-five percent of my answers aren't what clients want or expect to hear. We're quite brilliant at blinding ourselves to the real obstacles. But you're obviously uncomfortable, so we'll stop."

I looked down at my mug. "Thanks for trying."

"I appreciate you giving it a chance—I know it wasn't easy for you. But Jasmine . . ."

I met her intense gaze.

"I know you're pretty overwhelmed right now. Everything is new and crazy—and living with three boys probably isn't helping." She grinned. "But if you need to talk or just need a break from the testosterone, you're welcome here anytime. Even if it's two a.m.— I can't promise you *I'll* be coherent, but I know Veta will be."

"You guys have been ridiculously nice to me."

"Well, your guitar playing won over Veta. She can't stop talking about it or you. And I trust her judgment."

I let out a nervous laugh, not knowing how to respond. I'd never met people so open and trusting. It still seemed almost too good to be true.

Tina reached over and patted the back of my hand. "I'd offer you a hug, but something tells me it's not your thing."

"Not really."

"Fair enough. You can go ahead downstairs if you want. I'll get your mug."

I stood, tucking a lock of hair behind my ear. "Um, thanks for . . . you know."

She smiled and nodded. "I do."

Veta and Zoe were camped out on the white couch when I headed downstairs.

"Think Nick will come in today?" Veta asked Zoe.

"Don't know, don't care." She hunched closer to her book.

Veta hit her in the knees with a pillow. "You're blushing."

"Go away," Zoe said through her teeth.

I always wondered what it might be like to have a sibling. But in that moment, Veta made me glad I didn't have an older sister. I used to turn red just at the mention of boys.

"Hey," I said, folding myself in the rocking chair.

Veta's smile widened. "How'd the talk go?"

"It was . . . interesting."

"My mom's intense, huh?"

I nodded. "I can see where you got it from."

She batted her long eyelashes. "I take that as a compliment."

"What's going on, daughters of mine?" Tina asked, coming down the stairs.

The bell of the shop door jingled. Bryn and Sean wandered in with half smiles.

"Not much," Veta said. "We were just discussing Zoe's mega-crush on Bryn's little brother."

Bryn laughed. "What?"

Zoe threw her book down on the table and folded her arms across her chest. Her cheeks nearly matched Veta's hair.

"Leave her alone," Sean said, giving us a dirty look.

My mouth fell open. "I didn't do anything."

"I'm going out to lunch," Tina said. She ruffled Sean's hair on her way out. "Good to see you, *mijo*."

A giggle escaped my throat when he ducked away like an embarrassed twelve-year-old. His eyes matched the green logo on his black T-shirt today, and he wore a faded pair of jeans that probably flattered his butt. Not that I cared.

"Did Jasmine tell you she's working here?" Veta asked.

Bryn shook his head at me. "And you seemed so normal."

"Maybe she really needs the money," Sean said.

So much for Mr. Nice Guy. "I'm just the cashier."

"We're heading out to Bella Roma. Wanna come?" Bryn kept his eyes on Veta, like I didn't even exist.

"Nah, I want Raul's." She elbowed me. "You should take Jasmine."

Bryn glanced at Sean before giving me a quick smile. "Sure."

The last thing I needed was a pity lunch date. Plus, I didn't have the cash to eat at some fancy Italian restaurant. "That's okay. I'm not hungry."

Bryn shrugged and Sean excused himself, saying he needed to use the bathroom.

"By the way, don't make any plans this week," Bryn said. "We've got a gig at the Roach on Saturday."

I tried to keep from gaping at him. Was he on crack? "But I haven't learned most of the songs yet."

"Which is why we need to practice every night." His lips curved into a playful grin. "You got the chops, right? You'll pull it off."

"I don't know if I can—"

"Don't you think a show this soon is a little hasty?" Veta broke in, nudging my foot with hers.

Bryn held up three fingers. "We've got three weeks, okay? We need all the warm-up we can get."

"The Roach is a dive," Sean said, rejoining us. "We're lucky if thirty people show up." He met my gaze, an analytical glint in his eyes. "Shouldn't be too hard."

I looked down at my hands. "Okay."

"You want to get some pizza, Zoe?" Sean asked.

She catapulted off the couch, flinging her tangled blond hair over her shoulders. "Yes, please. Get me out of here."

"Later," Veta called after them as they piled out the door. She leaned back on the couch, letting out a long exhale.

Having less than a month to prepare was bad enough, but a week? I had to perform in front of people, like, *actual* people—not the line of stuffed animals on my bed I used to serenade as a kid.

"I don't know about this, Veta. What's the rush?"

"Bryn is devoid of patience. And I think he wants to test you."

"Does he always get his way?"

She raised her eyebrows. "Challenging the rank already, are we?"

"Just wondering if C-Side is a democracy or a dictatorship."

"It's supposed to be a democracy. But Bryn is the whole reason we're even opening for Luna's Temptation. He met up with them at a party, got them to see one of our shows. He keeps up our online presence and books our gigs—which aren't easy to get around here. So if he scores us anything, even at the Roach, we go."

"Nobody else helps?"

"We try, but me and Sean don't have the kind of time Bryn does. And Felix isn't really the go-getter type."

"Makes sense."

"Look, you practically nailed that song last night. You're going to pick the rest up, no problem. And, seriously, the Roach is comparable to playing at someone's birthday party." Veta nudged me. "It's not like it's your first time playing live. You'll do fine."

I nodded and turned away, every part of my body tensing. Maybe I should tell her. They wouldn't kick me out now, not with a show in less than a week. They'd hate me, though. And I couldn't do that to Veta, not after she fought so hard for me. Besides, I *nailed* last night's tryout. I could pull this off. Scratch that. I had to pull this off.

Chapter 9

My arms were shaking when I pulled my guitar out of its case, but not from nervousness this time. Veta had convinced me that I needed a yoga session with her and Tina after work. *It'll help loosen you up*, she'd claimed. The Downward-Facing Dog position kicked my butt; who knew holding your body up on all fours was so hard?

Sean stood in front of me, his green bass slung low on his hips. "Everything okay?" he asked.

"Yeah, why?" I dialed in a heavier sound on my Diezel. Sean had brought over my equipment earlier in the day. Nice of him, I guess.

"You're shaking."

"Veta bought me a double mocha, and I ended up finishing the rest of hers too." At least that much was true. I didn't want to admit how out of shape I was.

"Bit of an addict?"

I walked right into that one. "No."

He leaned in, giving me a musky whiff of soap and auto shop. "Your gasket will be here tomorrow, so your car should be ready by Wednesday."

How nice of them to be so expedient. "About that—"

"What are you two whispering about?" Veta asked. She was on the floor, scribbling down some last-minute lyrics.

Sean said, "Nothing important," and he moved to the other side of the room. I exhaled with relief. Now wasn't the time to talk anyway. Not in front of everyone.

"Are we adding 'Acceleration' to the set list?" Bryn asked Veta.

"I don't know yet. These lyrics are still really corny," she said.

"Why don't we just play it?" Sean asked. "Might sound less cheesy off paper."

"I keep coming up with really cool lines that don't go with the rhythm."

"It's always like that," Felix said. "Why do you think so many songs involve four-letter words?"

Veta laughed and stood up, taking her place at the mic. Bryn got behind the drums and started counting off. My heart thudded a little harder—I hoped wouldn't disappoint anyone.

The song began with Sean's fast and dirty bass line and a hard-nosed beat from Bryn. Veta joined them with a two-chord riff that made me feel like I was drag racing in the middle of a desert.

She grabbed the mic and belted out the lyrics in a throaty voice. "High thrust, low rev. Slick roads, back woods. Take me anywhere. My traction adapts."

I closed my eyes and felt a smooth gearshift in my hand. The engine growled with every jerking movement as I headed west on some dusty road. A gigantic sun dove behind jagged mountains.

I stomped on the delay effect, hearing an epileptic melody over the top of the song—high notes in irregular but quick succession.

"Tight curves, raw moves. Rough you up, bend the rules. I never play nice, 'cause I made up the game," Veta sang on. Her lyrics would sound ridiculous from anyone else's lips. But Veta had a voice that demanded attention, nearly pitch-perfect and raw in all the right places. Each word was like a sliver of broken glass, slight and cutting at the same time.

I picked my notes faster, trying to keep up with the volatile energy of the song.

And then Sean stopped playing. "Jasmine! What's with the Morse code?"

Our eyes met, but I looked away.

Bryn backed off the drums and the growl of Veta's riff ceased, leaving Felix's drum loop. He quickly shut it off. Sean really knew how to kill a mood.

"I know it's a little busy, but I think it works," I said.

"Not really," he said. "It's clashing with Felix's pad."

"His pad is a texture. It's not meant to be at the forefront. Am I right, Felix?"

Felix kept his eyes glued to his laptop, biting his lower lip. "Well, yeah . . ."

"Crank the distortion." Bryn looked at me as if he expected gratitude for the insight.

But I had my own ideas.

Bryn counted off, and we began again. I picked the notes slower, letting each ring out and bleed into the next. It sounded decent but lacked spunk.

Halfway through the chorus, Bryn stopped drumming. "Hold up." He yanked a rubber band around his dreadlocks and wiped a gleam of sweat from his forehead.

"It's still not working for me, Jasmine," Sean said. "The tone is too bright."

"Yeah, it's piercing as hell," Bryn added.

Veta rolled her eyes at me. "I thought it sounded better this time."

I gave her a thankful smile. "I can turn the volume down."

"Which will only make it softer." Bryn stuck a drumstick behind his ear. "It doesn't change the fact that it belongs in a New Age infomercial."

I felt my shoulders tense. What if I couldn't figure out something they liked?

Felix glanced over at me, his dark eyes filled with pity. "It wasn't that bad. Bryn's just on his period."

"No, I'm honest." Bryn flashed him a toothy grin. "You should be too."

Felix made a dismissing motion with his hand.

"I'll play with it a little more." I turned away, inwardly cringing at the quiver in my voice.

"Screw that," Bryn said. "Give us some teeth. Dirty it up. Do you guys remember the riff Teddy did for the intro? That was tight."

The humid air clung to my cheeks and fueled the anger building inside my chest.

"I like the cleaner sound," Sean said. The gentleness in his voice surprised me. I figured he'd be enjoying Bryn's reaming.

"I'll figure something out." My foot shook as I scrolled through my patches. Nothing fit.

"We don't have all year, Jasmine," Bryn said.

I stopped and faced him. "I'd be a lot faster if you'd back off." The words tumbled out despite how bad they sounded.

"Chill, babe," Veta said under her breath.

Bryn sat back on the stool, folding his bulky arms across his chest. "If you sound like shit, I'm gonna tell you. Better me than an entire audience booing you off the stage."

"You could try a little tact and patience," I said.

He shook his head, a smile brewing on his face. "That's not how

I operate. If you need buttering up, go cuddle with Felix after practice."

A hushed laugh came from Veta's direction, and Felix grinned despite his ears turning red. Sean smirked.

"I made a funny, Jasmine," Bryn continued. "Lighten up."

I forced a quick smile, trying to regain my cool. Jason always told me I was too sensitive, that half the time I defended myself against nothing.

"I'll try something with the EBow," I said. "Maybe you guys will like it better."

"At least you're willing to try other things," Felix said. "Teddy refused to change *anything*."

Sean clenched his jaw and turned away from the rest of us. "Count it off, Bryn."

The third attempt went smoother. Sean put more aggression behind the bass line, Felix added in a synth that sounded almost like an engine revving, and Veta sang her words with even more edge. The flutelike notes of the EBow rang over the top, mingling with Felix's pads to create a dreamy atmosphere behind the dark vocal melody. As much as I hated to admit it, the new guitar part worked better.

Apparently Bryn and Sean thought so too, because we finished the entire song.

Bryn roared, throwing his arms over his head. "That didn't suck. Thank you, God." He grinned. "And Jasmine."

Sean gave me a small nod. I guess that meant he approved.

The next song went pretty well. It called for a catchy, distorted riff—which Bryn liked right off the bat. I just hoped I could remember what I came up with; playing by the seat of my pants wasn't without its drawbacks. I'd lost count of how many melodies got away.

After we finished the second chorus of the last song, Veta

collapsed on the floor and dumped the rest of her water bottle over her head. "Okay, I'm done for the week."

My body felt like a vibrating bell. Playing guitar always got my adrenaline going, but jamming in a band gave me a buzz like nothing I'd felt before.

Bryn tore his shirt off and took an exaggerated whiff of his armpit. "Whew, I reek."

"Thanks for letting us know," Sean said, lifting his bass strap off his shoulders. His cheeks were flushed, and his hair jutted in various directions.

He caught my eye, and I pretended to be studying the wall behind him. Peeling green paint was fascinating.

"I'm going to make some ramen," Felix said. "Anyone want some?"

Everyone grumbled, but I practically jumped. "Me!" My stomach ached for nourishment.

Veta shot me a baffled look.

Hey, it was free food and I'd never had it before. My dad always kept us on a strict diet.

"I'm gonna hit the shower," Bryn said.

Felix followed Bryn out the door, and Sean attempted to pull Veta up. I carried my guitar over to the rack on the wall. Having a place to hang it made me feel good. I just hoped I'd fit in as well as my guitar did.

I attempted to watch an anime movie with Felix while we slurped salty noodles. A chick with gigantic eyeballs ran around fighting bad guys. Her boobs were about to burst out of her warrior outfit. Felix would go back and forth between a big smile and biting his lower lip. Sometimes he'd tap my shoulder and tell me that I just *had* to see this part.

Veta, Bryn, and Sean were upstairs shooting pool. Every now and then, Bryn hooted or Veta yelled, "Cheater!"

I checked my cell, frowning at the blank screen. No calls from Dad. He sounded so casual on the phone last night. Almost relieved.

The doorbell rang as I shoved the phone back into my pocket.

"Can you get that?" Felix asked, his eyes glued to the TV. "It's probably one of Bryn's special friends."

"Uh, sure." I got up slowly. It felt weird to be answering someone else's door.

My hand froze before I turned the brass lock. What would I say to this poor girl? "I'll probably never see you here again, but nice to meet you anyway"?

I ignored my thoughts and opened the door. A girl with a mess of dark hair stood on the porch, sizing me up. She had a striking resemblance to Clara Bow—if I ignored the tattoo sleeves, multiple facial piercings, and purple streaks through her hair. Definitely not a Mercedes-driving blonde.

"Who are you?" she asked. The voice fit her, bold and slightly raspy.

"Jasmine—I'm their new roommate."

Her brown eyes widened. "So you're the new Teddy, huh? That's interesting."

"Why?"

"The guys were pretty adamant about chicks not living here. Believe me, I tried." She looked at me expectantly. "You gonna let me in or what?"

Veta pushed herself in front of me. "What do you want, Amy?"

Her expression hardened. "I need to talk to Sean."

So this was Sean's ex. Not what I expected, but it made sense.

"Get the hell out of here," Veta said, keeping her voice low.

Amy rolled her eyes. "You're terrifying, Veta. Really."

I felt a warm hand on my back and realized it was Sean trying to get in front of me. I moved aside, and he nudged himself around Veta. "Let's talk outside," he told Amy.

Veta grabbed the sleeve of his T-shirt before he could squeeze himself out the door. "Don't fall for it."

He shrugged her off and followed Amy out into the yard. Veta slammed the door behind them.

"Calm down, babe," Felix said from the couch. "Maybe she wants to apologize."

Veta shook her head at him, a seething glint in her eyes. "Amy doesn't apologize." She grabbed my hand, dragging me into the kitchen.

"I guess you're still pretty pissed at her?" I asked.

Veta leaned against the island. "I know how Amy plays. It's why I didn't want Sean dating her in the first place. And did he listen? *No.*" She crinkled her nose in disgust. "If she had any heart at all, she'd leave him alone. Let him move on."

"Maybe she wants him back."

"Of course—until she gets bored again." Veta looked at the ceiling. "She promised me she wouldn't pull this with him."

I shoved my hands into my pockets and moved next to her. "Sean doesn't seem naive. He'll probably see through her crap."

Veta met my gaze, her eyes weary. "They were together for over a year—he was crazy about her. And he'd crushed on her for years before that."

A year seemed like an eternity to me; the longest relationship I'd had was about a week. Then again, making out in Eric Lamberti's stuffy Volvo during lunch break wasn't really a relationship. The guy liked onion rings and cigarettes—not exactly conducive to fresh-smelling breath.

Veta moved away from the island, a sadistic half smile breaking across her face. "I just had a really fun thought."

"Uh-oh." Somehow I knew this wouldn't be good.

She opened the fridge door and got out a carton of eggs. Then a tomato. Some wilted lettuce. A six-pack of beer.

"What are you doing?"

"Making a little smoothie." She winked.

"I highly doubt she'll drink that."

"Oh, I'm not planning on having her drink it." She dumped the lettuce and tomato into the blender. "Hey, Felix!"

"Yeah?" he called from the living room.

"Where's that fresh garlic you got the other day?"

There were a few seconds of silence followed by a very slow "Why?"

"I've got the munchies." She put her hand over her mouth, trying to cover a laugh.

Felix's heavy footsteps were his reply. "Veta . . ." He squinted at her as he made his way into the kitchen.

"What?" She gave him puppy dog eyes. "I'm starving."

Felix ran his hand through his fuzzy blue hair, eyeing the muck in the blender. "I'm *not* going to be part of this."

Veta used the edge of the counter to remove one of the beer caps. "Just give me the garlic."

"No way. Amy will kick my ass—that chick is scary."

"You're three times her size."

He frowned. "So?"

"Pussy," she muttered, pushing the GRIND button on the blender.

Felix rolled his heavily lined eyes at me. "Ask her what music she wants at her funeral." He padded back to the living room.

Veta waved me over. "Go up to your balcony and tell me where they are."

I really didn't want to be a part of this either, whatever it was. It would be childish and not my style. But I had my own curiosity about what was going on outside.

I ran upstairs to my room. Bryn's music and the clanging of weights sounded through the wall. Night vision wasn't one of my strong points—good thing there wasn't much to trip over. The balcony door made a creaking noise as I slid it back, but the hiss of the ocean probably covered it up. Or so I hoped.

I hunched over at the sound of Sean's voice and took slow steps toward the edge of the balcony. Then I squatted down, peering through the gap between the railing and the wall. Two shadowy figures stood inches apart in the yard below.

Sean moved away, turning his head toward the ocean. He mumbled something I couldn't hear.

"I know," Amy said. "But I told you—it's over."

"You just started a band together."

She exhaled. "He's the only good drummer I know, outside of Bryn."

"Good luck with that Dave guy, by the way. He's a real prize."

Amy tilted her head back. "So you *were* the other band. Dave said he turned someone down, but he wouldn't give us a name."

Sean let out a low chuckle. "And you believed him?"

"He's really good, even better than Teddy." Her voice sharpened. "What—are you saying you guys chose that little girl over him?"

My back stiffened at her comment. What was she—a year older than me, two at most?

"Yes. And she's my age."

"Oh yeah?" She pinched his arm. "Do you think she's cute?"

My breath caught in my throat.

"She's not my type."

A sagging feeling tugged at my chest, which irritated me. It wasn't like his words were a shock.

"You should probably know," Amy said. "We're playing before you guys at the Roach on Saturday."

"What?" Sean's voice went up a couple of notches.

"They were looking for a similar band to fill the slot, and they dug our demo."

"When the hell did you have time to put together a demo?"

She was silent for a few seconds. "I had a few songs worked out already—me and Teddy recorded them last week."

"The ones I helped you write?"

"You helped me work out a couple of bass lines, Sean."

"Fine, whatever."

"Pssst."

I jumped at the sound of the hiss behind me. Veta was crouched over, holding the blender. "You little spy. You were supposed to—"

I mouthed the words "shut up" and pointed down at Sean and Amy. She crept next to me and looked through the gap.

A big grin crossed her face when her eyes found Amy. "Perfect," she whispered. "She just needs to move a little closer."

I whispered, "Please don't tell me you're going to dump that on her head."

Her eyes had a devilish glint. "Maybe."

"Don't. Not from my balcony. Please."

She put her finger to her lips.

"Veta, seriously. This is stupid."

"Shh. I can't hear."

I peeked over again, tuning back into their conversation.

"I miss you," Amy said, moving closer.

Sean looked at his feet and said something I couldn't make out. Amy pressed into him, touching his cheek.

"Don't do it, Sean," Veta mumbled.

I'd seen enough.

I tried to stand up, but my legs had fallen asleep. They buckled, sending me right on my butt. A nice, loud *thump*.

Veta cussed under her breath. She hopped up and dumped the contents of the blender. There was the unmistakable sound of liquid hitting skin, followed by several four-letter words screamed in close succession.

It felt surreal, like I'd wake up any moment and laugh at the absurdity.

I pushed myself up and looked over the balcony. Most of Amy's head was covered in the brown goop, but Sean didn't appear to have much on him. At least Veta had fairly good aim.

Amy tried to storm into the house, but Sean wrapped his arms around her. "Let me go!" She elbowed him, getting sludge on his shirt.

Veta laughed. "Relax. It's just a little beer and eggs."

"That was real mature," Sean said, struggling to keep Amy in his grip.

"I didn't do anything—," I started to say

"Of course not." His voice was cynical.

Amy sneered at Veta. "Look at you, hiding up there like some scared little bitch. Why don't you come down here?"

"I've got nothing to say to you."

Amy shook her head. "You've got no right to judge me."

"Just leave, Amy," Veta said.

"I'll take you home." Sean tried to pull her toward the driveway.

Amy yanked her hand from his, still glaring at Veta. "See you at the Roach on Saturday." Her eyes flicked to me. "Can't wait to hear the new sound."

That's just what I needed. Sean's now-angry ex at my first live show, probably throwing broken bottles at our heads.

Sean kept his hand on the small of her back as they walked to his car. He grabbed a blanket from the back seat and tossed it at her. She wiped some sludge off her face before draping it over her head and getting in. They tore off in about thirty seconds.

"Feel better?" I asked. "We look like complete morons now."

Veta gazed at the ocean. The muted porch light made her face into a mask, shadowing her eyes. "She broke my brother's heart. I let her off easy."

"You seem pretty upset yourself."

"Amy was one of my oldest friends." Veta's voice sounded far-away, like her mind was elsewhere. "Messing with my brother is messing with me."

"Her band is playing before us on Saturday. I heard her tell Sean."

"With under a week to get songs together?" She shook her head. "I'd love to see them try." Her fingers shook as she lit a cigarette, letting a moment of silence pass. "I think I'm gonna head home."

"Okay."

"Sorry, bad energy. I need to clear my head." She faced me, flashing a tight smile. "See you at the shop tomorrow. Come in at noon. You look like you need the sleep."

With that, she turned on her heel and headed back into the house. I stayed on the balcony until she came out the front door, and I watched as her long legs carried her across the lawn. I'd known her for three days—seventy-two hours—and she'd pretty much saved my butt. But I still didn't know who the hell she was, what truly made her tick. Which meant I couldn't trust her. Not yet.

Chapter 10

Clanging pots and pans jolted me awake. Trails of golden light filtered through the dim balcony door, telling me it was way too early for that amount of noise. I squinted at my cell—almost 8 a.m.

Someone with heavy boots walked across the kitchen floor and headed up the stairs. Probably Sean. I really needed to talk to him and apologize.

I sat upright, breathing in the stench of citrus and garlic. How disgusting.

"Oh my God—what did he say?" Felix said, passing my door. The floor creaked as he moved around the loft. "Really?" He broke out in a laughing fit. Either that or he was having an asthma attack.

The door next to mine banged open. "Felix." Bryn's voice sounded demonic. "Shut up!" My room vibrated when he slammed his door shut again.

"Crap," Felix said in a loud whisper. "No, that was Bryn having a fit." His shadow passed under my door again. "I know—I wasn't even being that loud."

Fantastic. Why did I have a feeling this was a recurring event?

I pushed myself off the floor, my arms stiff and sore from

yesterday's yoga. Maybe I could catch Sean before he left for work. Although the thought of facing him made me want to hide in my room forever.

I tiptoed into the bathroom, which was muggy from a recent shower. The faint blueberry smell was blissful compared with Felix's breakfast downstairs. I pulled my hair into a ponytail and checked my face for anything embarrassing. A zit swelled above my right eyebrow. I dabbed a little concealer on it and reached for the mouthwash.

A few minutes later, I hovered outside Sean's room, clasping and unclasping my hands. Massive Attack's "Teardrop" wafted from his door, the ethereal vocals a soft whisper. A million opening lines swam through my head. *Good morning.* Too perky. *Sorry to disturb you.* Too formal. *Do you have a quick minute?* Too casual. *Hey, we need to talk.* I wasn't breaking up with the guy.

A door opened behind me, and I spun around to see a shirtless Bryn emerging from his room. He rubbed his eyes, narrowly missing the pool table.

"What's up?" he asked, his voice still hoarse.

"Not much." Just standing outside Sean's room like a freaky stalker.

"Did Felix wake you up too?"

"Uh, yeah. But it's cool." *Please keep walking, Bryn.*

"Are you waiting for the bathroom? 'Cause it looks open."

"I need to talk to Sean. I'm just waiting for a good time . . ."

Bryn walked past me and slammed his fist into Sean's door. "Hey!" The music inside cut off.

Sean answered, crinkling his brow at Bryn. He was already dressed for work—blue shirt with the sleeves rolled up, cargo pants, and boots. "What?"

"Jasmine said she's waiting for a good time. Does now work for you?" Bryn slapped Sean in the chest and sauntered off, chuckling his way down the stairs.

Sean's eyes widened at me, his lips parting. This was *not* the opening I had in mind.

"I, um, Bryn . . ." I paused, trying to find the words. "I can't believe he just did that."

He leaned against the doorjamb, looking away. "Yeah, well, that's Bryn."

I wiped my sweaty palms on my pajama bottoms. "I wanted to talk to you—about last night."

The side of his mouth quirked up, and I waited for him to unleash a mother lode of snark. But he opened his door wider and waved me in.

Sean's room smelled like vanilla, charcoal, and him. It made my stomach tickle. I noticed a drawing table covered in blackened paper. The sheet on top featured half a girl's face, but he flipped it over before I could make out more.

He plopped down on his neatly made bed, a gray comforter with matching pillows. There were two chairs, one in front of the drawing table and the other at his computer desk. The space was cramped but ordered. Even his drawing pencils lined up evenly. It was all very Sean, except the colorful posters of sea life on the walls.

"You're welcome to sit," Sean said, raising his eyes to mine. "My chairs don't bite—I promise."

I sat at his drawing table, folding my hands in my lap. The last thing I wanted to do was knock something over. "I didn't know you drew."

His pierced eyebrow rose. "Why would you?"

I shrugged, my mind searching for words. "Are you an art major?"

"Marine biology."

"Oh, cool."

"Yep."

The hum of his computer droned on.

So much for small talk. "I guess I'll get to the point. When Veta came out with the blender last night, I told her not to do it—"

"When she came out?" He leaned back on his hands. "So, what were you doing before that—stargazing?"

Heat crept up my neck. "She asked me to see where you guys went."

"But not to eavesdrop, right?" His upper lip curved up. "Because that would be creepy."

I looked down at my bare feet. "You're right. I'm sorry."

"Why is my personal business so interesting to you?"

"Why is mine? You think you know everything about me."

"Do I?"

"I didn't come in here to fight, okay? I know I should've warned you guys, but Veta's . . ." I trailed off, not knowing what to say next.

"Your friend?"

Was she? I'd never really had a girl friend, not a good one, anyway. "I guess, yeah."

We sat in silence, taking quick peeks at each other and then looking away. My hands gripped the armrests of the chair. Was he waiting for me to leave?

"I need to take off soon," he said finally. "Thanks for . . . apologizing."

"That reminds me . . ."

"Yeah?" He stood up and brushed past me, moving toward his computer desk.

"My car will be ready tomorrow, right?"

He nodded, shoving his iPod into his pocket.

Here goes nothing. "I was wondering if, um, I could pay you half tomorrow and then half when I get my paycheck next Friday."

He faced me, his expression anything but sympathetic. "Were you hoping an apology would get a favor out of me?"

Cunning people had plans. I just walked headfirst into things, like this situation. "No, God, no. I know how this looks, but I was going to say something at practice last night."

"It's simple. You want your car, you pay in full."

I stood up, backing toward his door. "Then I guess it'll be sitting at your shop until next Friday."

He shook his head. "We charge twenty-five bucks a day for storage."

"You can't do that."

"It was in the paperwork you filled out and signed. Try reading it next time." He walked toward me.

I put my hand on the knob. "I can't afford that—it'll take me even longer to pay it off."

"Why don't you ask your parents for the money?"

"I can't."

He moved closer, his eyes weary. "Why not?"

"Because I just can't. The why isn't your business."

"Yet you want a personal favor."

"Fine. I'll pay you, like, eighty percent tomorrow if you drop the storage fees."

"This isn't a negotiation—it's shop policy." A smile twitched at his lips. "Welcome to the real world, princess." He reached for the knob, but I shifted over, blocking it.

"What is your problem with me? And don't say it was something I did, because it started the moment you saw me on that curb."

"Yeah—where you snapped at me like I was a dog."

"I was having a bad day." My voice came out soft, defeated. I felt like a jerk. Then again, he'd implied that I was an idiot within a minute of meeting me.

"Are you going to move or do I have to pick you up?"

I rolled my eyes. "You wouldn't do that."

He was inches from me now, close enough for me to feel the heat off his skin. "Are you sure?"

My back pressed into the door, but I didn't look away. A sane person would probably move. "Do you need help at the shop—like someone to answer the phone? I'll work off the storage fees."

He tilted his head back, exhaling a soft laugh. "Now you've moved on to bartering? What's next—blackmail?"

My throat tightened—so much for not seeming desperate. "Forget it. I'll figure something out." I turned and left, hightailing it back to my room. There was no point in entertaining Sean any further.

An hour later, I was flipping my cell phone open and closed and tossing it between my hands—anything to avoid making the call. But when the options boiled down to calling Dad or robbing a bank, I needed to choose the slightly less evil one. Emphasis on the "slightly."

I took a deep breath and hit SEND. Part of me hoped I'd get his voice mail. Any excuse to postpone this.

"Hello?" he answered.

No such luck. "Hi, Dad."

"Jasmine . . ." The tapping of keys sounded in the background, meaning he was in his office.

"You never called me yesterday."

"Yeah, well . . ." He cleared his throat. "They overbooked my appointments and it was Brian Whitmore's birthday. You remember him, right? He and his wife came over for dinner a few times."

"A lot of people came over for dinner a few times." I leaned my head against the wall, lifting my eyes to the ceiling. Why was he acting like nothing had happened?

"What's going on?" His voice seemed cold—as if I were a patient asking for a prescription refill.

"I wanted to tell you that I'm okay—and I found a place." *Because you really seem to care.*

The typing stopped. "Where?"

"Santa Cruz." It pleasured me to say this. Dad hated Santa Cruz. He called it dingy and depressing.

"What's down there?" The clicking of his keyboard resumed, but I knew he was shaking his head.

"I joined a band."

"You could've done that at Stanford, or any college, for that matter."

Here we go. "The room I'm renting is really nice. I have a view of the ocean."

"Right. How are you paying rent?"

My hand tightened around the phone. "I got a job."

"Doing what?"

"I'm a cashier . . . at a souvenir shop."

He let out his dismissive chuckle. "I hope it's worth it."

"Do you even care that I'm okay?"

He waited a few seconds before answering. "Of course I do."

I swallowed the lump in my throat. "The car broke down . . ."

"Have you been changing the oil regularly?"

"It has nothing to do with that. Some part broke and leaked coolant everywhere. It's going to cost me eight hundred dollars."

"And?"

I gritted my teeth. "And I need a loan—like, three hundred or even two hundred would help. Just for food and bills. I get paid next Friday, so I can start paying you back then."

"I thought you had it all figured out."

"Dad, please—I told you that car had too many miles on it."

"Always so appreciative, aren't you?"

I rubbed my temple, wishing for a do-over. "I'm sorry. That came out wrong. Look, it'll be ready tomorrow. If I can't pay—"

"You want to rough it up in Santa Cruz—you go right ahead. But I told you, I'm not paying for it."

"It's a loan. I'd—"

"Tell me something, Jasmine. If you didn't need this money, would you have bothered calling at all?"

My throat tensed even more. "I'm not her. Don't talk to me like I'm her."

"Excuse me?"

"You heard me."

"Maybe your conscience is trying to tell you something," he said.

"At least I have one."

"Oh." He laughed. "That's right. I'm a heartless bastard. Haven't done a thing for you, have I?"

"Only when I do things your way."

"My way? You've talked about going to Stanford since you were five."

I closed my eyes, part of me just wanting to hang up. "Because that's what you wanted."

"Cut the dramatics, Jasmine. I'm not buying. You don't want to go to Stanford? Fine. Don't go. There are plenty of other colleges."

"Why can't you accept that I'm not ready?"

"I think you're scared. But you can't run from everything you're scared of."

"I'm not running. I'm right where I want to be."

"Really?" His voice rose. "You've been gone less than a week and you're already begging me for money."

"I'm not begging." My fingered hovered over the END CALL button.

"No? What do you call it, then?"

"God, why can't . . ." My fingers dug into the shaggy carpet. "Why can't you just—"

"Make it easy for you?"

"No . . . no! That's not what—"

"You want to have your cake and eat it too, Jasmine. I raised you better than that."

No, he raised me never to ask for anything. Even when I was tearing myself apart inside, trying to figure out why he wouldn't look at me after Mom left. He never told me it wasn't my fault. He never told me that I was okay. "So is this it, Dad?" I asked. "You're out of my life?"

"I never said that. I'm just not giving you money."

"You called me once, an hour after I left. And that was it. You couldn't be bothered after that. No, I had to call you—twice. I had to tell you I was okay. You didn't even ask."

"Because I don't know what to say! I've never been so disappointed in you—what you're doing, the way you're talking to me. It's pretty obvious you don't appreciate a damn thing I've done for you."

"I'm not doing this to hurt you. It's not about you!"

"You got that right. Because the only person you're thinking of is yourself. Wonder where you got that from?"

"I can't believe you just said that."

Silence lingered on his end, as if he were thinking of a way to cover his words. "Jasmine, I—"

"Go to hell." I snapped my phone shut and threw it down. It bounced off the carpet and into the wall.

My entire body was shaking. He'd never see me without seeing her. If I was running away from anything, it was being someone else for him. Someone he could forgive for being part of her.

By the time we closed the shop, Veta and I hadn't talked much. She kept giving me a look, like she wanted to say something, but a customer would come in or the phone would ring. And I was glad for the interruption, because I didn't want her to notice the storm going on inside of me.

I'd told my dad to go to hell. There was no going back from that.

"You were five bucks short," Veta said as we walked back to the house for band practice.

I dodged a wad of tourists aiming their cameras at the ocean. "Oh—sorry. I'll pay you back the difference."

"Don't worry," she said. "It happens."

I took a deep breath, letting the salty air coat my lungs. West Cliff Drive was full of life today. The sirenlike call of seagulls blended in with an array of noises—people on bikes, kids with ice cream–coated faces, couples stealing kisses, and dogs trotting alongside their owners, tails wagging. The knot of dread in my stomach made me feel like an alien.

"I guess you want to talk about last night?" Veta asked.

"Sure, if you want."

She did a double take. "Isn't that why you've been weird all day?"

"No—I figured you'd talk to me when you were ready."

Her arm bumped into mine. "Then what's up? Your energy is letting off some seriously bad juju today."

"If you say so."

She held her hands up. "Hey, I just call it like I see it."

I shrugged. "Just stressed about the show on Saturday, I guess."

"Ah." She kicked a rock down the sidewalk.

"The water looks pretty today. It's all glassy out there," I said, pointing to our left.

Veta didn't even look. "How come you never talk about your family?"

Heat rushed to my face. Tina had told her about my freak-out. "That was random."

"Can't help it." She made a churning motion with her hand. "Racing thoughts."

"There's not much to talk about. My dad's a cardiologist. Busy a lot."

"And you don't get along with him . . ."

My back stiffened. "I guess your mom told you about my reading?"

"Only because I asked. And she didn't say much—just that you closed up at the mention of your parents. Which wasn't a surprise. You did the same thing to me."

"Me and my dad want different things for my future. It's all pretty cliché. Whatever."

"What about your mom?"

"She left when I was five."

"That makes sense," she said softly.

"What does that mean?"

"Relax." She punched my arm. "You have a real masculine energy about you, like you're almost afraid of your femme side."

I rolled my eyes. "I don't bother to get all prettied up. Sue me."

"*Not* what I meant. It's your front, how you handle yourself." Her lips curved up in a playful smile. "Although, if I had a rack like yours, I'd flaunt it."

My arms pressed tighter into my sides. "It kills my back."

She shook her head, still grinning. "Don't be so afraid of your girl parts."

We headed up the driveway of the house, not a moment too soon.

When we walked into the studio, Bryn and Sean were bickering about something. Felix, as usual, hovered over his laptop, completely oblivious.

"Dude, she cheated on you," Bryn said. "Don't be such a sentimental douche."

"What's going on?" Veta grabbed her blue Gibson SG off the wall.

"None of your business," Sean said, tinkering with his E string.

She scrunched her nose. "You're still mad? Come on, she deserved it."

"Is that how it works in your newfound universe of peace and love?" Sean narrowed his eyes. "You can't punch anyone, but it's fine to douse them in salmonella."

Veta's grin faded, and she bent over to fiddle with her amp. "Don't be so dramatic."

I pulled my guitar off the rack and exchanged an uncomfortable smile with Felix.

"Move on, will ya? Amy isn't even that hot." Bryn tossed a drumstick at Sean's head.

Sean ducked, letting it crash into the wall. "Not to you. She has a brain."

I rammed a guitar cord into my amp input. Bryn apparently had ridiculous expectations. Amy wasn't supermodel material, but she was pretty in that rebel, pinup girl sort of way. I could only imagine what he thought of me.

"Natalie is bringing her friend by tonight," Bryn continued. "She'll make you forget all about Amy—trust me."

"Not interested," Sean muttered, his eyes meeting mine for a second.

A ping of gladness hit me, but it didn't stay long. He was too hung up on Amy to care about other girls.

"I think we should open with 'Encryption,'" Felix said. I admired his ability to block everyone out.

"Why?" Veta adjusted the height of her mic.

"I made an awesome intro for it last night." He rubbed his hands together like a mad scientist.

"Quit changing them up," Bryn said. "There was nothing wrong with the last one."

"Let's hear it," I said.

Felix didn't waste a second. A deep hum twirled around the room, followed by a drum loop that sounded as if it were playing underwater. A crisper beat kicked in with a staccato bass line, giving the song tension and drive. It made me want to forget everything else.

"Nice," Sean said, tapping his hand against his leg.

Felix cut the sound, giving Bryn a proud look.

"I love it," Veta said.

"Think you can nail it this time, Jasmine?" Bryn asked, his blue eyes playful.

I nodded and turned my back to him. It wasn't like I could forget my sloppy playing during the first tryout.

Felix started his intro again and Veta joined in with breathy vocals. "Lost in pictures. Writhing with conviction. You walk among the phantoms you breed." It sounded even more amazing than I remembered.

I turned up the reverb and chorus, recalling the arpeggio I'd come up with. There was no Dave watching my every move now. I could do it right this time.

By the chorus, I was in the zone, moving into a distorted riff. I glanced around the studio, taking pleasure in how focused everyone looked. Our timing was near perfect. Sweat formed on the back of my neck, but chills inched up my legs and arms. This was just what I needed.

I used a little EBow at the end, letting the hum of my guitar build into a slow scream. My chest relaxed and warmth tickled my stomach. If Bryn had issues with this, he needed his head checked.

I bit my lip and glanced in Sean's direction. He studied me like I was a complicated book. All intensity, no hint of a smile. Which could be good or bad. Some books were intoxicating, while others got thrown across the room.

"*That* was better than sex," Veta announced.

I tore my gaze from Sean's.

Bryn chuckled. "Speak for yourself."

Felix gave me a quick smile. "I love what you did."

"Thanks—I tried to mix it up some."

"Yeah, that was tight, Jasmine." Bryn twirled a stick in the air and caught it again. "Now we just need to work on your body."

"Excuse me?"

"What the hell, Bryn?" Veta asked.

He exhaled a short laugh and held his hands up. "I meant—you gotta loosen up. Try to look like you're having fun."

"But I was . . ."

"She's still learning the songs," Sean said.

"What shows did you say you played again?" Bryn asked.

None, I wanted to shout. But I could feel everyone's eyes on me, waiting, expecting. My throat tensed. "You never asked."

"I'm asking now."

Oh God, think. No big venues—that would be too unbelievable. Nothing too small, like a high school talent show. "Well, there's this yearly art festival in Woodside." True. "Me and Ja—um, my band played that a couple of times." Not so true. Bryn looked far from impressed. "And we jammed at this local club, Whiskey Hill, every Friday." The only *bands* that played there were retired executives doing cover songs.

"Never heard of it," Bryn said. "They get a decent crowd?"

"It's not bad."

"Maybe you can get us a gig there," Veta said, grinning at Sean. "I bet Aunt Linda and Jamie would *love* to see us."

Sean snorted a laugh. "Yeah, right."

"I'll look into it." Every lie made the lump in my throat bigger. If I could just rock this show, they'd stop questioning my ability.

We played a song called "Puppet Girl" next, a soft, childlike number. Felix's keyboard part made me shiver. It sounded like melting bells in a cathedral. My fingers slid up the guitar's neck, finding a nice middle ground between the synths and Sean's cloudy bass line.

"Your tongue is stale with lies and you're dead inside," Veta sang. "Puppet Girl. It's time to speak your mind."

My picking hand tensed at her seething tone. She rocked back and forth with the mic, her eyes shut and brow crinkled.

"Hold up!" Bryn said, ceasing his beat.

Veta shot him an annoyed glance and the rest of us stopped playing.

"Jasmine, are your feet glued to the floor or what?" he asked.

"Uh, no."

Bryn hopped off the stool and moved behind me, pushing my shoulders down. "Christ, you're like a Popsicle stick."

I twisted away, knocking my headstock into Felix's keyboard. "Sorry!"

Felix frowned and rubbed the corner like it was his own skin.

Veta giggled. "Shall we call you Grace?"

The room suddenly felt 120 degrees. A glance at Sean's smirk didn't help matters.

"What's your problem?" Bryn asked.

For a second, I saw my dad standing in Bryn's place. The disapproving gaze, the criticism. "I'm tired of you jumping all over me."

Bryn's mouth turned down at the corners. "You're going to bore the audience to death."

"What would you like me to do—stand on one leg?"

"That would be an improvement," he retorted.

"We all have to bring energy to the stage, babe," Veta said. "You'll stick out like a sore thumb if you just stare at your fret board."

"Sean doesn't move around much," I blurted out. Way to make him hate me even more.

"But he also looks completely at ease," Veta said. "His passion shows up in his face, his movements."

Felix chuckled. "Amy called it 'quiet sexy.'"

I peeked in Sean's direction. He was looking down at his bass, his cheeks more flushed than usual.

"I think you need to trust yourself a little more," Veta said. "Let that guard down."

My fingernails dug into the scratchy material of my jeans. "I'll work on it."

Bryn and Veta exchanged a significant look, but they let the issue drop. We got through the next couple of hours without further comment about my presence—or lack thereof. But Felix wasn't so lucky. Bryn called him out for a high-pitched pad he added to "Acceleration."

"It's like that damn mosquito tone," Bryn said.

Felix rolled his eyes. "You've got really sensitive ears for a drummer."

The argument might've continued, but the studio door banged open and two girls walked in. One was a leggy blonde wearing shredded jeans and a cami. The other was a petite but chesty brunette in a white babydoll dress and striped thigh-highs. Both had golden skin and rosy cheeks, like they'd been dancing in the sun all day.

"Ladies," Bryn said. "You made it."

"You could've mentioned you'd be in the studio, dork," the blonde said. "We were waiting out front for twenty minutes."

Bryn laughed it off and introduced the band. Their smiles lingered on Sean, but they barely acknowledged the rest of us.

"Your guitar is gorgeous," the dark-haired girl said to Sean. "It's, like, *emerald* green."

"It's a bass, but thanks," he muttered.

Veta batted her eyelashes at me and plastered a dumb grin on her face. I had to bite my tongue to avoid laughing.

"Let's play 'Encryption' for them," Bryn said. He nodded at the girls. "Tell us what you think."

"Sure!" they said almost in unison. The brunette whispered something in her friend's ear. They poked each other and laughed.

I kept my eyes shut through most of the song, but the presence of the girls burned into my skin. My fingers shook, causing me to miss a couple of notes. Still, they were probably too busy checking out Bryn and Sean to notice. The thought was enough to get me through the song without any major screwups.

The girls clapped and hooted when we finished. "You guys are awesome," the blonde said, making her way over to Bryn.

"How long have you been playing?" the brunette asked Sean.

The rest of us might as well have been invisible.

Veta wrinkled her nose at me as if she'd read my mind. "Looks like practice is over." She hung up her guitar and shook out her hair. "You ready to split, Felix? I need to eat and change first."

Felix held up a finger, staring intently at his laptop. "Just one sec."

I turned off my amp. "Where're you guys going?"

"Goth night at Club Mercury. It's eighteen and up, though," Veta said. "Unless you got a fake."

My stomach sank. "Yeah, right."

She shrugged and headed out. "Hurry up, Felix. I know where your keys are."

Felix took off after her, mumbling bye to me. I watched the door shut behind them. A night out at a club sounded a lot better than sitting in an empty room all night, left alone with today's events. At least I had the ocean.

The studio was filled with girlie laughter, mostly from Bryn's date, or whatever he considered her. She'd try to tickle him, and he'd grab her wrists. The other girl sat cross-legged on the floor, talking away to Sean. His eyes flicked to mine and his lips parted, almost like he wanted to say something, but I turned away and hung my guitar on the wall. I didn't want him to think I cared. Because I didn't.

"Hey, Jasmine?" Sean called as I reached for the door.

"Yeah?" I tried to sound casual, unconcerned.

"Are we still going to catch that movie?"

"What?"

His eyes widened expectantly. "You said it started at nine thirty, right?"

I glanced between him and the brunette. Her lips stretched into a tight smile. "Uh . . . yeah."

"Sorry, I gotta take off," Sean said to his admirer. "But it was nice to meet you."

Her face fell as she told us to have fun. I almost felt sorry for her. Sean waited for the door to shut behind us before he spoke.

"Thanks for the rescue."

"Do you usually need to be rescued from pretty girls?"

He shoved his hands into his pockets and shifted his weight. "Not really—no. I just didn't want to be rude."

"Since when?"

"It's easy with you. You've got an attitude."

"Oh, *I* do?"

His upper lip twitched. "I never said I didn't."

I bit back a smirk of my own. "So, now that I've saved you . . . how about cutting me a break on those storage fees?"

He tilted his face toward the sky, chuckling. "Nice try."

A squeal echoed from the studio, making us both jerk our heads toward the door.

"They're probably going to come out soon," I said.

"Are you hungry?"

"Sure." I wasn't, but I needed a distraction—even if that involved making ramen with Sean.

"Then let's get some dinner. I'll buy."

"Uh . . ." Was he asking me out? No, of course not. That would be insane. Maybe he was being sarcastic.

"We'd just be getting food—I promise. We're not getting deployed to the Middle East or anything."

"What?"

"You've got that deer-in-headlights look again."

"Oh, I didn't realize . . ." Warmth swelled in my cheeks. What was it about this guy that put me in moron mode?

He studied my face, his smile growing. "So, are you coming?"

"Yeah, sure. Why not?" Oh, only a million reasons, like the fact that we couldn't stand each other. But a little curiosity trumped common sense.

Sean's Camaro smelled like worn leather and the forest. One of those little air-freshener trees hung from his mirror.

He cracked the windows as we drove down West Cliff, letting the sea breeze comb our hair. I tapped my foot and tried to think of something interesting to say. All I could focus on was the growl of the engine and the way his fingers hovered over the gearshift. Maybe he was itching to go faster.

"What are you in the mood for?" He kept his eyes straight ahead and drummed the steering wheel to the harsh beat churning from his speakers.

"Anything edible. I'm not that picky."

"Do you like sushi?"

Leave it to Sean to pick the one thing I never wanted to try. "I don't consider raw fish edible."

"They've got veggie sushi."

"Didn't know there was such a thing."

He did a double take. "Did you grow up in a cave?"

"Close enough." Dad always had a specific list of what the nannies and housekeepers were allowed to cook. It was basically the American Heart Association diet, without an ounce of creativity or culture.

"We can go somewhere else if you want." His arm brushed my thigh as he shifted. "Sorry."

"It's fine." I scooted closer to the door. "Sushi's fine."

This pleased him enough to turn up the music and not say a word until we got to the restaurant. And then he only spoke to the hostess, who seemed to know him. She studied me curiously, but Sean didn't bother introducing us. Nice.

The restaurant was small but cozy. Paintings of surfboards, fish, and oceanic sunsets made it look more like a surf shop than a sushi place.

I scanned the list of foreign items on the menu. The rolls had cutesy names and baffling ingredients I couldn't pronounce. None of it sounded appetizing.

"Sorry I didn't introduce you back there," Sean said. "She's a nosy friend of Amy's. I thought she was off tonight."

I shut the menu, my stomach tightening. "You should at least tell her who I am."

"Why?"

"Well, I'm a girl . . ."

He raised an eyebrow. "Yeah? Congratulations."

"I mean, what if she thinks that you're—we're on a date or something."

He scanned the menu with a small grin. "Or something."

"Because from an outside perspective, it might look like we're on one." *Shut up, Jasmine. Don't dig yourself a hole.* "And you probably don't want her to think that. She might tell Amy."

Sean looked up, crinkling his brow. "Or we could just be hanging out."

I plopped the cloth napkin in my lap, wishing I could drape it over my head. "So, um, what's good here?"

His confused expression remained. "Why do you care about Amy?"

"I think there's been enough drama already, don't you?"

"Get used to it. My sister is the biggest drama queen I know."

"She was just trying to look out for you, I think."

He leaned back in his chair. "She doesn't give me enough credit. I know Amy better than she does."

"Don't be so sure." My dad certainly learned the hard way, and he never got over it.

"Do you know something I don't?"

I took a long sip of water, savoring the coolness on my throat.

Sean was the last person I wanted to share my life story with. "Sometimes you only see what you want to—and then the truth breaks you. It's better to expect the unexpected."

His eyes lingered on mine. "Are we still talking about me and Amy?"

I looked away. "I'm speaking in general."

"Right," he said softly, turning his attention to the menu. "I don't know why I'm looking at this. I always order the same thing."

I shrugged. "I do that too."

His lips curved up into another one of those subtle smiles. They were starting to grow on me. "I usually get the Pacific Fire rolls. Best thing on the menu—if you can handle spicy."

"I think I can manage."

He squinted at me. "We'll see."

Unfortunately, I lost that challenge after the first bite had me flailing for my glass of water.

He pushed the avocado-and-cucumber rolls toward me. "Those will go down a little easier."

"I'm fine," I squeaked. It hurt to inhale.

"Your little tough act doesn't work on me." He plopped another spicy roll in his mouth like it was nothing.

"You could've warned me about the green stuff."

He swallowed and laughed. "It's an acquired taste."

"Yeah, and it looks really good on your chin too."

His hand quickly swiped under his mouth. "Did I get it?"

I dabbed my finger in the wasabi and reached over the table. "It's right . . . here." I spread a little green paste below his lower lip.

"Real slick, Jasmine." He wrinkled his nose and wiped it away with his napkin. "Damn, that burns."

"Wuss."

"Says the princess."

"Are you ever going to stop calling me that?"

A playful gleam hit his eyes. "Hey, if the shoe fits . . ."

I attempted to give him my best evil look but ended up laughing about two seconds in. We were actually having a good time. Me and Sean. How was that possible? Maybe someone spiked the water.

Chapter 11

Tonight was the night. In just a few hours I'd be onstage, proving myself to an audience of strangers. But more important, I'd be showing the band that they'd made the right choice. I wanted to make them proud to call me the new guitarist of C-Side.

But I was falling apart.

I stood on the balcony, watching the sky turn into rainbow sherbet, when a scruffy black van pulled into the driveway and Sean eased his Camaro next to the curb. Bryn's uncle let the band borrow the van for gigs—if they could get it started. Apparently, Sean had worked his magic.

Bryn and Veta hopped out of the van and opened the rear doors before heading toward the studio. Sean jogged after them. They weren't wasting any time.

I called Jason with a shaky hand, wishing he could be that one friendly face in the crowd. It didn't seem right to do my first show without him.

"Are you freaking out?" he answered. He'd told me to call him beforehand if I really panicked.

"I can't do this," I whispered. "I need to tell them I—"

"Yes, you can. Even if you mess up, you can come up with impromptu stuff. It's what you're best at."

I paced back and forth, trying to breathe. "Not with an audience watching me."

"Picture them naked."

"I'll be the one feeling naked."

"Okay, then pretend your whole band is naked."

I crinkled my nose. "No!"

"How about just the bassist?"

"Would you stop bringing him up?"

"Sure. When you do." I could *hear* the Cheshire grin on Jason's face.

"Um, when was the last time?"

"Yesterday. You were, like—God, he's going to start charging me storage fees on Monday. He's such a jerk. But, oh—he made the best salsa ever. It was sooo good. I nearly had an orgasm eating it."

A laugh escaped my lips. "Shut up! I just said I liked it."

"Uh-huh."

"Whatever, it's not like that."

"Like what?" Jason put on his innocent voice.

Sean walked back out, carrying his amp. I put my hand over my face. "I hate you."

"There's the feisty bitch I know and love. Feel better?"

"A little."

Bryn appeared with his bass drum, tilting his head up at me. "Get down here, Jasmine! And drag Felix out of the bathroom on your way out."

I groaned into the phone. "I have to get going."

"Once you get lost in the music, you'll rock it. I know you will. Call me after, 'kay?"

"I will—if I'm still in one piece."

"Oh, and one more thing . . ." His voice got playful again.

"What?"

"Take a pic of the bassist with your phone cam and send it to me. I'm dying to see this guy."

I rolled my eyes. "Yeah, I'll get right on that. Talk to you later."

"Good luck!"

As soon as I hung up, the nausea came back. A second-grade talent show I'd participated in came to mind. I thought it would be a fun idea to sing "Cornflake Girl" by Tori Amos. Only it turned out I didn't know the lyrics as well as I thought I did. And I hadn't quite learned the concept of projection. The teacher ended up asking me if I wanted to lip sync.

Let's just say "Cornflake Girl" remained my nickname throughout the course of my elementary school career—and nobody meant it as a compliment.

I knocked on the bathroom door, and Felix answered in nothing but a blue towel. A very small blue towel. And as adorable as Felix was, I preferred him with clothes on.

"Um, they're loading the van. Bryn wants you to come down."

"Already? Christ, he's so type A." He studied me for a second. "Can I do your hair for the show?"

I hated when people messed with my hair, but I didn't want to seem rude. "Like, how? What would you do?"

Footsteps bounded up the stairs and Bryn appeared in the loft, slightly out of breath. He scrunched up his face at Felix. "Dude, close the door. Nobody wants to see that."

Felix brushed his blue 'fro, like he wasn't even bothered. "At least I have a towel on. Can't say you've given us the same courtesy."

Bryn shook his head. "That's what happens when you open my door without knocking."

I'd heard about enough of this. "I'm going downstairs."

After the van was finally loaded, the five of us sat on the front lawn, letting the ocean breeze cool our damp skin. The guys and I devoured two pizzas, while Veta slurped spaghetti. Singing and cheese didn't mix, apparently.

Veta and Felix debated what to wear.

"Whatever you decide, make the getting-ready part quick," Bryn said, tossing the crust of his fifth slice. "We should be there before nine."

"Then we better get started on Jasmine," Veta said, grinning at me.

"I'm fine like this." I motioned to my gray fairy tee and worn jeans.

Bryn crinkled his brow. "Are you kidding?"

"Um, no."

"Borrow one of Veta's schoolgirl skirts," he said. "That'd be hot."

I rolled my eyes. "We're not the same size."

"It's okay," Veta said. "I brought something special for Goldilocks. It's simple and tasteful—but sassy. Like her." She winked at me.

I stared down at my half-eaten slice of veggie pizza. My appetite was quickly diminishing. "I'd like to wear my own clothes."

"Babe, I'm not letting you go onstage dressed like Zoe," Veta said. "In fact, I think she owns that shirt."

Felix and Bryn chuckled.

"Let her wear what she wants," Sean said. "It's not a big deal."

I gave him a grateful smile.

"Actually, it is," Bryn said. "People dug Teddy. They're pretty skeptical about you, Jasmine. No offense."

My heart was starting to pound. "What are you getting at?"

"Like it or not," he continued, "people expect a certain something from us. You've already changed up our sound—which, hey, it works. Most of the time. But Teddy could dance circles around you in the performance area. It wouldn't hurt to wear something a little darker—sexier. Look like you're, you know, part of the band."

"Bryn . . ." Veta's voice sounded like a warning.

"When did we become sellouts?" Sean asked.

Bryn shrugged. "Hey, we need to keep the fans who *didn't* ditch us when you guys kicked Teddy out. It's a shitty reality, but it's reality all the same."

"Let me get this straight," I said. "You want me to dress like a piece of ass so people will forgive me for not being Teddy?"

Bryn sneered. "No. When the hell did I say that? I want people to see you and go, 'Check out their new guitarist—she's pretty bad-ass.' Not, 'What's up with their new guitarist? Is she twelve?'"

I swallowed the ache in my throat. He'd take Teddy back in a heartbeat if he could. "You were the one who made fun of me to Dave, weren't you? What was it you called me—a band geek doing her first talent show?"

"You said that?" Felix asked, his dark eyes wide.

"We were joking around," Bryn answered, looking away. "It didn't mean anything . . ."

"How can you—," I began.

Bryn stood, holding his hands up. "Jasmine, I'm sorry I offended you. I really am. You can slug me later. But we don't have time for this bullshit right now. Let's just get ready." He walked off, taking the pepperoni pizza box with him.

"He always has his panties in a bunch before shows," Veta said, putting her hand over mine. "Try not to take it too personally."

"What's his excuse the other ninety-five percent of the time?" I asked.

Nobody had an answer.

I let Veta and Felix attack me. They promised not to make me look slutty, and I didn't want to disappoint them. Especially when there was a good chance I'd blow tonight.

Now I was riding shotgun in Sean's Camaro, not feeling at all like myself. Veta meant well. She brought a wine-colored babydoll dress—one of the first she'd made. It was intended for her mom, but it never fit right. The dress had a black lace hem that fell above my knees, puff sleeves, and a not-too-low-cut neckline. Adorable, really. On someone else.

I also managed to stuff my feet into a pair of her mom's old knee-high boots. They were a half size too small, but Veta said they'd stretch. Right.

Then there was my hair. Felix curled it into golden ringlets that fell down my back. Which would be cute . . . on a doll. And my makeup. Veta called it cat eyes, but don't get me started on that.

Felix sat in the back seat, fretting over whether his crush, Samantha, would be at the show. Sean and I would just nod or tell him not to worry when we could get a word in.

"I still can't believe she kissed Rick the Dick. I hate that guy," Felix said. He yanked on a lock of my hair. "Doesn't Jasmine look gorgeous?"

Sean gave me a sidelong glance, a smile flickering at his lips. "She looks like a goth Goldilocks."

I rolled my eyes. "My thoughts exactly."

We stopped at a red light, and Sean's fingertips brushed my forearm. "Don't worry. You look cute."

Heat crawled up my neck and into my face. I was glad my hair hid most of it. "Thanks—so do you." That sounded kind of flirty. "I mean, I like your hat. It's very cute . . . nice."

He laughed and shifted into first. "Okay, thanks?"

Sean looked downright sexy in a gray fedora and a black button-down shirt with the sleeves rolled up. I liked the simplicity. His appearance wasn't screaming for attention or trying to mask anything. He was just himself . . . with a little flair.

Another light turned red ahead of us, and Bryn drove the black van right through it. He looked like he was going about fifty down Mission, a street populated with old houses, small businesses, and restaurants. It was part of Highway 1, the scenic route that snaked along the California coast.

Felix chuckled. "I bet Veta is ripping him a new one right now."

"What's his problem?" I asked. "We're not late."

"Everything involving the band is life or death for him," Sean said.

"C-Side is his life," Felix chimed in. "Well, that and surfing." He scooted forward and leaned toward my ear. "Which he kinda sucks at."

"He doesn't go to school or anything?"

"He's enrolled at UCSC," Sean said. "But he doesn't necessarily go."

"I know he comes off as superharsh, but he doesn't hate you or anything," Felix said. "He's just got no filter. If you met his uncle, you'd understand."

"Did his uncle raise him or something?"

"His uncle took custody of him and his little brother, because his mom . . ." Felix lowered his voice as if Bryn could somehow hear him. "She's kind of a druggie."

"Felix . . ." Sean glared at him in the mirror.

I nodded, not knowing how to respond. It wasn't easy having a parent who people like Felix whispered about in hushed voices.

"Anyway, his uncle is worth millions—he was some hotshot back in the dot-com days," Felix rambled on. "He's pretty much like a big kid, though. Buys them lots of stuff, but he doesn't really do the dad thing."

"What are your parents like?" I asked, turning to face Felix. "Do they live around here?"

A sheepish grin crossed his pale face. He'd done himself up like a geisha tonight, red and black smudged around his eyes and butterfly clips in his hair. "They live in Placerville—that's where I grew up. It's this old gold rush town on the way to Lake Tahoe."

"Old Hangtown." I grinned. "I'm familiar."

"Ha—yeah, that *never* gets old. Anyway, Dad is cool—pretty mellow. But my mom is superconservative and a huge control freak. It's so annoying."

"Have you noticed that Felix spends half the day on his cell?" Sean asked.

"Yeah."

"It's his mom—she calls him about forty times a day."

Felix punched the back of Sean's seat. "She does not!"

We pulled behind a gray building that looked like it should've been condemned. The back featured graffiti-drawn stick figures and a broken window. Veta and Bryn were already unloading the van.

"This is the Roach?" I asked.

Sean turned off the ignition. "What'd you expect—the Ritz?"

"Well, no but—"

"Ooh! Open the door!" Felix shoved my seat forward and squeezed out of the car, mumbling an apology. He ran up to a short blond girl who was smoking near the back entrance.

"That would be Samantha," Sean said.

"Ah." I scanned the few people standing around. Dark clothing and bold hair. Tattooed hands bringing cigarettes to pierced lips. A couple of them looked older. A lot older.

Nothing I could do would impress these people. They'd see me just like the band saw me—a privileged little girl with no scars to show. A high school band geek.

"Hey." Sean touched my shoulder. "You okay?"

I forced a smile. "Fine."

His eyes reminded me of his sister's right then, that forklifting-information-from-my-head look. "You sure?"

"Yeah, it's just my first show. With you guys, I mean. New crowd."

"Don't worry about Bryn, okay? It's not you he's pissed at."

I looked down at my clasped hands. "He wanted Dave, didn't he?"

"It doesn't matter. You're the person we decided on."

I thought I could do this. I really did. But my chest was getting tighter by the second. "We should help them unload." I climbed out and didn't look back.

We joined the crowd to watch Newton's Whore perform after assembling our equipment backstage. Boots and worn sneakers took up almost every inch of the sticky black floor, and Rob Zombie's "Superbeast" growled from the speakers. The air reeked of sweat, booze, and sly drags of cigarettes and pipes. I caught myself holding my breath.

Bryn and Veta charmed a group of pancake-faced girls in front of me. Their makeup glowed under the blue lights. Felix huddled over Samantha, whispering in her ear. They both giggled a lot.

"Hey, deer in headlights," Sean said, his warm breath tickling my neck.

I shook my head. "You guys and your nicknames."

His lips stretched into a small grin, and he leaned toward me again. "It's a family thing. We can't help ourselves."

A guy with a bleached Mohawk squeezed between us, his elbow catching me in the ribs.

"Watch it," Sean said.

The guy turned, a cruel smile on his broad face. "Or what, Ramirez? You gonna cry to the bouncer and have me kicked out?" He laughed and shoved his way to the front.

Sean folded his arms, his jaw tensing.

"Nice guy," I said.

"That's Nate—one of Teddy's friends," he muttered.

As if on cue, several people up front started chanting for Teddy to get onstage. One would think he was the only person in that band.

I stood on my toes and brought my mouth to Sean's ear. "This can't be easy for you."

He shrugged, but his eyes never left the stage. "I'll live."

Amy strutted out, carrying a blue Music Man bass. She'd paired a red and black tulle skirt with a tactical vest, and matching dread extensions protruded from her head like pigtails. I wasn't sure if it was her first time playing live, but she looked like Xena up there— menacing and gorgeous.

A lanky guy gave us a wolfish grin before getting behind the drums. The infamous Teddy, with long, dyed-black hair and a dragon tattoo above his left pec. It was obvious originality was the last thing on his mind.

Dave was all prettied up in a torn fishnet shirt and those tall boots with a million buckles. He gripped his pointy black guitar, testing his pedals. Not that he used much variety.

The Felix of the band hid behind two keyboards and a laptop. I couldn't tell if this person was male or female, but I envied them. At least nobody could see if there was fear in their eyes.

"What's up?" Amy's voice boomed out to us.

The crowd answered with hoots, whistles, and a remark about her tits. A comment like that probably would've sent me running off the stage, but Amy grinned wider.

"Thanks, they're real," she said.

"Can I check?" the annoying pervert asked.

Amy's pierced eyebrows rose. "Only if you want my boot up your ass." She'd have no problems overcoming the scrawny guy, either; her tattoo sleeves didn't hide the sinewy muscles in her arms.

I glanced at Sean, but his expression hadn't changed. He just stared straight ahead, like he was trying to see through her.

A dirty synth and a kick drum started up, vibrating the floor and every part of my body.

"We're the newly birthed Newton's Whore," Amy's husky voice echoed. "And this first song is 'Contagious.'"

Teddy launched into a full beat, and Amy stomped her boot in rhythm, her fingers plucking the E and A strings. The bass line was fast and sporadic, almost punklike. Dave followed with quick but controlled power chords.

Amy's staccato vocals fell somewhere between singing and spoken word. Her eyes flirted with the audience, and her upper body moved with the grace of a snake. "Strip down. Overload me with your sensory infection. Strip down. Filter yourself through me."

Amy oozed sensuality, much like Veta. But she lacked sincerity. Her performance felt deliberate, a couple of notches away from being over-the-top.

Teddy resembled a rabid animal behind the drums. The audience ate it up. People were starting to thrust their arms in the air and push forward.

Dave practically did the splits, headbanging like some '80s butt rocker. All I could see of the keyboardist was the top of his/her bobbing head.

Hell broke loose during the chorus. Amy's vocals turned feral as she writhed back and forth with her bass. "All you are is a twisted disease. Contagious, methodic. You fuck me up. You knock me down. You spread yourself around, and then you do it again."

Despite the pumping fists in front of me, I wasn't fooled. Amy had a healthy dose of angst and a catchy bass line. She knew how to suck people in and fire them up. But she didn't know how to sink her teeth into them. Not like Veta did.

Dave jumped around the stage now, chugging his guitar in any position he could muster. He came up behind Amy and she slumped against him, tilting her head toward the ceiling. A guttural roar escaped her throat.

Teddy's black hair fell across his sweaty face, his arms stuck on fast-forward. Every movement was jerky and furious—as if he were inhaling Amy's rage.

A warm body shoved me forward, sending my forehead into a girl's back. She shot me an annoyed look and shouted something I couldn't make out.

Arms encircled my waist, gripping me harder than necessary. "Sorry, baby!" a male voice hollered into my ear. "You all right?" His breath stank of vodka and smoke.

I turned my head to find a set of unfamiliar eyes. They belonged to a guy not much taller than me but at least twice as wide.

I ripped myself out of his grasp and moved away.

Sean wedged himself between us. People were jumping and slamming into him. A flailing arm knocked his fedora off, but he managed to catch it.

"There's a pit forming." Sean's lips brushed my ear as he spoke. "Did you want to be in it?"

"No!"

Newton's Whore finished "Contagious," and the crowd roared around us.

"Didn't think so." He put his hat back on, grinning.

"Don't start. It has nothing to do with being a princess."

"So you admit to being one?" Even though his voice was low and gentle, it was all I could hear.

I turned back around, watching Amy tune up for the next song. "No, but I know that's what you're thinking."

"You've got no idea what I'm thinking."

The heat thickened around me, making my throat tense. I closed my eyes. "I want to enjoy the music, not give and receive black eyes."

"Don't worry. I got your back."

"I'm fine, thanks," I said. But I didn't want him to move.

Amy let out a brutal scream, drowning out anything Sean might have said. She danced with her blue bass, dark strands of hair sticking to her cheeks. The rest of the band joined in at breakneck speed.

I could feel Sean taking blows from behind. He'd grab my shoulders to steady himself and then drop his hands. I kept wishing he'd hold on.

His mouth brushed against my ear again. "Move up and to the left a little."

I did as he said, slipping into a tiny gap between bodies. Sean's warmth bled through my clothes, and my head rested against his chest.

His fingers ran over the curve of my shoulder, tangling with one of my curls. "Sorry." He brushed it aside and stroked my upper arm. "You okay here?"

I nodded, experiencing a rather embarrassing shiver. Being so close to him was like the buzz I got from a great song. Every inch of me felt alive.

Amy's fingers stabbed at her bass strings. "You're in my head. You're in my bed. You fill me with dread. You wish I was dead." She scanned the audience, pausing on Sean. The guitar and bass dropped out, leaving a soft beat and a pad that sounded like a busted piano. Amy's voice fell into a whisper. "I want to forget . . . just let me forget." She hunched closer to the mic. "The taste of your lips, your breath on my skin, how we'd drive for hours and laugh at the world . . ."

Sean's chest stiffened. Amy's dark eyes narrowed at us before she turned away and screeched out the chorus.

She was going to make my first show hell . . . I could feel it.

My arms shook as I attempted to lift my Diezel amp head. One slip and this beast would crush my toes. Bryn had helped me unload it, but he and Sean were hustling to get set up onstage. Felix kept running to the bathroom every five minutes with his nervous bladder, and Veta just wandered off with some tall brunette, leaving the three of us to do the bulk of the work.

Newton's Whore took their sweet time packing up. Teddy kept stopping to talk to people in the audience, and Amy got involved in a ten-minute conversation with the sound guy. Bryn said they were doing it to screw us out of time.

Amy packed up her bass a few feet away. She flipped her hair back, revealing two Spanish words tattooed on the side of her neck. The thought of needles anywhere in that region gave me chills.

"It's Jasmine, right?" she asked.

"Yeah." I lowered my amp head back down, but I let go a little too fast. It thudded onto the cement floor.

She snorted a laugh, standing up. "Problems?"

I shrugged, hoping she'd keep walking. But she stopped in front of me and opened her mouth to speak.

"I'm sorry about what Veta did," I cut her off. "It wasn't my idea."

Amy's eyes widened. "Okaaay."

"I just wanted you to know that." If only I could find a hole to crawl in right about now.

Her burgundy lips quirked up. "How'd you score the Diezel?"

"I bought it."

"No shit?" Her smirk grew. "I thought maybe you boosted it."

"I had a savings—"

"That must've been one hell of a piggy bank."

"It wasn't a—" I rolled my eyes. "Whatever."

"Where're you from?"

I tried to shove my hands into my pockets, only there were none. Stupid dresses. "Over the hill."

She gave me a once-over. "Saratoga?"

Here we go again. Saratoga was considered one of the richer areas of the South Bay. "Does it matter?"

She exhaled a laugh and shook her head. "Dave said you were an uptight bitch."

"He—what?"

Sean came backstage, shooting us a weary look. Amy gave him a little finger wave before turning and making her way outside.

Sean grabbed a cable and draped it around his arm. "Ignore her. She's just trying to get under your skin."

"Why? I haven't done anything to her." I picked up my amp head again, hunching over with the weight.

Sean grabbed the other end, making my arms grateful. "Because you're easy."

"I am not." We shuffled onto the stage, which overlooked at least a hundred faces. My heart thudded.

"You need a thicker skin or you're going to find yourself pissed off a lot," Sean said as we plopped my Diezel on top of a speaker cabinet.

"Nobody wastes time being polite around here, do they?" I gave him a significant look.

"Come on, Jasmine. Does this look like a debutante ball?"

I folded my arms. "I wouldn't know. I've never been to one."

Bryn came up to us, his forehead moist with sweat. "Where the hell is Veta?"

"She went out back with some girl," I said.

Bryn cussed and stormed off, more than likely in search of her. Felix hunched over his keyboard, biting his nails.

"Everything okay?" I asked Felix.

"It will be," he said, his expression not mirroring his words.

Dave, Teddy, and the guy with the bleached Mohawk huddled together in front of the stage. Dave's eyes flicked to me, and he said something that made the others laugh.

I turned and shuffled backstage, my breath quickening. The pizza churned in my stomach, just as it had the night we went on the roller coaster. *Get it together. You can handle this. You have to handle this.*

A hand touched my shoulder. "Hey," Sean said.

I spun around and made eye contact, but no words came out. He couldn't see me like this. I needed to get to a bathroom, run outside—do something other than stand here like a trembling idiot.

His green eyes combed my face, and his half smile faded. "Sometimes I meditate before a show. It helps."

"You don't seem like the type."

He looked at his feet, shrugging. "My mom got me into the habit. I prefer running, but that's not always possible."

"I thought the crowd would be small."

"It is."

Was he kidding? "You said thirty people."

He took off his fedora, running his hands through his long bangs. "'Cause sometimes it seems that way. But the crowd is bigger than usual tonight. I know Bryn has been really milking the Luna's Temptation thing online."

"Oh."

His brow crinkled. "More people is usually a good thing, Jasmine."

Oh, yeah. More people to see me have a meltdown or pass out. "I need to finish setting up."

Bryn sprinted past us, but he didn't say anything. I hoped that meant he'd found Veta.

"Hang on a sec." Sean cupped my face and slid his thumb along my cheekbone.

My body tensed. "What are—"

Veta came bursting through the back entrance, stopping me mid-sentence. She raised her eyebrows at us.

"Relax." Sean dropped his hand. "Your eyeliner was running." He put his fedora back on and walked off.

I rubbed my cheek with the back of my hand.

Veta ran up to me and put her hand on my arm. Her cheeks were flushed, but *her* makeup was perfect. "I just hooked up with the sexiest girl, oh my God." Her head tilted back. "My legs are still shaking."

I held my hand up. "Wait, you did this just now?"

She punched my arm and giggled. "All we did was make out, but her lips—holy crap. I think I'll be high off them for hours."

"Where'd you go?"

"The van—there's a mirror in there, by the way. If you need it." She must have seen something on my face, because she grinned wide. "But you don't."

Bryn jogged backstage, his eyes like blue flames. "We've got five minutes!"

Veta grabbed her Gibson and followed him. "Take some breaths, Bryn. You look like you're going into labor."

He flipped her off.

I lifted up my hair, fanning the back of my neck. Five more minutes. I had a million things left to check, but I couldn't even think of where to start.

Chapter 12

The guys hustled onto the stage, but I froze. Tina's boots ate into my baby toes and the balls of my feet.

Veta linked her arm with mine, leaning toward my ear. "You ready?"

I was supposed to go out there and know what I was doing. But I couldn't even remember my opening guitar part for "Encryption." Not to mention, the audience hated me by default. I wasn't their precious Teddy.

Felix's phased drum loop started up, followed by a rumbling bass synth.

Veta's eyebrows pinched together. "Babe?"

I squeezed my eyes shut, my throat locking up. "I—I can't . . ."

"Come on, girl. We gotta get out there." Veta yanked me forward, but I tore myself from her grasp.

"No—I'm . . ." My head felt airy, and the floor moved like a ship on rocky seas. "I can't remember my part—my opening."

"Jasmine, look at me."

I focused on her wide hazel eyes. Felix's loop kept repeating. It sounded like bubbles underwater, racing toward the surface.

"It will come back to you," she said. "You just need to get out there and start playing. You'll be fine."

I shook my head—no, no, no. I couldn't do this to them. I couldn't do this to myself. But my knees felt like jelly.

"You've played live before and nailed it, right?" Veta continued. "This won't be any different."

"I lied." The words poured from my mouth. I couldn't keep them in anymore. "I've never done a show in my life." There was this feeling of watching myself from the outside. I couldn't actually be spilling my guts in a quavering voice, like some lost little girl. I'd never be that pathetic.

Veta's mouth opened, and her eyes widened. "Please tell me you're kidding."

Bryn and Sean appeared in front of us, both of them looking frantic. Felix's loop cut off.

"What the fuck is going on?" Bryn's cheeks were getting redder by the second.

"She's freaking out," Veta said, her voice tense. She moved back from me, folding her arms.

"I'm sorry. I thought I'd be okay. I thought . . ." There was that whimpering voice again. This wasn't me. I was stronger than this.

"She lied," Veta said. "This is her first show. Ever."

Bryn ran his hands through his dreads. His glare moved from me to her. "I told you we shouldn't have—"

"Bryn," Sean said. "Don't make it worse, man." He was the only one of the three who didn't look angry. His face was almost emotionless, but I knew he expected this from the start.

"What's the holdup?" a guy from the audience hollered.

Bryn moved toward me, his jaw clenching. "Get out there and suck it up, Jasmine. You owe us that much."

"I know." *Just give me five more minutes. A little more time, that's all I need.*

Bryn shook his head at Veta and me, probably wishing he could slug us both. But Veta didn't deserve his anger.

"It's not her fault," I told him.

He shot me another disgusted look before following Sean out.

"I could've helped. If you'd trusted me." Veta backed toward the stage. "But now all I can tell you is—don't stop. I don't care how bad you screw up—just keep going." With that, she disappeared around the corner.

I glanced at the exit. It would be so easy to walk out that door. Never have to face these people again. But where would I go? Back to Dad? Right. I knew him. He'd say "I told you so" and probably slam the door in my face out of pride. There was always the Greyhound station, a one-way ticket to another city. Another place full of strangers. Another place without a home.

No. That would be the coward's way out. My mother's way out.

"Sorry about that," Veta's voice echoed out to the crowd. "I met this really hot girl, and they had to pry me away from her. It wasn't pretty."

People answered with laughter and whistles. Felix started up his drum loop and synth again.

I sucked in my breath, putting one foot in front of the other. Every step pinched and throbbed. Shadowed faces fanned out toward the club entrance, some of them looking right at me. My hands went cold.

"What's wrong, honey?" someone shouted. It sounded like Dave's voice, kind of nasally.

I threw my guitar over my shoulder and stared at the ground.

"Here's a little something you haven't heard before," Veta said.

Sean launched into his pulsating bass line, and Veta perched her guitar against her hips, swaying in time to Bryn's kick-heavy beat. Felix ran his swirling pad in the background, his smile glowing under a blue light. Even Sean, who didn't seem like the performing type, looked incredibly comfortable up here. His eyes fluttered shut as his long fingers slid up and down the neck of his bass.

I scanned the audience. Heads bobbed in time, arms pulsed, and bodies swayed. Then my gaze locked with Amy's. The edge of her mouth curved up in a sly smile, and she nudged Dave, motioning to me. He laughed, and she batted her eyelashes, flicking her hair in an exaggerated way.

Veta curled over the mic and sang in a breathy voice. "Lost in pictures. Writhing with conviction . . ."

Shit. I'd missed my cue, leaving nothing but Felix's dreamy pad to back her up. The flickering lights made me feel as if I were moving in slow motion. Nothing felt real.

I focused on Veta's sexy lyrics, waiting for a good place to ease in my arpeggio. My stiff fingers found the twelfth fret and my right hand began picking the notes, clean with a little chorus effect. They sounded like melted butter behind her vocals. Perfect.

Veta lurched forward, chugging out the first chord of the chorus. I hit my pedal to switch to a more distorted sound. The notes came out, but they still sounded clean. I stomped on the pedal again. Nothing. This couldn't be happening. *Please, please. Work.*

Veta looked over her shoulder at me, mouthing "go." She thought I'd missed my cue again. Heat inched up the back of my neck. If I didn't get this to work before my solo, we'd all be screwed. I pressed the pedal one more time, my mind racing. No luck.

It had to be the MIDI—I must've plugged it in wrong during the rush. I could either walk over to my amp and change the channel manually or squat down and fix the connection. Both options would make me look like a complete moron.

Screw it. I dove for my amp, nearly tripping over my guitar cord on the way over. There wasn't a need to look at the crowd—I could feel their laughter burning into my skin. I changed the sound and got back into position. Felix glanced over at me and bit his lip. He looked horrified.

"You rise above it all. Press my back against the wall," Veta belted. She jabbed her thumb toward the ceiling, which meant she couldn't hear herself. The sound guy scrambled. At least I wasn't the only one having problems.

I banged out the end of the chorus and then switched back to my clean channel. But the guitar cord ended up wrapped around my legs again. I twirled out of it, all the while stumbling to play the verse arpeggio in time.

Veta grabbed the mic off the stand and squatted on one foot, her other leg stretching out to the side. She reminded me of a slick panther, hunting for prey. "You think you're the only one with whispers like chocolate. And I think I'm the only one . . . who knows you're full of shit." She blew a kiss at the crowd.

My hand slid up to the third fret, and I hammered out a fast melody. Veta moved in rhythm, every note jolting her body. She arched her back until the top of her head nearly reached the floor.

It was almost time for my solo. I switched channels again and grabbed my EBow for the lead-in. The violin-like squeal of my guitar took over the song, and I shut my eyes, begging myself to nail this. My fingers were slick and I hit a sour note, but I had to keep going. No matter what.

Veta danced around the stage, bumping hips with Felix. He put his arm in the air and swayed.

I ditched the EBow and charged into the solo. Either Bryn was playing faster or I came in too late—maybe both. I paused for a second and dove in again, but this threw Sean and Veta off, both of them speeding up. Felix's pad hummed in the background, like some lonely baby bird. Any worst-case scenario I'd imagined couldn't top this.

I changed up my lick to coincide with Bryn's beat, tapping my foot to get into the groove. We jelled together again—just in time for the song to end.

"No, I can't hear a thing. But your sweet . . . sweet . . . encryption!" Veta pulled back from the mic, her face serene.

Bryn finished by slamming his snare with more effort than necessary. I didn't dare look at him.

"C-Side's new guitarist, ladies and gentlemen!" a guy announced with a laugh. The voice came from the front, right where Amy and her band stood.

I could hear chuckles and see grins on various faces. Other people eyeballed me like I had the plague. Voices and clapping morphed into a distorted hum, making it hard to distinguish words. Probably a good thing.

"Hey, Blondie!" a girl called out. "Get some guitar lessons—and a brush."

I squatted to fix the connection on my effects processor, wishing I could cover my ears.

"You wanna get up here and try it?" Veta asked, her voice lighthearted but firm. "Didn't think so."

Every inch of my face burned, and I had to stop myself from smoothing my hair. It always frizzed out in damp, hot places. Ducking behind my amp for the rest of our short set seemed like a great plan.

Sean's boots appeared in front of me. "Remember," he whispered, "thick skin."

By the time I got the nerve to look up, he'd returned to his side of the stage. I appreciated his intent, but thick skin didn't grow overnight.

"Some of you already know this one—a little ditty called 'Puppet Girl,'" Veta said.

This got a few happy sounds from the crowd, much to my relief. I hadn't killed the show yet. But that girl's comment kept repeating in my head. Everyone in the club thought I was a fraud. How much worse could it get?

Felix's melting bell synth filled the stage, and Sean's flange-tinted bass line followed, creating a dreamy atmosphere. I closed my eyes and tried to be anywhere but here. The smell of hot equipment and sweat consumed every breath, and ice ran through my veins. Here it was for all to see, my insecurity under a spotlight.

My fingers pressed the right strings at the right time, every pluck numb and cautious. I sacrificed my edge—what made my playing mine—to avoid making another mistake.

Veta began strumming a power chord, adding dimension. "Seen, but not heard. You take your cues from shadows. Puppet Girl. It's time to speak your mind."

She broke away from the mic and danced around me during the bridge. I kept my eyes downcast, too afraid to move or to even blink. Respect for Veta and the band kept me on that stage, but every inch of me wanted to bolt.

I hit too many bad notes during the next couple songs. Each one felt like an electric shock down my spine, paralyzing me for a few seconds. Veta got a little pitchy near the end of "Acceleration," but her performance didn't miss a beat. She moved like a contortionist, using her guitar as a prop. Sometimes she'd teeter on the edge of the stage and draw in a knot of people. They'd reach for her with hungry eyes and parted lips. Other times she'd feed off Felix or Sean, making them graceful dancers in their own right.

But she couldn't crack me tonight.

"I don't know about you guys, but I feel like shaking things up," Veta said before our last song.

A few "woo hoos" and "yeahs" followed. Someone commented on Bryn's "hotness."

"Oh, come on. That was weak!" Veta threw her hands up. "Do you guys want to stir shit up or not?"

The cheers got louder and several people shoved themselves to the front.

"Lose your pants, Bryn!" a girl yelled. Several voices, both male and female, howled their support of the idea.

"Not what I had in mind," Veta said. "But why the hell not?"

An already-shirtless Bryn stepped out from behind the drums, a big grin on his face. He walked toward the edge of the stage and began doing some awkward stripper dance. Veta played a little riff and sang, *"Bow chica bow bow."*

Oh God, he wasn't actually doing this.

I hugged my guitar and peeked over at Felix and Sean. They both kept their eyes down but had little grins, like they'd been through this before.

Bryn pulled off his black jeans and twirled them over his head. Thankfully, he had boxers on underneath.

People, mostly girls, toppled one another to move toward Bryn. He threw his pants into the crowd, creating a tangle of outstretched arms and bobbing heads. Then he took a bow and flexed his guns—as if he were the only guy with biceps.

"Hey, Jasmine! Let's see you dance." Amy. I recognized her husky voice. She smiled, but her dark eyes challenged me.

I contemplated taking off Tina's boots and throwing them at her head. At least my feet would stop hurting. But all I could do was stand there and clutch my guitar, my body shaking.

Bryn reached for my arm.

"Don't!" I twisted away, ready to whack him with my headstock if necessary.

Bryn leaned his face toward mine, his eyes cold. "You've already made us a joke tonight. Might as well humor them."

I gritted my teeth, my heart pounding. "I'm doing the best I can."

"Yeah? Well, your best sucks." He stalked off toward the drums.

My entire body sagged, nausea creeping toward my throat. I always did better on tests than I'd expected. Every grade was a pleasant surprise, proof that I doubted myself too much. Not this time.

The band launched into "Back-Seat Love Affair," Sean's quick and dirty bass line driving the crowd into a frenzy. I joined in with my James Bond–like lick. It was fast and awkward—easy to screw up. I bit my tongue, my mind repeating *don't mess up* like a mantra. My chest felt tight, every breath smothered. I was better than this, damn it. I had to give these people more than they expected from me.

Pressure grew behind my eyes. My fingers ground into the strings, playing harder, faster. But I kept fumbling, my brain wanting one thing, my hands doing another. The more I tried to keep it together, the worse the notes sounded. Sloppy, contrived . . . amateur.

The pick fell between my fingers and evaporated into the floor. I tilted my head back, sucking in my breath, wishing I could disappear with it.

Veta glanced at me over her shoulder, her full lips turned down at the corners.

And I knew. I'd just blown my last chance.

Bryn took apart his drum kit like it was on fire. He'd managed to locate another pair of jeans and a black Mindless Self Indulgence T-shirt.

I packed up my gear, avoiding eye contact with everyone. Felix helped Veta haul her amp back to the van, both of them whispering as they went.

"Damaged" by Assemblage 23 blasted out of the speakers, which turned voices into an indistinguishable hum. But I could feel a chill between my shoulders, imagining the cruel remarks being flung at me.

My mouth felt like cotton, my lower back ached, and weakness preyed on my limbs. Failing wasn't something I did. Ever. Unless I counted that talent show in second grade. Maybe I should've taken the hint then. But I always thought one day I'd be good enough. One day I'd get up on a stage and finally be seen and heard and respected. All the years in Jason's hot garage, the infected blisters, the days when playing guitar was the only thing keeping me sane, the moments I'd master a new technique or find a melody that gave me chills—it was all supposed to lead me to a night like tonight.

I'd imagined a mind-blowing high. The pulse of the audience would run through my body, daring me to play better and harder than ever before. My melodies would heal and inspire, make people feel as if I were speaking directly to them.

This was supposed to be the night I could call myself a real musician.

"You want help with your amp?" Sean asked behind me.

"Sean," Bryn said, his voice thick and charged. "Get over here."

Sean jogged over to help Bryn haul the drums offstage, leaving me alone with the buzz of conversations below. I scrambled to wind up my cords.

"Hey!" a guy called, slapping his hand against the stage. He sounded like the idiot who'd harassed Amy. I kept my back to him. "Hey, chicky—I wanna ask you something."

Chicky? What a tool.

"Why'd they pick you?" His laugh cut above the music. "Do you give really good head or what?"

Every muscle in my back tensed. I imagined myself whirling around and smashing the toe of my boot into his face, but I just grabbed my guitar and ran. Through the sweltering backstage area. Out the door. Into the cool night breeze.

The rest of C-Side stood in a tight circle outside the van. Bryn made wide gestures with his hands, his lips moving fast. Veta's arms were folded and Sean's head was down. Felix saw me and put a finger to his lips. He broke away and ran back into the club, like he knew something big was about to go down. Something he didn't want to stick around for.

Sean turned and headed toward me, leaving Bryn and Veta staring after him. "Go ahead to my car," he said. "I'll get your amp."

"I can help—just let me put my guitar away."

He glanced over his shoulder and turned back to me, exhaling. "You don't want to walk into that right now. Trust me."

"We're going to the same place. I've got to walk into it at some point."

"Bryn's having a party tonight. He'll be distracted."

And I'd rather get this over with. "Thanks, but I'll be fine."

"Suit yourself." He shook his head and moved past me toward the club.

My hand tightened around my guitar case handle, and I held my breath. The edge was close enough to taste, bitter and acidic in my throat. It wouldn't take much to push me over now.

Bryn jabbed an accusing finger at me as I approached. "You're out. I want you gone by the end of the month."

His words slapped me in the face, making me freeze.

Veta held her hands up at him. "Bryn, not now, okay? We'll deal with it tomorrow."

Bryn tilted his chin up, rolling his eyes. "I'm gettin' real tired of the Jasmine defense campaign."

"I'm not defending her." Veta kept her gaze down, away from me. Not that I blamed her. If I were her, I'd hate me too.

The midnight air probed at my skin, sending goose bumps up my bare arms. "I—I know I screwed up, but—"

"You lied and you took us down with you," Bryn said. "I don't give a fuck what your excuse is."

I let my guitar case slip to the pavement and wrapped my arms around myself, holding tight. Every part of me wanted to scream, but I couldn't. I had to hold it in, keep my cool. "I'm sorry—I really am. It wasn't supposed to happen like this."

"What did you expect, Jasmine?" Veta said. "Lying creates bad karma."

I looked down at a flattened cigarette. It had a red lipstick stain around the filter, just like the ones Mom used to leave on the patio. "Karma had nothing to do with tonight. I wanted to be ready, but I wasn't. I don't have an excuse."

Sean walked by with my amp, his cheeks flushed. He glanced at Veta and me before loading it in the van.

"So much for your hippie-dippy psychic intuition, huh, Veta?" Bryn let out a bitter chuckle. "Me and Sean called this on day one, and you said no, no, she can do it. Give her time to warm up to us."

Sean hopped out of the van. "Bryn, come on."

"I give people the benefit of the doubt," Veta said. "So what?"

Bryn folded his arms. "Get your head out of your ass, Veta."

"Stop talking to her like that," I said.

Felix walked by with a bunch of cables, his eyes widening at me.

"Would you prefer I lie to her?" Bryn asked. "Is that what real friends do?"

"You're crapping all over her for something I did."

He waved me off. "I got nothing more to say to you, Jasmine. Go back to band camp or wherever you came from."

I moved toward him. What did I have to lose anymore? "Having a rich uncle doesn't make you God, Bryn. It just makes you a spoiled brat with a nice house and a cushy job you didn't earn."

"Oh my God," Felix blurted out, covering his mouth.

Bryn's eyes narrowed. "Are you seriously—"

"I'm not done," I continued, the pressure in my chest ready to burst. "It doesn't give you the right to talk to people the way you do or bark orders at the band like they're your fucking employees."

Bryn slammed his fist into the rear door of the van, making Felix jump back. "Do you ever shut up? *Do you?*"

Sean grabbed Bryn's shoulder. "Chill, all right?"

Bryn shook him off. "You do not get to talk about me or my family, you got that?" He moved forward, staring me down. "You know dick about us!"

I wanted to push him down. I wanted to curl up in a ball and hide. I wanted to take it all back. Everything was sitting inside my throat, waiting to escape. "All I know is what I see."

"And you know what I see?" He jabbed his finger at me again. "I see a—"

I knocked his hand away. "Get your finger out of my face."

Veta stepped between us, her back to me. "Whoa, okay." She nudged Bryn backward. "I think we're done for tonight. Let's just get out of here."

Bryn moved around her. "I see an insecure little girl who'd rather pretend to have the chops than do what it takes to get them."

The ache in my throat became unbearable. I felt like I was drowning, losing complete control of myself. I needed to get out of there. Now.

I snatched up my guitar case and jogged in the opposite direction, wincing at the stabbing pain in my feet.

Newton's Whore and a few other people stood near the back entrance, watching. "Uh-oh—that doesn't look good," one of them said. Others laughed.

"Those boots weren't made for running, sweetheart!" Amy said.

"Jesus—just leave the poor chick alone already," a guy with long black hair said. Teddy. I didn't need his pity.

"Jasmine!" Veta called. "Where are you going?"

I ducked behind a brick building, hoping she wouldn't come after me this time. She didn't.

A half moon illuminated only slivers of the alley ahead, and the air reeked of urine and sour meat. I walked faster, closing my eyes. My boot hit something glass. It shattered against a building, ringing through my ears.

My chest heaved, like I was going to vomit. I dropped my guitar case and sat down on it, running my fingers through my hair. A thudding drumbeat from the club and the hiss of cars were the only sounds filling the space around me.

I tried to scream, but my throat muscles tensed, letting out just a rush of air. It felt wrong to let go. Anyone could be lurking in the shadows. Anyone could hear me.

"Get it together," I muttered to myself. "You have to get it together."

I wanted to call Jason but my stuff, including my phone, was in Sean's car. Because I had to wear this stupid dress. This stupid dress that was meant for someone else. And for what? To fit some ridiculous image Bryn had in his head? An image I'd never live up to.

Footsteps echoed down the alley. I jerked my head up and saw a lean figure walking toward me.

"Jasmine?" Sean called, the moonlight outlining his hat. He squinted at me as he approached. "What are you doing?"

I shielded my face with my hands, staring down at shards of glass and a Coke can. "I have no idea—isn't that obvious?"

His boots stopped in front of me. A few seconds went by. Then he shifted his weight. "Are you crying?"

I looked up at him over my fingertips. "I don't cry."

The side of his mouth quirked up. "Right."

"Honest. Not since I was five."

He put his hands in his pockets and rolled the Coke can under his Doc. "Why's that?"

"I just can't."

"Can't or won't?"

I looked away. "It doesn't really matter, does it?"

He sighed. "Okay, tough girl. You ready to go?"

"I can walk. It's fine." *Barefoot if I have to.*

"It's after midnight, Jasmine."

I shrugged. "Good thing I'm not Cinderella."

He squatted down, making our eyes level. "I'm not just going to leave you here."

"I can take care of myself."

"By sitting alone in a dark alley that smells like ass?"

I folded my arms, feeling a smile twitch at my lips. "Good point." I met his gaze. "But you don't have to play nice anymore. I'm out of the band."

"Fine." He stood up. "Quit being an idiot so we can get out of here. That better?"

"A little."

He held out his hand. "Come on."

I slipped my fingers through his and let him pull me up. Part of me wished we could hide in this smelly alley forever. At least then I wouldn't have to face whatever came next.

Chapter 13

My heart sped up when Sean pulled into the West Cliff house driveway. It was just the two of us in the car. Everyone had already taken off by the time we came out of the alley.

Strange people mingled in the yard, and more cars than usual stretched down the street. The party had begun.

"They didn't waste any time," I said.

Sean yanked his keys from the ignition, twirling them around his finger. "Nope. They never do."

My palms pressed into the cold leather seat. "Any chance I can spend the night in your car?"

"Only if you don't mind your room becoming a cheap motel."

"Seriously?"

"It's been known to happen, yeah."

"Great." I tapped my fingers against my leg, biting my lip.

He rested his head against the seat, peering over at me. "You won't have to deal with Bryn tonight, if that's what you're worried about. He's probably already got his tongue down some chick's throat."

"It's just . . ." *I've got nowhere to go. No money. No car. My best friend in the world is across the Pacific Ocean. My father hates me. And I probably just lost the first real girlfriend I've ever had. Help me. I'm freaking out.* I looked down at my hands, swallowing that lump of reality. "Never mind."

He studied me for a few seconds but didn't say anything. I hugged myself and watched a couple of vivacious girls tackle a guy on the lawn.

"Hey," he said finally.

I faced him. "Yeah?"

His lips parted but closed again, like whatever he saw in my expression made him clam up. He reached for the door handle. "You ready?"

"Yep." I pushed the door open and got out.

Laughing people, booze, and clouds of smoke haunted most of the normally spacious living room. Skinny Puppy's erratic "Pro-Test" growled out of Bryn's surround-sound system. Parties weren't my thing. Too loud. Too much talking. Too much . . . everything.

"Sean!" A sprite of a girl threw her arms around him. "Ha, got you before you could sneak upstairs. You were *awesome* tonight."

He returned the hug. "Thanks."

I scanned the crowd, looking for the quickest path of escape.

"And I love the hat," the girl continued. She plucked his fedora off and put it over her short dark hair. "Can I have it?"

Sean gave her a playful smile. "Only if you give it back."

She batted her eyelashes. "Of course."

"This is Hazel," Sean said, nudging me. "Best mastering engineer on the planet and one of our biggest fans."

She grabbed my arm, giving it a little squeeze. "My heart went out to you tonight, sweetie. Been there, done that. But it's nothin' a beer and a little nookie won't cure."

Right. "Um . . . thanks." I forced my lips into a smile. Guess word hadn't gotten around that I was no longer in the band.

She dropped my arm and started talking to Sean about a singer named Amph and his large ego. I kept hoping he'd turn to me and ask if I wanted to escape and hide out upstairs.

A guy moved in front of me, handing Sean a beer. "What's up, man? Long time, no see."

"Hey," Sean's voice rose. "Did you make it out to the show?"

So much for that fantasy.

I slipped away, moving toward the kitchen. I needed water. Bad. Most people I passed seemed to look right through me, but a couple gave me smirks or dirty looks. Felix danced around the couch with a bag of Doritos, and Bryn nuzzled up to the blonde who'd dropped by rehearsal the other day. Veta was nowhere to be seen.

A few people milled around the kitchen, mixing drinks and eating corn chips and salsa. The corn chips I bought for *me*.

"Is that her?" a girl whispered behind me.

"Shh," hissed another, giggling.

I snatched a water bottle off the island, tore the cap off, and chugged. Then I speed-dialed Jason.

It rang. And rang.

I exhaled, closing my eyes.

Jason's cheery recorded voice answered. "You've reached Jason. Spill it." *Beep.*

"I screwed up. Bad." I slumped against the island, shielding my mouth. "They kicked me out, Jason." A girl squealed a laugh loud enough to break every dish in the kitchen. I considered dousing her with the rest of my water. "I miss you . . . so much. Call me when you get this. Please."

"Hey," a male voice said.

I looked up, hoping to see Sean. But a guy with spiky black hair stared down at me. With an off-kilter nose and plump lips, he was what Jason and I would call quirky-cute. "Um, hi?" I straightened.

His hazel eyes flicked to my chest for the quickest second. Slick. "How's it going?"

"It's going. Did you . . . need something?"

"Yeah." He grinned. "You're standing between me and my SoCo."

"Oh, sorry." I moved away, folding my arms. "Wait, your—what?"

He reached over and held up a bottle of Southern Comfort. "Bottled apathy."

"Bad day?"

He poured the amber liquid into a shot glass, pursing his lips. "You could say that. Got suckered into working the late shift. Missed my friend's show. And then got fired." He checked his cell. "Twenty minutes ago."

"Ah. I got fired from my band."

He handed me a shot glass and poured, nearly overflowing it. "What's your name?"

"Jasmine. Yours?"

"Kirt." He raised his glass. "Cheers, Jasmine."

We clinked glasses and he downed his, closing his eyes.

I stared at the liquid wobbling in my shaky hand. I'd never gotten drunk before—just a little buzzed off Jason's mom's wine coolers and some Boone's Farm his boyfriend brought over once. But apathy sounded pretty damn good right now.

I brought the glass to my lips and downed it. Well, more like choked on it. The stuff felt like battery acid oozing down my throat and esophagus. "Whoa," I croaked, hand on my chest.

Kirt laughed, pouring himself another shot. "Guess I forgot to mention—it's a little strong."

Heat moved into my cheeks. "Yeah." I coughed.

A group of loud people, one of them Felix, made their way into the kitchen, debating which brand of macaroni and cheese tasted the best. I gave Felix a weak smile and said hi, but he turned away, continuing his conversation.

Kirt snatched up the bottle. "How about we take this outside?"

A heavy feeling settled in my stomach. "Sure."

We went out the back entrance and ended up sitting against the outside wall of the studio, the bottle of Southern Comfort between us. Part of me knew this wasn't the greatest idea. That part told me to go up to my room, close my eyes, and pretend tonight never happened.

But I'd just lie there, feeling the throb of music below me, going over every mistake I made on that stage tonight. Again and again. Wondering if I just lost the best opportunity I'd ever be given. And then I'd think about tomorrow.

I couldn't deal with tomorrow.

Kirt lit a cigarette and blew a trail of smoke into the darkness. "So, what band were you in?"

I took a swig from the bottle, wincing. "The one I'm not in anymore." He was obviously one of the few people here who didn't see my disaster of a performance. Why fill him in?

"Okay then."

I rested my head against the wall, staring up at the clear night sky. "Why'd you get fired?"

"Got caught hooking up with the boss."

A giggle escaped my throat. "Really?"

He stretched his legs, taking a long drag. Then he laughed, sending puffs of smoke out his nose. "No. This dick stiffed me on a tip after him and his family of, like, eighty stunk up the place for two hours. Then he comes back in and asks me for directions to 17. I told him to shove it."

For some reason, I found this really funny. Enough to catch the attention of the couple making out on the lawn. I covered my mouth.

His eyebrows rose. "Getting a little buzzed there?"

"No, I'm good." And I was. A little hot and lightheaded, but still with it. I could probably stand on one foot and touch my finger to my nose. "Where in town do you live?"

"Why?" He scooted closer, his shoulder touching mine. "You wanna come stalk me?"

"Oh, you wish." I took another drink. It tasted like maple syrup with a bitter kick.

"I'm staying with my parents in Scotts Valley. It's temporary." Kirt flicked his cigarette and grabbed the bottle from me. He started going on about his nagging dad and his pushover mom. How he'd be getting an apartment with a friend soon—once he found another job.

I took a few more sips, thinking about my dad. He'd have a fit if he saw me right now, and then he'd wave his finger and say, "I knew it. I knew you'd end up just like her." Because he was always right. Dad knew *everything*.

My feet felt numb. I stared down at Tina's black boots. "I want to throw these boots into the ocean."

"Why don't you?" Kirt's hot breath, ripe with menthols and booze, hit my ear.

I cocked my head, grinning up at him. "They're not mine."

"So?"

"It wouldn't be very nice." I untied the left one, ripping out the laces. Then I hurled it onto the lawn, nearly hitting the kissing couple. "Oops." My chest heaved with giggles.

Kirt reached over and unlaced the right one. "I won't tell." He yanked the boot off. "So where do you live?"

"Nowhere. Everyone keeps kicking me out."

He laughed, pressing his arm harder into mine.

The stars blurred into a soapy film, masking the sky. "It's not funny."

"Aw, I'm sorry." His lips brushed against my neck. "You smell really good—you know that?"

I shoved him away. "Don't."

He leaned toward my ear again. "Don't what?"

I pushed him back again, but my arm felt like it weighed a hundred pounds. "Just stay over there—on your side."

"My *side*?"

A pair of scruffy black Converse shoes stopped in front of us. "Hey, Kirt—what are you doing, man?" the owner asked.

My eyes moved up, meeting Bryn's smug face. Not who I wanted to see.

Kirt raised our bottle. "Just chillin' with, uh . . ." He looked over at me.

"Jasmine," Bryn said.

"You two know each other?" Kirt asked.

"That's who kicked me out." I snapped my fingers. "Just like that. No regrets."

"She's wasted," Bryn said to someone next to him.

"No, I'm not. I know where I am, who I am." But I couldn't control a damn thing that came out of my mouth.

"She's fine," Kirt said.

Sean knelt in front of me, his brow crinkled. "Get lost, Kirt."

"Oh look, it's Veta's kid brother." Kirt flicked a lit cigarette at Sean's knee, chuckling. "You still afraid of cigarettes?"

Bryn grabbed Kirt's arm, pulling him up. "Come on, Lushy McGee. Let's go."

"What? Why?" Kirt asked.

Bryn led him away, talking in a low voice.

I buried my face in my knees. My head felt like it was floating and spinning at the same time.

"I've been looking all over for you," Sean said.

I tilted my head up. "Why?"

"Found her other boot on the lawn," Felix said, dropping it in front of me.

Where the hell did he come from?

Sean picked up the Southern Comfort, sloshing the alcohol around inside. It was more than half empty. "Jesus, Jasmine. How much of this did you drink?"

"I don't know—a few sips."

"Right." He handed it off to Felix.

Felix scrunched up his face—at least I thought he did. "How bad is she?"

"Oh my God," I said. "I'm not in inventive care—intensive. Whatever."

Sean studied me like I was his friggin' patient. "Bad enough to nuzzle up with Lushy McGee."

"Ew." Felix held up the bottle. "I'm gonna put this away. I'll be right back." He headed inside.

"I didn't nuzzle up with anyone."

"Then what were you doing out here?" Sean asked.

"Talking." I ran my fingers through my tangled hair. "It's not like anyone else will talk to me."

Sean sat down, draping his arms over his knees. "I was talking to you. You disappeared."

"I needed to call Jason."

"Who's Jason?"

"My best friend. He's like my family—my only family." I looked at my cell phone in my lap. It stared back, green and silent. "But he didn't answer."

"Try him again. Does he have a car?"

"Yeah. Why?"

"Ask him to come by."

I laughed, imagining Jason doing the butterfly stroke across the Pacific Ocean. "Yeah, right."

Sean shrugged. "What—he won't drive an hour to help you out?"

"That'd be kinda hard from Maui."

Sean's mouth opened, but Felix returned, squatting next to him. "Where's Veta?" Felix asked.

"She said she was going to the beach with some people." Sean rubbed his temple. "One of her bonfire things—I dunno."

"Maybe we should call her," Felix said. "She kind of knows her better."

I waved a hand in front of his face. "Hello? I'm sitting right here. You can talk to *me*."

"I know." He still wouldn't look at me.

"I'm not a bad person, okay?" The words flew out of my mouth faster than I could think. "I tried tonight. I really did. I'm always trying."

"Um . . ." Felix bit his thumbnail.

"I've got this," Sean said, nodding behind him. "Go find Samantha."

Felix crinkled his nose. "You sure?"

"Yeah, yeah. It's cool. Nothing I haven't dealt with before."

Felix patted him on the back and shot me a quick glance as he stood. "Feel better, Jasmine." He ran back to the house like he couldn't get away fast enough.

"I'm not drunk."

Sean smirked. "Then you're a great actress."

"I've been around drunk people. They slur, and they act like morons, and they puke everywhere."

"And let me guess—you've never been drunk before?"

"Nope." I moved to my knees and stood slowly. "See, I'm fi—whoa." I thrust my hand against the wall, balancing myself. "Okay, maybe a little dizzy."

Sean got up and wrapped his arm around me. "You're kind of a klutz sober too."

I moved away, leaning against the wall. "Shut up."

"You feel like watching a movie? I got a bunch on my computer."

"In your room? With you?"

He exhaled a laugh, looking down. "That sounds really bad. But yeah—unless you want to go to bed."

"I'm not tired." I tried walking forward, but it was like making my way down an airplane aisle during turbulence. My limbs shook and the ground moved up and down.

Sean appeared alongside of me, putting his arm around my waist. I leaned into him this time. "You're not picking me up."

"Only if you pass out—I promise," he said, guiding me forward.

We waded through endless people, their loud voices making my head spin more. I tripped halfway up the stairs. But somehow I got to his room without breaking anything, object or body part.

I fell back on his bed, letting my legs dangle off the side, and stared at the plastic stars on his ceiling. Some of them seemed to vibrate. "You got the whole galaxy up here."

"I wish." He went over to his computer. "What kind of movie are you in the mood for?"

"How come you're being so nice to me? I mean—you hated me before. And now . . ."

"I never hated you, Jasmine. I'd have to know you better for that."

Of course he didn't know me. Nobody outside Jason did, really. Even Jason didn't understand   because he had a loving mom. A great boyfriend. A home.

"I've got nowhere to go," I said.

Sean moved onto the bed, sitting against his metal headboard. "What do you mean?"

"My dad kicked me out—because all he sees is her. It doesn't matter what I do. Even if I went to college."

"Who's *her*?"

I sat upright, putting my hands over my face. "I don't know. I don't know what I'm saying. There's too many things. Too many thoughts in my head."

The bed shook as he moved closer to me. He rubbed my back, sending a tickle across my skin.

"I didn't have a plan." Heat built behind my eyes. I squeezed them shut. "It was just supposed to work, because I wasn't going to *let* myself screw up. Music is all I've got, you know?" My breaths quickened. "And I blew it—I blew everything. Told my dad to go to hell. I—"

"Whoa, Jasmine. Just slow down." His fingers kneaded the back of my neck. "Nothing is set in stone."

The warmth of his touch cascaded down my shoulders. "Then why do I feel like this?"

"Partly because you're drunk. And partly because you hold in way more than you should. The two don't go together."

I looked over at him. "I don't know what the hell I'm going to do."

He put his hand over mine, giving it a little squeeze. "You don't have to figure it all out tonight."

My fingers weaved with his, and I found myself leaning into him. I wanted to rest my head against his chest and feel his arms around me, like at the club.

He pulled back some. "Do you want to lie down?"

My eyes focused on his mouth. I liked the shape of it, fuller than average. Kissable. I ran my thumb along the soft line of his lower lip.

"What are you doing?" he asked.

"I have no idea." I craned my neck and inhaled, pressing my mouth against his.

His lips parted, like he was going to return the kiss, but he nudged me back. "Jasmine . . ." His eyes were wide, searching my face.

My heart thudded. "I—I'm sorry." I turned away, scooting to the foot of the bed.

"It's okay," he said softly.

The knots in my stomach turned into a wave of nausea. A chill ran through my body. "I think I'm gonna—oh shit."

Sean scrambled off the bed and put a small trash can in front of me. All I thought was *Thank God it's lined with a plastic grocery bag* before an acidic liquid seeped into my throat. And then it felt like the entire day came spewing out of me, my body wrenching and shaking. Every time I tried to inhale, more came out, choking me. Sean stroked my hair, telling me I'd be okay. It would end soon.

But it didn't. My breath went ragged and my eyes watered. I'd never felt anything this intense in my life. This awful. My gut jerked upward until there was nothing left but air and a bitter taste on my tongue.

And then I fell back against Sean's warmth, closing my eyes. My cheek rested against his chest, and his fingers ran up and down my arm. We just stayed like that, neither of us saying a word.

Chapter 14

The ring tone version of Placebo's "Meds" interrupted my dream of flying over the ocean. I felt around for the phone until I realized it was in the clutches of my other hand.

"Hello?" The roof of my mouth tasted like chalk.

"Did I wake you up?" Dad asked.

"Mmm-hmm." My eyes flashed open. "Dad?" The sun-filled room made my temples ache. A room that wasn't mine.

"I was hoping we could talk."

A tattooed arm wrapped around the gray pillow next to mine. Sean was lying on his stomach, facing me, his eyes fluttering open. "Oh my God," I said.

"Oh my God what?" Dad asked.

"Um, there's a spider in my bed."

Sean crinkled his brow, his lips twitching.

"So kill it," Dad said.

The back of my throat felt as if it had been ripped apart and stitched together again. "Sorry, Dad. I—I have to call you back." I snapped the phone shut and sat up, gawking at Sean.

He rolled over, draping his arm over his forehead. "A spider? Really?"

Tina's dress still clung to my body, as did the black panty hose. I racked my brain to remember last night. Got kicked out of the band. Party. Bittersweet alcohol. Something about boots in the ocean. "What—why—*what* am I doing in here?"

"You got drunk and passed out," he said.

"In *your* bed?"

He dropped his arm, squinting up at me. "You don't remember anything?"

I yanked his black sheets off me. "Obviously not the important parts."

"I would've slept in your room, but, um, a couple of people already found it."

"Are you kidding me?"

"Remember what I said about unclaimed rooms becoming motels?"

I climbed out of the bed, hugging myself. "Great."

Sean sat up and the covers slid off, showing his naked chest.

I tore my eyes away. "Are you—do you have any clothes on?"

"Yes, pants. Relax. Nothing happened with us." He looked down at his hands. "Well, except you—"

"What? What did I do?" My body tensed. Please don't tell me I hit on him or something.

He searched my face for a few painful seconds. "You told me some stuff, that's all."

Was he trying to give me a heart attack? "What stuff?"

"Just about your friend Jason. And your dad."

I raked my fingers through my hair, remembering puking in a trash can and Sean's soothing voice. God, this was humiliating. "I—I have to go."

I opened his door and bolted, nearly ramming into Felix.

His eyes flicked from me to Sean's door, his mouth making an O.

"*Not* what you think."

"Are you feeling better?" he asked.

I glanced over my shoulder at Sean's room. He hadn't come out. "How bad was I last night?"

Felix crinkled his nose. "You were pretty drunk. I mean, we found you with Lushy McGee and you guys looked . . . close."

"Who?" The name sounded familiar, but I couldn't see a face. Not a clear one, anyway.

Felix shuddered. "He's a huge manwhore—like, worse than Bryn. Be glad we found you when we did."

"Um, thanks."

"Do you need the bathroom?"

I rubbed my face, getting black smears on my hand. "Yeah—and bad, from the looks of it."

"Just let me pee first." He rushed in.

I walked to my room, afraid to see what was behind the white door. Images of naked strangers and a circus flashed through my mind. *Please let my laptop and clothes still be here.*

I shoved the door open and winced, hoping for the best.

The first thing that hit me was the odor, a mix of sweat, booze, and . . . salsa? My sleeping bag and pillow were on opposite sides of the room and several beer bottles lined the turquoise carpet, but it was people free.

I opened the closet. Everything was still inside. A miracle. Then I unraveled my sleeping bag. Shards of corn chips fell out and something red and lumpy was smeared inside. Either puke or salsa—I didn't want to know which. Two condom wrappers were strewn nearby, one with something stuffed inside. It made my skin itch just to look at it.

I grabbed a tee and a pair of jeans from the closet and made a beeline for the shower.

* * *

A half hour later, I roamed the cliffs overlooking the Pacific. The sea was the closest thing to a god for me. Jason and I swore by coming down here to get rid of colds or a broken heart. I remembered calling him last night—why hadn't he called me back?

I climbed the rocks, searching for one that was nice and flat, like a bench. It didn't take long to find; there was always at least one.

Soft mist hit my cheeks as I sat, and my skin and tense muscles drank up the sun's warmth. I shut my eyes, pretending there were no houses or slowing cars behind me. No tourists speaking fifty different languages. Not even any robo-joggers or squeaky baby strollers. I had the ocean all to myself.

And then I took a deep breath and called Dad.

"Did you get the spider?" he answered.

"Um, not exactly." I shaded my face with my hand. "So, what did you want to talk about?"

"I wanted to see how you were."

Neither of us was great at apologies. "I'm fine." I squeezed my eyes shut, shaking my head. "Actually, I'm not. Things are pretty bad." I was tired of pretending everything was okay.

"Why's that?"

A large wave crashed against the rocks, dampening my face. It lessened the throbbing in my head. "I messed up my first show with the band. They kicked me out—and I need to be out of the house by the end of the month." I took a breath. "And before you tell me it's my fault—I know. I'm not making excuses."

"Where are you going to go?"

"I don't know."

"Do you still have that cashier job?"

Did I? Tina gave me the schedule yesterday. Before the show. "I have today off."

"What about your car?"

Oh man. "I don't know."

"That sounds like a lot of uncertainty."

I swallowed hard. Bryn owed me the $650 I gave him for July. But it would have to go toward a new place. "I've got no money. What am I supposed to do?"

"It's not so easy out there, is it?"

"Spare me the I-told-you-so lecture, Dad. Please."

"Then what is it you want to hear?"

I stared at the faint outline of a boat on the horizon. It looked peaceful and lonely. "That there's hope. If I talked to the band and apologized. Maybe they'd give me another chance."

"Apologize for what—messing up your first show?"

"They needed someone with live experience. I told them I had it, because—well, at first I really wanted the room. And then I heard them play, and they were so good. Me and the lead singer, Veta, hit it off right away. It just felt right, you know?"

"So you lied."

I knew what he was thinking. "I had to. They wouldn't have let me in if—"

"Nobody *has* to lie, Jasmine."

I drew spirals into my jeans with my finger. "You lied to me."

"What are you talking about?"

"About Mom—you told me she left to take a job in London."

"You were five. What was I supposed to say?"

"It's not like I didn't overhear Grandma and Aunt Sari's comments, or notice how they looked at me."

"So you're saying it's my fault you lied?"

My hand clenched into a fist. "No!"

"Then tell me what you're getting at, Jasmine."

"Do you have any idea what it's like to do everything you can *not* to be someone?"

"You're being cryptic."

"I've got her eyes, her love for music. Grandma couldn't look at a single picture of me without saying, 'You'd better watch this one. She's got Michelle's smile.'"

He let a few seconds go by before exhaling into the phone. "You can't dwell on the past forever."

"Our last conversation ended when you said I reminded you of her."

"Your actions, not you. The good thing about actions is you can change them."

"By doing what? Going to college right now? You may think I'm being selfish, but not going to college isn't a crime."

"No, but you're putting yourself in a desperate situation. And for what? You've got options, Jasmine!"

An ache formed in my throat. Why didn't he get it? "I feel like I've been trapped in a classroom my entire life. In junior high, it was all about taking the advanced classes, getting into Peninsula Hills. And Peninsula Hills was *like* going to college. That's what they prided themselves on. I never had enough time for music. But I kept telling myself I would—someday. That's what kept me going."

"There's no reason you can't take music classes in college—even major in it."

I rested my forehead against my hand. "I don't want to experience it through theory books and lectures. It just wouldn't be the same."

"If you don't go this year, you'll keep putting it off."

"I need to see this through, whether I fail or not."

"I just don't understand you, Jasmine."

"Obviously."

Neither of us spoke for a few moments. Two seagulls glided over the water, weaving around each other.

Dad cleared his throat. "Well, the ball is in your court. I'm here if you need to talk or want advice, but that's it. I'm not—"

"Giving me money. I got it."

"I wish you could see what I see."

"Ditto." What more could I say?

"I guess I'll talk to you later, then," he said.

"Wait . . ."

"Yes?"

"I . . . I don't want you to hate me." I shut my eyes, fearing what he might say next.

"I don't. I just wish you'd wake up."

"I know."

A car door closed and an engine started on his end. "I've got a meeting to get to. But you know where to reach me."

"Yep."

"Bye, Jasmine."

"Bye." I snapped the phone shut, sucking in my breath. That was about as close to an understanding as Dad and I got. But I'd take it right now. Despite everything, I wanted him in my life— even from afar. And that surprised the hell out of me.

I watched a group of surfers try to cling to a wave. They were a mess of bobbing heads, arms, and feet. Maybe Bryn was out there. I wondered if he'd even talk to me at this point, or hear me out.

"You're on my rock," a voice said, followed by the crunch of footsteps.

I shaded my eyes and saw Sean hovering over me, the sun a halo behind his head. "I didn't see your name on it."

He held something small and shiny out to me. "I come in peace."

I took the object from him. It was hard and wrapped in silver foil. Chocolate. "What's this for?"

"Generally people eat it. Can I sit down?"

I shifted over, giving him plenty of room. "It's your rock, apparently."

His arm brushed mine as he slid next to me. "You should try it—best chocolate in town."

I unraveled the foil and took a small bite. It tasted exactly how good chocolate was supposed to—potent and creamy. "It's great. Thanks."

I studied his profile, wishing I could read his thoughts or have some idea what to say. His nose was straight and defined, unassuming like his voice. Uneven bits of stubble ran along his jaw, as if he'd rushed shaving. It made him seem less together, more human.

He glanced over at me, and I turned away, biting my lip and hoping he wouldn't ask what I was gawking at, or—worse yet— give me that "take a picture, it'll last longer" line. Kyle Larson said that to me in the eighth grade. I never got over it.

"Have you ever been surfing?" he asked, finally breaking the silence.

"No. Have you?"

"Yeah, I suck at it. But I was pretty good on a skateboard. Can't figure that one out."

"I'm not athletically inclined at all. But I guess that's kind of obvious."

His lips twitched. "I dunno. You sure hauled ass down Ocean with those guitars."

"You saw that? Great." I looked away. "Veta said your mom doesn't tolerate lateness, so . . ."

"It's true. She's pretty kick back, but she's got her buttons."

"I like her—your mom. I mean, your whole family is great. You and Zoe seem a lot alike."

He smiled out at the water. "I hear that a lot."

I took another bite of chocolate and let it coat my tongue. He didn't seem to be in a rush to bring up what happened. Maybe he was waiting for me.

"So I'm sorry about last night," I said. "The show, whatever happened afterward. I think it might have involved puking."

He scrunched his nose, looking down. "Yeah."

I put my hands over my face. "I'm such an idiot."

"Don't worry about it. We all have our moments, trust me."

I folded my arms, keeping my focus on the waves. "You said I talked about my dad—what did I say exactly?"

"You weren't all that coherent, to be honest. You said he kicked you out because all he sees is *her*."

My back stiffened. "I talked about my mom?"

"Is that who 'her' is?"

"Yeah." I let a breath out.

He looked in my direction, like he was expecting me to say more. But I didn't. Couldn't think of how to start.

"I've been meaning to tell you I'm sorry," he said. "For being a dick when we met. You caught me on a really bad day—or week, actually. I kind of hated the world." A half smile brewed on his lips. "More than usual."

I hugged my knees to my chest, thinking of Jason. How he'd stuck by me year after year, even when I got weird. "Teddy was your best friend, right?"

He leaned forward, resting his elbows on his legs. "Since second grade. I miss him as much as I hate him."

"Did they just hook up once—he and Amy?"

He nodded. "Me and Amy had a fight—and I went for a drive. She decided to take refuge in Teddy's room with a bottle of vodka."

"Did you catch them?"

"Amy was sitting on my bed when I got back. She told me."

"Wow."

He shrugged, a burst of air escaping his lips. "Sounds like a bad reality TV show, right?"

"Sounds like two crappy friends who don't deserve you."

"That's what Veta said."

"I don't know what a breakup is like. That would require having a relationship, which I've never had because . . . well, who knows." I rolled my eyes. "My point is, I know what it's like to be screwed over by someone you trust."

"Your dad?"

My lips parted. How much did I want to tell him? Sean was really growing on me. Maybe I even had a little bit of a crush. Okay, more than a little. But I needed to forget that.

"I'm not going to judge you," he said. "I promise."

"It was my mom, actually. She took off when I was five."

He nodded. "My dad left after I was born—decided he couldn't handle the family thing. All we saw of him after that was his child-support checks—and that was only because my mom didn't let up."

I smiled. "Good for Tina."

"Do you know where your mom is?"

The waves roared in my ears, and a thick breeze painted goose bumps down my arms. Saying who my mom was out loud made it real. But I wanted to know Sean. I wanted him to know me—even if I couldn't work things out with the band.

"She's in prison." My chest deflated as soon as the words slipped off my tongue. I'd said it. It was done.

He didn't say anything for what felt like the longest time. "What did she do?"

My eyes tilted to the clearing sky. "Whatever kept the money coming. My dad never told me much about her—like where she came from. I know she ran away with her boyfriend at fifteen and ended up homeless. I know she was a bartender at this bar my dad and his friends always went to during their residency. She told him she wanted to study fashion design but couldn't afford it." My fingers dug into sharp edges of rock. "I once heard my grandma say that Dad knew she had problems but he was smitten. He wanted to give her the world."

"Did he?"

"Not the one she wanted, I guess. She cleaned out their bank account and then basically disappeared. We didn't know where she was until this identity theft ring got busted in Vegas five years ago. She was one of the people they arrested."

"What do *you* remember about her?"

I closed my eyes, trying to see her face. Dark curls. Red lipstick. Big brown eyes. "She'd smoke on the patio—Camels, I think. She always had music playing—'80s hair metal bands, usually. It was pretty terrible."

Sean chuckled. "Yikes."

"She had a soft voice, almost sweet. And she always took me to this one park. It had a weeping willow she loved to sit under—she liked trees. She talked about them as if they were people."

"You remember a lot."

"Just insignificant details."

His fingertips brushed my arm. "They sound pretty significant to me."

I hugged my knees tighter. "I wish I could forget her."

"But your dad won't let you?"

"I deferred my acceptance to Stanford. I'm not ready. He doesn't get that—he thinks it's just laziness."

"You got into Stanford?" He shook his head. "Shit."

"I kind of snapped during my graduation ceremony. My friend Jason and his boyfriend were whispering together about their trip to Hawaii. Everyone around us was talking about freedom, parties, bad college food. But all I could think about was another four years of *this*. Feeling like I can't breathe." I shook my head. "I think he's afraid I'll end up like her."

"Lying to get in a band won't prepare you for a life of crime." He nudged me. "I don't think."

"I really love playing with you guys, especially Veta. She's amazing."

He rolled his eyes, grinning. "She's a total attention whore. But, yeah, I guess maybe there's a little talent in there somewhere."

I punched his arm. "I wish I knew what to say to her. Hell, I wish I knew what to say to Bryn."

"Show them you're worth the trouble."

"What if I'm not?"

"If you don't believe it, neither will they. Just like the audience didn't buy you last night."

I rested my chin against my arms, watching a large wave ax another surfer. "Last night was a nightmare."

"You can let it scare you off or take it on. Trust me, it won't be your only bad show."

I gave him a sidelong glance. "I told you—I'm not a wuss."

He leaned toward me, his breath hitting my ear. "Prove it."

My shoulder curled up. "You really want me to?"

"We won't find another Jasmine."

"Since when is that a bad thing for you?"

His lips twitched. "Don't fish for compliments."

I shoved him, laughing. "Shut up."

"Make me."

"Don't say that."

His eyes lifted to mine. "Why?"

"I'm stronger than I look."

"So you keep saying."

I got up on my knees, planting my hands against his chest. "I'll push you right off your rock."

He pressed his shoulders back. "Go for it."

Just how exactly *would* I manage this? A surprise attack, maybe.

"I'm not ticklish, so don't bother," he said.

My eyes narrowed. "You think you got me all figured out."

I waited a few seconds before lunging at him. He grabbed my wrists, holding me off. I twisted my hands out of his grip and went for him again, which made him laugh.

Okay, that wasn't working. So I tackled him, a full-on body slam. I didn't care if we both landed on our butts—just as long as I proved my point.

He fumbled to grip the rock, his eyes widening. "You're nuts, you know that?"

I didn't budge. It was a little awkward—feeling his warmth against me, our faces inches apart. Mostly because I liked it. A lot. "I just hate losing."

The corner of his mouth curved up. He wrapped one arm around my waist and used his other hand against the rock as leverage to sit upright. Which pretty much left me straddling his lap.

"You still haven't shut me up," he said, keeping one arm around me.

That annoying blush crept up my neck again, but I kept my eyes on his. "Um . . ." I didn't have anything witty to say. All I could focus on was the yellow around his irises, his dark eyelashes, and the faint scent of his shaving cream and blueberry shampoo.

"There's that deer-in-headlights look again." He brushed his fingers through my hair, pushing it over my shoulder.

My heart pounded a little harder. "Find another gum wrapper?"

"Maybe."

His fingertips followed the contours of my cheek, like he was doing a hesitant sketch, and he leaned into me. My eyes fluttered shut—terrified we'd knock teeth. His lips met mine, but I couldn't even remember how to move my mouth, much less breathe.

Just as he started to pull away, I wrapped my arms around him and returned the kiss. His fingers slid down the back of my neck, drawing me closer, and I tasted a hint of cinnamon on his tongue. Part of me knew this was a bad idea, but every nerve tickled, not wanting it to stop.

I'd made out with guys before, but it was more because they weren't completely disgusting and they happened to notice me. Sean was different. And not just because he knew how to kiss—quite well, I might add. He was the first guy I actually wanted to kiss.

Which kind of scared the shit out of me.

Our breaths quickened and my hands slid under his shirt. We'd yet to come up for air, but stopping would be awkward. We might actually have to talk about what we were doing.

"Yow!" a guy called behind us. "Go for it, dude."

Someone else laughed.

We pulled apart. Moment ruined.

The voices came from two boys—probably around fourteen. They ran off when Sean glared over his shoulder at them.

"Little bastards," he said.

I looked down, letting my hair fall over my face. "Yeah."

He tucked a lock behind my ear. "What's wrong?"

"I wasn't expecting this."

"Me neither. I'm sorry if I—"

"No, I wanted to." I laughed, scrunching up my nose. "I just thought . . . I thought I wasn't your type."

"You're not. I mean, you're not like Amy." This time it was his turn to wince. "That didn't come out well."

I climbed off his lap, my limbs shaky. "It's okay—I get it. She's all badass and tattooed—and I'm . . . boring."

"You know what's boring? All the scenesters in this town. Everyone trying to out-weird each other. The same faces at every show, every club. The same drama. Amy thrives on that bullshit. I don't. Never did."

I wrapped my arms around myself. "Then why were you with her for so long?"

"Because when it was just me and her, we got each other. She's really not as hard as she pretends to be." He glanced over at me. "Kind of like you. She's got rich parents too."

"Seriously?"

He laughed. "Yep. Oceanfront house—it's huge."

"Never would've guessed."

"Yeah, she prefers it that way." He ran a hand through his ruffled hair. "I'm not the best with words. But I do like you—if that isn't obvious."

"Why?" I sucked on my lower lip. It still tingled from our kiss.

He tilted his head back. "Did you not hear what I just said?"

"I'm a girl who likes reasons."

He sighed. "Okay—the way you play guitar, for starters. I've never seen anything like it. Your methods, the way you move— none of it makes sense to me, but it works really well. I like how you let yourself get lost in the music when you think no one is looking. You close your eyes and you get this little smile on your face . . ."

I looked away, not able to hold back a grin. "Shut up."

"You need to get yourself back in the band."

"I know," I said. "I need to pay for my car too."

He put his hand over mine. "That's true."

I exhaled, closing my eyes. "Yeah."

Chapter 15

I wanted to make damn sure I got to work early the next morning, which meant running the whole way. Veta hadn't called me or dropped by yesterday, not surprisingly. And Bryn was out all day. Which was a relief. After that kiss with Sean and cleaning my disaster of a room, I wasn't ready to deal with anyone. And I needed to do this right.

I burst through the door to find Veta on the white couch, reading another guitar magazine.

"You're early," she said without glancing up. "Why?"

"I still have a job here, right?"

"Why wouldn't you?"

I shoved my hands into my pockets. "I just figured after everything—that you might fire me."

She flipped a page. "I know how to separate band issues from work, Jasmine."

"That's not . . ." I shook my head. "Can we start over?"

"I don't have a time machine, babe."

I sat in the rocking chair across from her. "How about a reading?"

"You got twenty bucks?"

"If you want me to pay, I'll pay."

She tossed the magazine on the coffee table and folded her arms. "Why do you suddenly want a reading?"

"I thought maybe . . . I don't know. I'm sorry. I know those are just words, but I really am."

She exhaled, her face softening. "Look, Jasmine, I get why you did what you did. Why you might not have been comfortable fessing up to the guys, especially Bryn. But you waited until the last minute to tell *me*. And that was only because you were freaking out."

"I didn't want to disappoint anyone, especially you."

"Well, you disappointed me *and* pissed me off. Congratulations."

I swallowed, looking down at my hands. "I wanted to tell you—almost did a couple of times."

"But you didn't, and that's my point. I respect that you're guarded and all that, but this was something that affected all of us."

"I know." I met her gaze. "I don't like asking for help."

"Why?"

"If a class was hard, my dad always said, 'Figure it out on your own. You won't have a tutor to walk you through life; why start now?'"

Veta crinkled her nose. "That's ridiculous."

"I know, but that's how I feel too. It's bad to need anything I can't give myself. Because I don't want to end up like . . ."

She looked at me expectantly.

My body tensed. If I could tell Sean, I could tell her— she was my friend too. I owed her that much. "My mom."

"She's the superdependent type, huh?"

"You could say that." I told Veta briefly how my mom left and where she ended up. "It's not something I want the world to know. I wish *I* didn't know. Because, that's my mom. No matter what I do, I'll always be part of her."

"You're not her, though. You're you. If anything, I'd say you have a lot more of your dad in you."

I shook my head. "We're nothing alike—that's why he kicked me out."

Her sandal tapped against the hardwood floor. "So the fact that you're telling me all this—does that mean you trust me?"

I nodded. "I think you're a good person. You're true to the people you care about."

She relaxed against the couch, sighing. "I don't exactly have a halo over my head, believe me. I make a shitty girlfriend. And I have a mouth—I've said a lot of mean things."

"I can't see you being shitty to anyone . . . unless you're protecting someone." I grinned, thinking about the sludge she poured on Amy's head.

"Remember that ex I mentioned—Sophie?" she asked.

"You said she moved to New York, I think."

"She got into NYU—film school. I was supposed to go with her." Her eyes lifted to the ceiling. "But my life is here. NYU and all that was her dream, not mine. I didn't have the guts to tell her— hey, I don't love you enough to give up my dreams."

"She shouldn't have expected you to."

"Well . . ." Veta looked down, picking at her nails. "I told her I cheated on her."

"Why?"

"It was the one thing I knew would make her glad to go to New York without me. I didn't want her to have regrets. Because if I told her the truth, I was afraid she'd decide to stay and resent me for it." Her forehead crinkled, like she was trying to hold something back. "I suck at love."

"We all suck at something."

She shrugged. "So you see? I'm no saint."

"Who is?"

She studied me for a few moments. "Why haven't you had a boyfriend?"

"Ask guys."

Her eyebrows rose. "It's all them, huh? Not your back-the-fuck-off 'tude?"

"Well, apparently I'm good enough to make out with. That's about it."

"Or maybe that's all you want."

"I didn't really like them much . . ." *Not like Sean.* I broke eye contact, focusing on the magazines.

"Speaking of guys . . . Did you really sleep with my brother?"

My mouth dropped open. "What? No. I mean, yes." I held my hand up. "But—"

"I know. Felix told me what happened at the party. And Sean knows better. Even if he thinks you're cute."

"He said that?"

She rolled her eyes. "I know my brother. His biggest crushes have always been musician chicks."

"Oh, right—Amy."

"Don't forget Dolores O'Riordan—singer of the Cranberries."

"Really?"

"Oh my God. He was, like, smitten when he was little. He had every album and a gajillion posters."

"Interesting. I thought he'd be more into dark, gothy singers."

"He had this obsession with everything Irish. I think it made him feel closer to our dad somehow."

Heels clacked down the stairs. "What are you doing, ladies? It's after nine—chop, chop." Tina clapped her hands.

I bolted up. "Sorry, I lost track of time."

Tina grinned. "I'll let it slide this once." She walked back to the supply closet.

"Hey," Veta said. "We're having a band meeting tonight."

"Yeah?"

She grinned. "In case you wanted to show up and fight for your cause."

"Thanks—I'll be there." I headed for the supply closet—probably the first time I'd ever looked forward to cleaning. Just the thought of confronting Bryn again filled me with dread.

I was behind the counter by myself when Amy showed up. She looked like a gothic G.I. Jane in a wifebeater and cargo pants cut off at the knees.

"Need something?" I asked, keeping my tone cool. Why bother with politeness?

She rested her elbows on the counter, her lips curving up in a half smile. "Veta here?"

"She's doing a reading right now—should be done in a few."

Her expression didn't change. "Heard you're out of the band."

I really wanted to wipe off that smug look. Or maybe just punch her. "You heard wrong."

She squinted. "Hmm, that's funny. Bryn just put the word out that they're looking for a new guitarist."

"Yeah, well, Bryn isn't the whole band."

"We talking about the same Bryn? 'Cause he seems to think he is."

I shrugged. It wasn't like I could argue with that. "It's probably more comfortable to wait on the couch."

"More comfortable for who—you or me?"

"Both. You obviously have a problem with me—for reasons I

can't figure out. And I think you're a bitch." The words slipped out before I could stop them. But, for once, I was kind of glad.

"Ooh, feisty." Her lips stretched into a wide grin. "With nothing to show for it."

"I had a bad night—so what? It was my first show."

Amy gave me another one of her quick scans, like she was assessing me for defects. "I bet you're one of those girls who carried around a skateboard just to snag skater guys. The kind with the shiny, unused wheels." She folded her arms. "Me and Veta used to pound fakers like you."

"I've never touched a skateboard. And if you're implying I play guitar to impress guys, you don't know what the hell you're talking about."

"You're just another chick who can't play her instrument but thinks batting her eyelashes is gonna make up for it. It's a shame, too. You've got some nice gear."

I bit my tongue, wishing I could jump over the counter and drag Amy outside by her overdyed hair. Those were funny words coming from someone who couldn't actually sing. Who was passable at bass—but not great. And what was left? A bitter girl with a lot of holes in her face. The largest one being her mouth, of course.

"Get out," I said finally. Kicking out the losers *was* part of my job description. And I wasn't going to let this girl intimidate me anymore.

"Are you serious?"

"Yeah, I am. Get out."

"Or what?" She laughed. "You'll call the cops?"

I moved out from behind the counter. "That would take too long."

"Don't tempt me, sweetheart."

I'd never been in a fight. But in that moment, I didn't care. I just wanted a shot—any shot.

Voices echoed behind us. Veta headed our way with one of her regulars, a hippie college student named Sage. Sage gave Veta a hug and handed me a twenty before leaving.

Veta's eyes locked on Amy, her smile fading. "What are you doing here?"

"I wanted to talk to you," she answered.

"About?"

Amy's eyes flicked from me to Veta. "Can we at least go upstairs or outside?"

"I'm working—in case you haven't noticed."

Amy shrugged. "This won't take long."

"Fine—outside." Veta rolled her eyes at me before following Amy out.

I let out a breath, grateful that Veta interrupted us before things got ugly. I'd been tempted to slug obnoxious people before—who hasn't? I just never came that close to actually doing it. There was something about Amy that inched under my skin and made me boil inside.

Zoe came barreling in from outside and went for the couch. She cracked a book open, her small mouth puckered and tense.

"Hey, Zoe—everything okay?" I asked.

"Yeah, fantastic," she muttered, casting a weary eye toward the entrance.

The door jingled again and a trio of giggling kids sauntered in, two girls and a boy about Zoe's age. The boy had jagged dark hair and a skateboard tucked under his tanned arm. He headed toward the counter while the two girls huddled together, giggling at Zoe. Zoe ducked her face behind her massive book. Poor girl. I wished I could tell her it got better.

"Hi," the boy said to me. "Are you Jasmine?"

"Yeah—who are you?"

He pushed his shades on top of his head, revealing wide brown eyes. "I'm Nick. Bryn's little brother."

I glanced at the girls ogling him. I should've guessed. "Nice to meet you. Those your friends?"

He shrugged, wrinkling his nose. "That's Stacy and Lindsey. They followed me in here."

"We did not!" one of them called back.

"What can I do for you all?"

"I was trying to catch up to Zoe, but she ran in here first," Nick said. He looked over his shoulder at her. "Hey, Zoe."

A green eye peeked over the cover of the book, and a barely audible "hello" followed. Apparently Nick wasn't put off by this, because he walked right over and sat next to her.

"She's so weird," one of the girls whispered.

"I know," the other said.

"If you girls want a place to hang out, the Boardwalk is across the street," I called over to them.

The redheaded girl sneered in my direction. "We know."

Just then Veta breezed back in. "What is this—a slumber party?" She stopped in front of the redhead. "You buying something this time, Stacy?"

"I'm Lindsey," she replied.

"Whatever. Leave," Veta said.

The other girl pointed over at Zoe and Nick on the couch. "What about them?"

"She lives here. And he's not standing around, blocking our entrance." She made a waving motion toward the door. "*Adiós!*"

They rolled their eyes and trudged out of the shop, whispering to each other again. Veta looked at Nick and Zoe, a persnickety smile forming on her face. She walked behind the counter and leaned into my ear. "I should probably kick him out. But that is just too cute."

Zoe was pointing at her book and explaining something to Nick, and he was listening intently—or at least doing a good job of seeming like he cared.

Veta propped her elbows on the counter, resting her face in her hands. "I'm so tired of drama."

"Amy sure brings it, doesn't she?"

She stood, sighing. "Maybe you should sit down for this."

My stomach tightened. "Just spill it."

"Okay, so Dave and Teddy's friend Nate—" She rolled her eyes to the ceiling. "Nate's this—"

"Jerk with a Mohawk. I saw him at the show."

"Right. Apparently, they bashed C-Side on the Luna's Temptation message board last night and posted a cell-phone video, starring you."

Heat rushed into my face. "What?"

"During 'Encryption,' I guess. When you were having sound problems."

"Oh my God." I slumped against the counter. How much more of this bullshit did I want to take? "And Amy dropped by to rub it in?"

"She claimed that she and Teddy had *nothing* to do with it."

"It was probably her idea. You should've heard the crap she said to me." I went over the gist of our conversation, including Amy's comment about her and Veta *pounding fakers like me.*

Veta tilted her head back and laughed. "Oh, please! That was a million years ago. Look, Amy has always been competitive, and you're a threat—that's all it is, babe."

"How? She saw me play at my worst."

She smirked. "Sean."

I looked down at the hardwood floor, hiding my expression. "What do you mean?"

"Oh, come on, Jasmine. Even I noticed how cozy you and Sean were at the Roach, and I was pretty distracted."

"We were just hanging out."

"Well, Amy doesn't know that." She put her hands on my shoulders. "But you don't need to be worrying about her right now. If Bryn saw their comments, he's not going to be feeling generous tonight."

I gritted my teeth. "Wonderful."

I stopped in front of the studio door, hearing animated voices inside—mainly Bryn's. The meeting had started a few minutes ago, but I kept finding reasons to linger in the main house. Needed to comb my hair. Got thirsty. Felt like a granola bar.

My cell phone went off. The sound echoed across the backyard and the voices stopped inside. Of all times for Jason to call me back.

"Where've you been?" I whispered.

"I'm so sorry! I left my cell on the beach—just found it." He laughed. "It's crunchy, but it still works."

"Can't talk right now. About to do damage control."

"Good luck!"

"Thanks." I snapped the phone shut. Now or never.

All eyes fell on me when I walked in. The band was in a circle on the floor. Veta on her stomach, feet swaying in the air. Felix sitting crossed-legged. Bryn with his legs spread out wide in front of him. And Sean against the wall, one knee tucked into his chest, the other stretched out. He gave me the kind of knowing smile you give someone you share a secret with.

"Hi," I said, clasping my hands.

Veta scooted over and patted the space next to her. I could see the resistance in Bryn's shoulders as I sat.

"Why are you here?" Bryn asked.

My heart sped up. I guess we'd be diving right in. "I want to stay—in the band."

"That's nice, but it's not happening," he answered.

"Bryn . . ." Sean said.

I tucked my knees to my chest, wishing they could shield me from Bryn's glare. "I'm sorry for what I said after the show—about you being spoiled. I don't know you or your family. I had no right to make assumptions."

"I appreciate the apology, but it doesn't change anything."

"I'm not done," I said. "I could've worded it better. But I do think you can be pretty harsh with the band."

He shrugged. "I don't get you. You don't get me. But you know what? This is my house, my studio, and I started this band with Veta and Sean. That makes you shit outta luck."

What the hell could I say to that?

"But we're not *your* band," Sean said, his voice almost too soft to hear.

"What's your point?" Bryn asked.

Felix glanced between the two guys, biting his nails. I wondered if he'd ever experienced confrontation before joining the band.

Sean leaned forward, as if he was preparing for something. "What Jasmine said about you treating us like employees was pretty dead-on."

Bryn stabbed his drumstick into the floor. "This from the guy who makes C-Side his lowest priority. Who misses at least one practice a week because he'd rather study the sex life of fish."

"It's more complicated than that. But thanks for the astute summary."

"You're welcome, Jeeves."

"We get that this is your house, Bryn," Veta said. "Even if you didn't remind us constantly. We get that you devote a lot more time than the rest of us."

Bryn's eyes bugged out. "I'm the only reason anyone knows who the fuck we are. I book the shows. I'm the one with the mastering studio hookups. I handle all the promotion now that Teddy's gone—over a bunch of petty, high school b.s."

"Petty?" Sean asked. "You haven't been with a girl for more than five minutes. What would you know?"

"I'm smart enough to know better," Bryn said. "Who the hell needs to settle down before they're twenty? Twenty-five, even? Do yourself a favor and live a little."

My fingers dug into the rough material of my jeans. "I didn't mean to start this—I should've just kept my mouth shut."

"You didn't," Felix said. "This was brewing before you got here."

Bryn jabbed a finger at me. "She lies and makes us all look like asses, but I'm the one on trial. That's pretty good."

"Nobody is on trial," Veta said. "Stop being so dramatic."

Bryn put a hand to his chest. "Oh, *I'm* dramatic?"

"Yeah," Veta continued. "You can dish it, but you can't take it."

"Oooh!" Bryn tilted his head back. "You are such a hyp—"

"You know what?" I hollered over them. "This isn't solving anything—this is just a bunch of yelling."

"And you're adding to it," Bryn said.

"Okay, what can I do?" I asked, meeting his stare. "If you want me to work on my stage presence all night, every night—I'll do that. If you want help with promotion, I'll do that too. I'll clean the entire house from top to bottom."

Bryn's eyebrows rose. "You can't even clean up after yourself,

Jasmine. You left my cheese out all night. After you ate three-fourths of it."

My mouth dropped. "What? Why would I touch your cheese? I hate sharp cheddar."

"But someone here eats it like candy," Sean said, nodding at Felix.

Felix's ears turned red. "Um . . ."

"I asked you point blank, man," Bryn said. "You told me you saw Jasmine eating it last night."

Felix scrunched up his face, doing that shy thing he did so well. "Sorry, Jasmine. I only did it because I thought you were leaving and . . ."

I rolled my eyes. "It's fine—whatever."

"Awesome," Bryn said. "I live in a house full of liars."

"Gee, Bryn, I'd offer you some cheese with that whine, but apparently Felix ate it all. Can we move on now?" Veta asked.

Bryn folded his arms tight across his chest. "Fine."

Veta rubbed her temples. "The Luna's Temptation show is in less than two weeks. And if you didn't notice last time, pickings for *industrial rock* guitarists are pretty slim."

"Give me a break," Bryn said. "Everyone and their brother plays guitar, okay? We just need to find someone decent who kills it onstage and nails it in the studio. How hard is that?"

I hugged my knees tighter, wanting to break in. Wanting to tell Bryn that I was decent.

"Maybe that's all you're looking for. I want more than that," Veta said.

"I know this guy—Eli—kickass metal guitarist," Bryn said. "I mean, this guy kills. His band just broke up, and I know he's looking. He might be into it."

"Oh, sure," Veta said. "Until the next hot metal band picks him up."

I waved. "Hello? I'm still here. And I *am* a decent guitarist. I can work on the stage thing."

"There are too many cons with you, Jasmine," Bryn said. "For one thing? I don't want a guitarist I have to babysit at parties."

He just had to remind me of that, didn't he? "That will never happen again."

Bryn laughed. "Yeah, I've heard that one before, but it doesn't matter. We've got bigger problems. Do you have any idea what people are saying about you on the boards? About us?"

I looked down at my hands. "I heard about the video."

"Yeah, and guess who sent me an e-mail about it this morning? Ajay."

My eyes fluttered shut. Ajay Yamada was the drummer for Luna's Temptation. I didn't want to hear this.

"He said they've been finalizing dates for a summer tour—starting in August. And they want to bring an opening band. We're one of the bands they're considering."

"Oh my God." Felix's hands hovered over his mouth. "That's huge! Right when our new album comes out too."

"Yeah, except we need a guitarist to finish it. We can't exactly use Teddy's shit. And Hazel can only master so fast," Bryn said. "Not to mention, between losing Teddy and Jasmine's smashing performance up on YouTube, Luna's Temptation is a little concerned. Can't say I blame them."

"So we rock our show with them, and Jasmine records her guitar parts," Veta said. "Problem solved."

Bryn motioned to me. "I don't see her vastly improving in two weeks. She needs at least a few gigs under her belt."

His words hit me right in the stomach, but I had to stay here. I had to fight for this.

"We'll do another show at the Roach," Sean said.

"No dice," Bryn said. "Newton's Whore cockblocked us and snagged the only available slot for the next month. And Dave is working Zia on the LT message board. She's already agreed to go to their show on Saturday."

"Ugh." Veta clenched her teeth. "I hate that guy."

"Veta has a big crush on Zia," Sean said to me.

"So? The woman is perfection," Veta replied.

Zia Martin was the lead singer of Luna's Temptation. She defined the word "enigmatic" with her bizarre answers to interview questions and her unpredictable performances. I saw one show that resembled a scene out of *Moulin Rouge!* and another that was as dank and sterile as an insane asylum.

"Do you think Dave knows about the tour?" I asked.

"Luna's Temptation announced plans last week," Bryn said. "And I'm guessing Dave knows they're looking for an opener. Nothing stays under wraps for long."

Veta shrugged. "So what? Newton's Whore formed a week ago. They aren't ready for a tour. They haven't even finished an album!"

"You know Amy," Sean said. "Chance like that? She'll make sure they're ready."

Just hearing her name, especially from Sean's mouth, gave me that feeling of *ick*. "Then we'll make sure we're even more ready." I caught Bryn's eye. "Or you guys will."

"We don't have the time to dick around, looking for other guitarists," Sean said. "What if the next one doesn't work out? Jasmine knows the songs."

I mouthed "thank you" to Sean. But Bryn didn't look convinced.

"I can't take back what happened," I said, "no matter how much I wish I could. Believe me, I've never been more disappointed in myself—or humiliated. And I can't promise you miracles. But I'm still here. That should count for something."

"Just *being here* isn't going to get us on tour with LT," Bryn said.

"Neither is sitting around and squawking like a bunch of old hens." Veta stood, brushing off her black jean skirt. "The way I see it, we're out of options. She's staying."

"Seriously," Felix finally spoke up. "This is giving me a headache."

"She's got my vote," Sean said.

Bryn ran his fingers through his dreads, his eyes weary. "If she costs us the tour, I'm going to—"

"Come on," Veta broke in. "Anything could cost us the tour."

He looked around at everyone else. "She screws up again, she's gone. You got that? It's still my house."

"Fair enough," Veta said, while Sean and Felix nodded.

"Great." Bryn's eyes fell back on me. "Then I guess you better get to work."

I hopped to my feet, nodding. But there was still a nagging doubt in my gut. The part that said I didn't belong on a stage. The part that couldn't even imagine letting go.

Chapter 16

I grabbed my acoustic guitar and headed for my balcony after another grueling yoga session with Veta. She swore it would help me with my stage fright, but all I felt was sore.

No meditation could beat the pinch of strings against my fingertips. Or the sight of the ocean merging with a crisp blue sky. Too bad this couldn't be my stage.

I plucked out the chord progression of one of the few songs I'd written and actually remembered. It was in a minor key, a little somber, but cozy at the same time. As the song built, I hummed along, muttering lyrics here and there—whatever thought happened to be racing through my mind. It didn't really matter since I couldn't sing on key.

A knock echoed through my room. Maybe Bryn wanted me to stop singing. Served him right, though, considering the noise he subjected me to in the middle of the night.

"Door is open," I called.

Sean appeared on my balcony a few seconds later, hands in his pockets. "Hey."

"Oh, hi." Why did this have to feel so weird?

He shifted his weight. "We need to talk about your car."

"You can sit." I motioned to the plastic chair next to mine and laid my guitar back in its case.

He plopped down, drumming his hands on his legs. "I miss sitting out here."

"Why did you give it up?"

"Memories, I guess."

"Oh, right." Memories that involved Amy, obviously. Nothing I wanted to hear about.

"And it's nice not having Bryn on the other side of the wall," he added.

I rolled my eyes. "Tell me about it."

We both let out a half-assed laugh and then went silent.

"So," I began. "My car."

"Pete asked me what was up. We're getting smashed right now, with tourists and whatnot. Not a lot of space."

"And you really need me to pay and get it out of there."

He kept his eyes focused on the ocean, nodding. "I told him a little about your situation. He said he'd be okay with you making payments."

I studied his serious expression. "What's the catch?"

"I kind of promised him we'd get your car tonight."

"And bring it back . . . here?" That didn't sound much like a catch.

He chuckled. "No, I figured we'd drive it to the wharf and push it over the side."

"Dork." I gave him a little shove. "I can give you a couple hundred now. And more when I get paid Friday."

"Sounds good to me."

"Thanks for this, Sean. I owe you—big time."

He rested his head back, a little smile still on his face. "Don't thank me. Thank Pete. And, yeah, you owe me eight hundred and sixteen bucks."

"Wait, what's the sixteen for?"

"Sales tax on parts, princess."

I looked away, scrunching up my face. "You must think I'm a real genius."

"Well, you did get into Stanford. But standardized tests don't really measure real-world IQ."

"Shut up."

"I'd tell you to make me, but we saw how that turned out."

What was that supposed to mean? "Right. Wouldn't want a repeat of that." I peeked over at him. "I guess."

He shrugged. "You've been avoiding me ever since."

"No, I . . ." Okay, maybe a little. I hadn't made much effort to talk to him, and I'd turned Veta down when she offered me shotgun in Sean's car. "I'm sorry. I just . . ." *Don't want to like you too much.*

"It was one of those things—whatever." He faced me. "We don't have to talk about it."

But I kind of wanted to. "I don't want things to be weird."

"A little late for that."

Silence.

"Should we get the car?" I asked.

"We don't have much time—I was thinking after practice."

"Okay." I tried to think of something else to say—something to make him more comfortable. "Have you ever been to Monterey or Carmel?" I pointed at the strip of land across the glittering blanket of water. Santa Cruz made the northern tip of what was referred to as the Monterey Bay.

"Sure."

"My dad took me to Carmel a lot when I was little. I thought it was the most boring place on earth."

"There are some amazing beaches over there. Rugged, quiet. The clouds keep the sun bunnies away," he said.

"I'd probably like it better now." I glanced over at him. "Have you ever been to the wharf in Monterey?"

"Yeah, we used to skateboard over there and wreak havoc."

"My dad always took me to see the dancing monkey there. Highlight of my trip," I said.

"I loved that monkey."

We smiled at each other. He had a certain spark in his eyes, the kind that tickled my stomach.

"What were you playing out here?" he asked.

"Just this song I've been working on forever. It's still not done."

"I'd love to hear it."

I nudged him. "And I'd love to see your drawings."

"Only if you promise to play me that song when it's done."

"Deal," I said.

"There's one drawing I could use your opinion on."

"Go get it."

He looked down, like he was rethinking the offer for a second. But then he stood. "I'll be right back."

After he left, I got up and walked over to the railing, watching boats of varying sizes dodge each other. I hoped he didn't suck. But I couldn't imagine him being bad at much.

Sean returned a minute later and stood next to me, sketch pad in hand. It had already been flipped open to a page of his choice. "Don't freak out, okay? I like to draw people, but usually I make them up."

"I won't." I took the pad from him.

A series of delicate lines formed the shape of a girl's profile. She stood on a rock, staring at the ocean. Gentle marks with an eraser made her hair look like silk floating around her face. She wasn't smiling, but her hands were laced together—as if she was at peace with herself. An open guitar case sat on a rock behind her, waiting patiently. I recognized her determined squint; she was contemplating a million things and gathering the strength to accomplish every single one of them.

"Wow." Once again, he'd left me speechless. I wanted to tell him it was beautiful, but that would be like calling myself beautiful. And I never saw myself that way.

"Is 'wow' a good thing?" he asked.

I looked up at him, taking in his flushed cheeks and the uncertain curl of his lips. The way his hair kind of stood up in the back, as if he'd been lying on a staticky pillow. And then I rose to the balls of my feet and kissed him, tucking the sketch pad under my arm.

He wrapped a shaky arm around me, pulling me closer. His lips tasted like salt and cinnamon, a combination that made me feel warm all over. I reached up, weaving my fingers through his hair, but he slipped his pad out from underneath my arm and broke the kiss.

"I guess that means you like it?" he asked.

"Love it." I moved toward him again.

He rested his forehead against mine. "We shouldn't do this out here."

Bryn was slinging weights around in his room, and Veta and Felix were watching some anime movie downstairs. But any one of them could suddenly decide to run out into the front yard. They weren't the most predictable people in the world.

We moved inside my room, where he set his sketch pad on the carpet and started kissing me again. I ended up on my back, my crumpled sleeping bag beneath me. He kissed a trail down my neck, his breath sending tickles across my collarbone. Our hands roamed under each other's shirts, all sloppy and excited, until I finally yanked his off.

A loud thud sounded behind the wall, followed by a loud clanging noise and Bryn cussing. We both laughed into our kiss.

Sean broke away. "We need music."

My fingers traced circles against the soft skin of his back. "We could go to your room."

"We could," he whispered, his lips closing in on mine. "But . . ."

"Yeah . . ." That was about all I got out before his mouth was on mine again. This felt way too good. And judging from the pressure against my thigh, he thought so too.

He edged my shirt over my head, his eyes widening at my black cotton bra. Or, more likely, what was underneath.

"What—you haven't seen boobs before?" I asked. I hoped he wouldn't be like other guys, who basically forgot the rest of me once they saw my chest.

He smiled, his eyes meeting mine. "I won't look if you don't want me to."

"I—"

The sound of my door flinging open interrupted me. I looked over Sean's shoulder to see Veta gawking at us, mouth agape. This could *not* be happening.

"Oh, for fuck's sake." She blocked her eyes and slammed the door closed.

Sean cussed and rolled off me. "Why is it so hard to knock?" he called.

I fumbled for my T-shirt and threw it over my head. Sean did the same.

"Get your ass out here, Sean," Veta said through the door. "Now."

"Give me a second," he said, his cheeks pink. We both knew why he was stalling.

We sat there for a few awkward seconds, me clutching part of my sleeping bag, him looking toward the ceiling like he wanted to fly through it.

"Any day now," Veta said.

"She sounds pissed," I whispered.

"Don't worry." He gave me a gentle peck on the lips. "She'll only hit me." With that, he grabbed his sketch pad and went for the door.

Veta smacked the back of his head as soon as she saw him. "*Pendejo.*"

"Ow." He shut the door, muffling the harsh whispers that followed.

I heard Veta say something like "What the hell are you thinking?" before they moved away, probably toward his room.

I was annoyed at myself for not locking my door. At Sean for being so irresistible. And at Veta for making such a huge deal out of this. Mostly because I knew she was right. The last thing we needed was more band drama.

Another knock at my door made me jump. "Can I come in?"

I took a deep breath at the sound of Veta's voice, preparing myself. "Yep."

She walked in and sat on her heels. "Hey."

I looked down at my fingers, weaving them in and out. Anything not to face her. "You're not going to hit me too, are you?"

"No, but I am going to tell you that you're an idiot. Bryn was leery about you living here for a reason."

"It just happened, okay?"

"Doesn't it always?" She moved off her heels and sat cross-legged. "It's not like I didn't know you had a crush on Sean. I just thought you knew better than to act on it."

"I do—did. But I didn't expect him to be so . . ." Amazing.

"Wow, you really like him."

I tucked a lock of hair behind my ear. "Whatever. I barely know him."

"Jasmine . . ." Veta gave me her warning voice.

"Fine." I let a smile slip. "He's turning out to be a lot more than I expected."

Veta covered her face, shaking her head. "Oh, dear God." She dropped her hands. "Band stuff aside. He's not over Amy, babe."

"I know." I folded my arms. "We've just kissed a couple of times. It's not like I'm expecting to be his girlfriend."

"But you like him more than other guys you've met."

"Maybe—yeah, a little."

She studied me in that intense, Veta way. "Then you shouldn't be messing around with him."

"It's not all me, you know."

"Why do you think I smacked him?" She shook her head again. "You're on thin ice with Bryn as it is."

"I know, Veta." I closed my eyes. "Believe me, I know."

"I'm just saying . . . you've got a lot more to lose than Sean does."

I swallowed. "You're right."

Bryn's door opened. "Practice time!" he called.

"You ready?" Veta asked.

"Yep." I gave her the biggest smile I could manage, not wanting her to worry. I'd already made her stress enough this week.

Bryn's plan for curing my stage fright was inviting his groupies over to see our practices. About five girls stood against the wall, most of them smiling in Bryn's direction.

We started with "Encryption," the first song I butchered at the show. I closed my eyes, trying to think only of the music, the moment. My fingers danced through the verse arpeggio without faltering, but I was also being cautious. That fear of messing up began to swell in my throat.

When we hit the chorus, Sean made his way over to me and we

played in rhythm, leaning toward each other. My fingers fed off the vibration of his bass notes and the heat of his skin. I tilted my head back, letting the melody break me down from the inside.

"Your eyes don't match your words," Veta sang. "But I can't hear a thing. No, I can't hear a thing but your sweet encryption."

I took a peek at our mini audience. A couple of the girls were dancing together, arms in the air, while another watched us intently, bobbing her head. They all looked entranced, as if the song had taken over their minds.

This was what Saturday night should've been.

When we finished, the girls clapped and hooted, asking for more.

"What'd you ladies think of Jasmine?" Bryn asked. Somehow I doubted they were looking much at *me*.

"She's good," a girl with short dark hair said.

"Yeah, you and the bassist have a cool energy," another said, grinning at Sean and me.

"What's your secret, man?" Bryn asked Sean. "You opened her right up."

Sean laughed and shook his head. "It wasn't me."

Veta cleared her throat, a smirk twitching at her lips. "Well, *something* is bringing you out of your shell."

I looked down, feeling an odd mix of relief and unease. I didn't have to hide anymore. I could just be myself. The girl who finally decided to come out of her best friend's garage and join the world.

And then there was Sean . . .

Our audience lasted for half the set before they bailed. Not that I blamed them. Band practice couldn't be fun to watch with all the stopping and starting. Playing the same song over and over. The bickering over a seemingly petty element.

"I've got news," Bryn said after we plowed through "Back-Seat Love Affair." "Didn't want to say it in front of them."

Uh-oh. I'd come to fear Bryn's *news*.

"We're doing another show on Saturday."

Not again.

"This Saturday?" Felix's eyes widened.

"Bryn," Veta began. "I—"

"Here!" Bryn broke in. "We're doing a casual show here—in our studio. And then I'm throwing an after-party."

"But I have a date with Samantha," Felix said.

"So invite her and go out after," Bryn said.

"Isn't Newton's Whore playing the Roach on Saturday?" Sean asked.

"Yep," Bryn said. "Perfect night for a party, huh? Luna's Temptation being in town and all?"

"Oh, Bryn," Veta said. "You're pure evil, you know that?"

Bryn gave her innocent eyes. "What? I throw good parties."

Those pesky knots started forming in my stomach again. "Luna's Temptation is coming *here*?" I asked.

Bryn nodded. "It was Ajay's idea. He thought it would be cool to drop by and see us practice. Like I said, it'll be a casual thing. Just a couple of songs."

"Great," I said.

"It wasn't like I could say no."

I knew he was right. You didn't say no to a band like Luna's Temptation—even if they wanted you to play in your underwear.

"You got through your first show—which is huge," Veta said. "It will get easier. You're already improving."

"I just hope I don't psych myself out again," I said.

Bryn shot me an annoyed look. "Then don't."

"Don't overthink it. You'll drive yourself nuts," Sean said.

"I'm warning you guys now," Veta said. "If Zia shows up, I might be forced to have a total fan-girl moment."

"Samantha says she's straight," Felix said.

Veta waved him off. "Everyone thinks they know who Zia is, but nobody really does."

"Ajay said she shows up to practice in her pajamas," Bryn added.

Maybe I could learn a little something from the lead singer of Luna's Temptation. She sounded like my kind of girl.

Sean and I barely spoke on the way to the auto shop. He'd cranked up "Frozen" by Celldweller, which reminded me of early Nine Inch Nails. A sexy bass line slithered behind breathy male vocals and a distorted riff weaved in and out, adding texture.

After we parked, Sean turned the ignition off, but he didn't make a move to get out. "You got any plans tonight?" His tone was a little too casual, like we were work buddies or something.

"No. You?"

"I'm thinking popcorn and *Grosse Pointe Blank*."

I tried to contain my goofy grin. "Me and Jason worship that movie."

"Yeah? I've probably seen it a hundred times." He drummed his steering wheel. "You want to watch it with me?"

My rational side told me this was a bad idea. But how could I resist Sean *and* John Cusack? "I'd like that."

Sean smiled, reaching for his door handle. "Cool."

We got out and exchanged payment and keys without saying much more.

The steering wheel of the Jetta felt cold and foreign, and the engine was quieter than I remembered. Even the smell was different, mustier somehow. All my memories in this car were with Jason and my dad, my old life. A life I could never drive back to. It made me a little sick inside. With sadness, though—not regret.

I pulled up along the curb and followed Sean inside the house, wondering where we were going to see the movie. Downstairs was the safest bet, but I kind of hoped for his cramped room—maybe cuddling on his bed. *Bad idea, Jasmine. Bad.*

I leaned against the island as he put a popcorn bag in the microwave. It looked like the movie theater–butter kind, my favorite.

"You can go on up to my room and stake out a spot," he said.

"Oh—we're going to watch it up there?" I had to at least *act* like I wasn't thinking about it.

"Yeah, I told you—all my movies are downloaded on my computer." He shook his head. "Actually, you probably don't remember. You were drunk."

I rolled my eyes. "I'll see you upstairs."

He turned his attention to the inflating bag in the microwave. The smooth scent of butter teased my nostrils all the way up the stairs. The loft was quiet and dark, but I doubted Felix or Bryn had gone to bed.

I slipped inside Sean's room, pondering where to sit. The bed seemed too forward—like I was saying, "Hey, let's hook up." The chairs were too distant, definitely not convenient for popcorn passing. Maybe scooting a chair next to the bed would do the trick. Friendly, but not within kissing distance.

Sean pushed the door open, a bowl of popcorn in one hand and two small bottles of cherry cola tucked under his arm. "Still contemplating where to sit?"

"No, I was just checking out your fish . . . posters."

"Right." He set the bowl and drinks on his bed and went over to his computer.

Oh, screw it. I sat on his bed against the headboard, cross-legged and folding my arms. Didn't want to take up too much space.

Sean propped his pillow and slid in next to me, moving the bowl between us. We both smirked at the opening scene, where John Cusack's character, a hit man, argues with his nutty secretary over an invitation to his high school reunion. She wants him to go. He wants no part of it.

Our hands bumped inside the bowl, and we took turns peeking at each other. I wanted to get the popcorn out of the way and tackle him. But I kept reminding myself of the many reasons why I shouldn't.

Halfway through the movie, I laid back against the pillow, stretching out my numb legs.

Sean held up the bowl. "You done?"

When I nodded, he leaned over me and set the bowl on the floor. His arm touched my thighs, sending warm tickles all the way down to my toes.

"Excuse you," I said.

He sat back up, smiling down at me. "Sorry."

"Yeah, right." I stuck my tongue out at him.

He raised an eyebrow.

Then we just stared at each other for a minute, ignoring the voices coming from his computer speakers. He brought his face toward mine and I inhaled, wanting nothing more. As soon as our lips touched, all rational thought disappeared.

Sean seemed to know what I liked—not too much tongue and no cheesy moves. Some guys tried too hard, period. Not that I'd kissed many.

He pulled back. "I thought we could at least get through an entire movie."

"You started it."

"I can stop."

"Do you want to?"

"No," he whispered, running a finger along my cheek. "But . . ."

"But?"

"You know this is a really bad idea, right?" His mouth inched closer to mine.

Yes, but did I care at the moment? Not really. I wrapped my arms around his neck.

"Hang on a sec." He climbed over me and walked to his computer, stopping the movie. He pulled up the iTunes window and clicked on a playlist. The violins in Björk's "Jóga" filled the room, playing a soft, rich melody.

The song was perfect—a little too much so. He moved back alongside me, propping himself up on his elbow.

"Slick," I said. "Is this your hook-up playlist?"

He grinned, cupping my face. "Shut up."

Our lips melted together and our movements mirrored the song, building in urgency and then slowing down again. I rolled on top of him, my eyes fluttering shut as his hands ran up my thighs and followed the curve of my back. He pulled my shirt over my head, and I returned the favor. Goose bumps spread across my exposed skin, but my chest felt warm against his.

Sean ended up on top of me again, kissing his way down my neck, my chest, my stomach. It tickled and sent my heart pounding. His fingers teased the skin underneath the waistband of my jeans and he looked up at me, as if asking for permission.

Jason said the first orgasm you have with another person changes *everything*. And I'd never even had sex—of any kind. The closest I'd ever come was Eric Lamberti sticking his hand down my jeans in his stuffy Volvo. It wasn't pleasant. At all.

But I was curious. Really curious.

I unbuttoned my jeans and Sean slid them off, leaving me in nothing but black underwear and a bra. I couldn't even remember the last time I'd shaved. Yesterday, I thought. *Please let it be yesterday.*

"You all right?" he asked.

"Yeah, why?"

"You look freaked out."

"I've never had sex." Shit. Did I have to blurt it out like that?

His hand tensed on my arm, and his eyes looked uncertain, like he didn't know quite what to say.

"Not that I thought we were going to have sex," I rambled on. "It's just—I haven't done the in-between stuff either."

His brow crinkled. "The in-between stuff?"

"You know—more than making out, but not actual intercourse—sex." What was I—twelve?

His lips twitched.

"Don't laugh," I said.

"I'm not—you're just cute."

I winced. "Shut up."

He kissed the tip of my nose. "I meant it as a compliment. Honest."

"I'm assuming you and Amy have . . . um . . ." Why did this feel so awkward? I had no problem talking about this stuff with Jason.

"What?" He tried to hold back a smile, but it didn't work.

I rolled my eyes. "You know what I mean."

"Are you asking if we had actual-intercourse sex?"

I pushed him away, laughing. "Jerk."

He moved onto his back, staring up at the ceiling. "Sorry, couldn't resist." His expression turned serious. "Yeah—we did."

"Was she your first?"

He nodded.

I folded my arms over my bare stomach, feeling cold. "Do you miss her?"

"Sometimes," he said softly.

"I figured." My voice came out angrier than I wanted it to. He was just being honest.

He propped himself on his elbow again, peering down at me. "Not enough to want her back."

Those gorgeous green eyes made me want to believe him. God, he was turning me into a mush ball. *Not* good. I pulled his face to mine, losing myself in the slow electronica song whispering in the background. A woman sang about falling hard—her voice a mix of innocence and passion. His fingers slipped under my bra and I found the zipper of his jeans.

He broke our kiss. "Maybe we should slow down."

"Why?"

He hesitated, his eyes searching my face. "You're a virgin for a reason, right?"

"I haven't met anyone I liked that much."

He combed his fingers through my hair. "Sounds like a good reason."

"I'm not going to do anything with you I don't want to do."

"Promise?"

"Yes." I poked his mouth. "Now less talking, more kissing."

He smiled and brought his lips to a spot just beneath my earlobe, making me shiver. "That better?" he whispered.

I closed my eyes, murmuring something resembling "yes."

Sean's mouth found mine again, and his hand slid up my thigh. My damp palms glided against his skin, making his muscles tense. I kissed him harder, my breaths coming out in short bursts. All I could think about was this moment—his warmth and the taste of his lips. How I didn't want it to end.

What felt like hours later, we spooned under his covers, our fingers laced together. His slow breaths tickled my ear—he'd already fallen asleep.

My virginity was still intact, but I felt different. There was this deep tickle inside my stomach, the kind I got when a song found me. Every now and then I'd be messing around on my guitar, and the right notes would merge together, creating something incredible. Something I never knew I was capable of.

Unfortunately, a lot of those songs were like comets—they'd light up my world for a night and be gone when I woke up.

Chapter 17

My schedule for the rest of the week went like this: Work. Eat. Practice until after midnight. Sneak in a few kisses with Sean. Sleep.

Despite this, Saturday came way too soon. Tina let us off work early, because Bryn demanded that we have another practice before *the* practice. He was probably more nervous than I was, which didn't exactly make me feel better.

Sean and I sat on my balcony, slurping down bowls of Cinnamon Toast Crunch, while Felix and Veta hogged the bathroom and prettied each other up. Veta was on makeup job #4 last I'd checked. Bryn paced around the loft, arguing with someone on his cell. He kept saying things like "chill" and "No, I didn't."

"You doing okay?" Sean asked.

I swallowed a mushy bit of cereal. "I could use a real dinner."

He grinned. "There's always Felix's baguette."

"Yeah, we'd need a saw to cut it." None of us were very good at grocery shopping, especially this week. And Bryn said he'd tackle anyone who tried to eat the food he'd bought for the party.

"You impressed Bryn last night," Sean said before slurping the rest of his milk.

"That's funny. All I remember is him bitching about that part I added to 'Puppet Girl'—or maybe that was Thursday. I can't remember. Sleep deprivation and all."

He draped his arms over his knees, looking out at the water. "He said, 'Jasmine actually seemed like part of the band tonight.'" A smile twitched at his lips. "Then he questioned his sanity."

"Lovely." I shook my head. "It's a step, I guess."

"You're going to be fine tonight." He massaged the back of my neck, working his way across my shoulders.

I tilted my head forward and closed my eyes. "Keep doing that and I'll buy anything you say."

"Really?"

I elbowed him. "Don't get any ideas."

We still hadn't talked about us, and I didn't know how to bring it up. How did one say, "I know you just went through a messy breakup and Bryn would kill us, but would you ever consider being my boyfriend? Not now, of course. In the future. The *near* future, maybe. Because I'm really starting to like you. A lot."

It embarrassed me that the *b* word was even entering my thoughts. I'd done fine without one for seventeen—almost eighteen—years. But I was tired of being the girl to kiss and forget. I wanted something real. I wanted to matter.

My bedroom door opened and footsteps padded across the carpet. Veta appeared on the balcony, staring down at us, her eyebrows raised.

"What?" Sean asked.

She folded her arms across her chest. "Must you two be so obvious?"

"He's just helping me relax," I said.

Her lips quirked up. "Oh yeah? Bryn looks like he could use a little relaxation." She winked at Sean. "Maybe you can help him out too."

Sean dropped his hand. "Har, har."

Veta flipped her hair back and did a little turn. "What do you think, Jasmine? Too much?" She had on a short black dress with thigh-highs and tall boots. The term Dominatrix Barbie came to mind. Zia, gay or straight, would surely notice.

"You look hot," I said.

She grinned like she knew it. I had to admire confidence like that. "Now we just have to do you."

"No." This time I'd be playing as myself—faded Taylor tee, ponytail, and all.

Her lower lip stuck out. "Not even your hair? We could do little buns on the sides—you'd look so pretty."

"She looks pretty now," Sean said.

I shot him an appreciative smile but hoped it didn't show the giddiness I felt inside.

Veta sneered at him. "I never said she didn't."

"You guys ready?" Bryn hollered from the loft.

"Yeah!" Veta called back, and then groaned. "God, I hope Zia shows up."

I did too. Although, I was pretty nervous to meet her and the rest of the band. What if they were total pricks?

Luna's Temptation said they'd drop by around seven. It was seven thirty. And Newton's Whore was supposed to go on at nine, according to Bryn.

The five of us plus Samantha sat on the floor of the studio, gulping water and munching on a bag of cheese puffs. It was meant for the party, but Bryn got hungry and let us chow down. Practice had gone as well as it could. Minimal arguing that was mostly between Bryn and Felix. Bryn still hated the "mosquito tone" synth in "Acceleration."

Felix and Samantha huddled in a corner together, whispering and giving each other little pecks. It was really adorable, but I couldn't help feeling envious. Sean and I kept exchanging these smiles through practice. All I wanted to do was run my fingers through his hair and kiss him.

"You did tell them to come back here and not the main house, right?" Veta asked.

Bryn rolled his eyes. "I'm not an idiot. And Ajay has my cell."

"When was the last time you heard from him?" Veta asked.

"Still yesterday, Veta. That hasn't changed in the last hour," Bryn said before cramming a handful of cheese puffs into his mouth.

"What exactly did he say?" she continued.

"I didn't memorize the e-mail." His words were distorted by chewing.

"She wants to know if Zia is coming," Sean said, a smirk twitching at his lips.

"Ajay said he and Nile were coming for sure—that's all I know."

Nile Morel, the brooding keyboardist, was considered by many to be the male eye candy of Luna's Temptation because of his long brown hair, angular jaw, and lanky frame. A couple of Jason's goth friends were obsessed with him and plastered pictures of him all over their desktops and bedroom walls. I couldn't imagine him standing in *this* stuffy little studio. Maybe that was why they hadn't shown up. It wasn't supposed to happen.

Bryn's cell phone started blasting "Dance Hall Girl"—one of Luna's Temptation's most popular songs. We all kind of froze, looking wide-eyed at one another. Were they here?

Bryn fumbled for his phone and nearly dropped it. "Hello?" His eyes flicked to the door of the studio. "Don't worry about it, man. We're just hanging out."

"Are they coming?" Veta whispered.

Bryn put his hand up, looking down at his feet. "Yeah. Okay. Sounds good."

"Is Zia coming?" Veta continued.

He waved her off. "All right, later."

"Well?" Veta's hazel eyes bugged out.

"They got caught in traffic and Ajay got hungry." Bryn stuffed his phone in his pocket. "They're about five minutes out."

Sean and I exchanged an uneasy look. Was this really happening?

"And *they* would be?" Veta asked.

"Obsessed much?" Bryn asked, standing and crumpling the bag of cheese puffs.

Felix laughed. "Do you have to ask?"

Samantha squealed in the corner, her cherubic face stretching in a wide grin. "I can't wait!"

Felix gave her a kiss on the cheek.

The rest of us stood, all looking around like we suddenly didn't know what to do first. My hands shook and my heart thudded.

Sean came up behind me, putting his hand on my shoulder. "I'll play next to you if you want."

I leaned toward his ear. "I might like that a little too much."

He grinned. "That's the idea."

Veta cleared her throat as she walked past, giving us a warning look. We pulled apart and kept ourselves busy, tuning our instruments and checking equipment. As if we hadn't already set everything up.

The studio door opened what could've only been a couple of minutes later. Samantha crouched down next to me, Felix put his fingernails in his mouth, Veta stood taller, and my hands tensed around my guitar. At least I was only slightly nauseated this time.

Three people walked in. Ajay, the drummer, was the shortest of the bunch, not much taller than me. Jagged dark bangs framed his face, but his hair was short and spiky in the back. He nodded and waved at us before leaning against the wall.

Nile, the keyboardist, moved in next to him, his steely eyes settling on me. His stare seemed to burn through his pictures, but the in-person effect was even more intense.

I turned my attention to Zia, who loomed by the door. She looked almost angelic with wispy bleached hair, big blue eyes, and a white crocheted dress that fanned out over her legs. Veta gawked at her, a dopey grin on her face.

Bryn gave Ajay and Nile "guy" handshakes. "What's up?"

"This place is dope," Ajay said. "How much rent do you pay for that view?"

Bryn shrugged and laughed it off. "Enough, man. Enough."

Veta and Sean exchanged a smirk.

"I, like, *love* you guys," Samantha blurted out, standing up. "It's so cool to meet you."

Zia responded with a cool nod, while Ajay and Nile gave her polite smiles. Samantha took this as license to bound up to them and start gushing over their last show. Bryn shot Felix a death glare—as if Felix had control over the situation.

Samantha pulled out her cell phone and started snapping pictures of Ajay and Nile. Zia ducked outside, like this was all too much for her. She hadn't said a word since she got here—which made her either shy or a total diva. Hard to tell which.

"Bryn looks like he's about to shit glass," Sean whispered in my ear.

I bit my lip, trying not to laugh.

"Felix." Bryn clenched his teeth.

"What can I do?" Felix mouthed.

Bryn threw his hands up, as if he were saying, "Grow a pair!"

"Um—hey, Sammy?" Felix called in a too-soft voice.

When she didn't respond, Bryn put a firm hand on her shoulder. "We need to get started, okay? They've got a show to get to."

"Oh." Samantha covered her mouth. "Sorry. I'll just, um . . . I'll go outside and let Zia know."

"Don't—" Bryn started, but she was already out the door. "Sorry about that," he said to Ajay and Nile.

Nile chuckled—it came from deep in his chest, like he meant it. His eyes rested on me again. "That's a sweet ax."

My lips stuck together, preventing me from saying "thank you." Nile Morel was speaking to *me*. How was this happening? I stretched my mouth up, hoping it resembled a smile.

Bryn grabbed his sticks and plopped in front of his drum kit, while Ajay checked Veta out and whispered something to Nile.

Sean leaned into my ear again. "Is Nile making you tongue-tied?"

I gave him my best *whatever* look.

"Thought so," he muttered, focusing on his bass.

"Should we wait for Zia to come back?" Veta asked, lowering her guitar strap over her shoulders.

"She'll probably come back when she hears the music," Ajay said. "Conversation—when she's not in the mood—makes her *wander.*" He exchanged a knowing grin with Nile.

Veta cocked her head. "Wander?"

Nile answered this time. "Yeah. She calls it refueling or some shit. Sometimes she'll just disappear in the middle of a conversation. Don't take offense—it's not personal. Zia is just . . ."

"Zia." Ajay chuckled.

I wondered if she regularly did that to fans. Then again, it probably didn't matter. They were Luna's Temptation. She could flip everyone off at a show and people would give the gesture some deep artistic meaning.

We'd decided to start with "Back-Seat Love Affair" this time. Veta figured something hard and catchy would get their attention, especially my Bond-like guitar part. They were counting on me to nail it—which I had no problems with during regular practice. Unfortunately, my mind kept focusing on who was standing against that wall, watching.

A thick drum loop started up, calling for my lick. I closed my eyes and let the rhythm seep inside me and take over my hands. But I didn't let myself breathe until I joined Veta with the power chords leading up to the first verse.

When I opened my eyes, Sean smiled at me and leaned back with his bass, tapping his boot like this was the most casual thing ever. I followed his lead and let my head bob to Bryn's beat. I didn't care how dumb I looked—better to get lost in the moment than to hesitate and screw up.

Veta swayed in front of the mic, her voice breathy and controlled. "Come into my little world. Where twilight reigns and kisses taste like novocaine."

Zia had managed to sneak in without me noticing. She stood next to Nile, focusing on Veta. Her expression was completely neutral—almost aloof. Eyes that expressed interest, but not too much. Mouth set in a calm line—not smiling or frowning. I wondered if she practiced that look in the mirror.

Veta widened her stance, taking us into the chorus. "Back-seat love affair, with that leather stare. Hardened ecstasy. You'll never come down." Her voice was spot-on tonight—with just enough grit to cut through our distorted guitars.

I caught Nile's gaze and the corner of his mouth perked up. An icy feeling ran through my veins—was he laughing at me? Did I look really dumb? Did I play a sour note?

Sean pressed his arm into mine, and the friction of his movement awakened my every nerve. I closed my eyes, forgetting everything but his warmth and the familiar smell of his skin, a mix of citrusy deodorant, cars, and sweat. His fast and steady bass line hummed through me, and I moved with him, my fingers sliding between the twelfth and fourteenth frets.

Sean's lips brushed against my ear. "Nice." He moved away, picking the frantic bass notes of the bridge.

Veta rocked back and forth, her sultry vocals turning into a snarl of rage and desire. "Come on, ride with me. We'll strip off our masks and leave no regrets."

I wanted to go to this place Veta sang about—a place where I was free to be me. Where I could love without consequence. Just for a little while. Long enough to impress the hell out of Luna's Temptation, at least.

I tipped my head back, inhaling everything around me—the heat, the growl of our guitars, Sean's steady rhythm and presence, Felix's squealing synth and goofy grin, and Bryn's no-nonsense beat. My fingers glided right into my solo just like they used to in Jason's garage. The melody screamed everything I felt—excitement, uncertainty . . . lust.

Veta faced me with a grin, chugging out a fast and tight riff. She let her eyes drift to the ceiling as if she were getting lost herself.

I played off her energy—even adding in a couple of unexpected notes. There was this incredible sense of power brewing inside of me. I bent the last note, letting it build in the air like a siren.

And from then on, I was in the zone—even when I messed up a part in "Acceleration." I was enjoying myself, dueling with Sean, jamming with Veta. For the first time, I really felt like I was part of this band.

Ajay held his hands up after we polished off "Puppet Girl." "We gotta split. But listen—you guys sound hot."

Sean and I exchanged an excited glance. We pulled this off. *I* pulled this off?

Nile looked in my direction. "What happened Saturday?"

Oh God, he'd seen the video. "Off night," I said.

"Obviously." He grinned. "Hope you don't have too many of those."

I eyeballed my feet. What to say, what to say . . .

"There still a party going on tonight?" Ajay asked, saving me the trouble.

"You know it," Bryn said, walking over and holding his hand out.

Ajay shook it and slapped him on the back. "Cool, we'll talk more then." He nodded at the rest of us. "Thanks for letting us listen."

"It was a pleasure," Veta said, her eyes landing on Zia. "I've been dying to meet you—all of you."

Ajay gave her a flirtatious smile. "Take care of that voice, huh? It's killer."

She wiped a bead of sweat off her forehead. "Thanks."

Zia gave her a stiff smile but didn't comment. The three of them waved and shuffled out the door in what seemed like record time. I hoped they weren't *too* excited to see Newton's Whore.

We waited a minute before jumping around and squealing like

children—well, Felix, Veta, and I did, anyway. Bryn collapsed to his knees and rested his forehead against the floor. Sean watched all of us in amusement.

"So I did okay, right?" I asked. Just to make sure I wasn't dreaming or in denial.

Veta threw her arms around me. "You. Were. Awesome."

She'd caught me off guard, but I hugged her back, letting myself relax. "So were you." I laughed. "I think Ajay wants you."

"Good for him." She pulled out of our hug, a playful gleam in her eyes. "Nile seemed to like you."

"No, he liked my *ax*."

"Well, it's a nice ax," Sean said with a smirk.

Veta rolled her eyes and fell back against Felix, fanning herself.

I took in Sean's messy hair and flushed cheeks. Why did he have to be so cute after he played? Why did he have to be so cute . . . period? Yikes. I needed to stop this. I sounded like a lovesick girlie girl.

"Hey," he said. I knew the look in his eyes—intense but hesitant. It was the same one he'd give me before we were about to kiss.

I pulled my guitar strap over my head. "Hi."

"Where's Samantha?" Felix asked, bringing me back to reality.

Bryn sat up, squinting at him. "Maybe Zia bound and gagged her."

"Very funny." Felix took off out the door. "Samantha?" he called, his voice fading. "*Samantha?*"

"Maybe he should whistle for her while he's at it," Bryn said.

Veta shoved him with her foot. "Ass."

"Well?" Bryn shook his head. "Listen to him. Who does that?"

We all looked at one another and said, "Felix."

* * *

The party was in full swing by eleven, and Veta insisted on introducing me to a sea of faces. Too bad it only amounted to a few awkward hellos and nods. People still saw me as that girl who choked onstage. What were they supposed to say?

The living room turned into a mosh pit when Luna's Temptation arrived. If people weren't shoving one another to talk to one of the band members, they were staring and pointing at them.

Veta and I sat on the stairs, chugging Coke out of plastic cups. She gazed longingly in Zia's direction.

"If I didn't know better, I'd say she makes you nervous," I said.

She shook her head and sighed. "I can talk to just about anyone, you know? I always have something to say."

"But she makes your mind go blank."

"It's her energy. It's so . . ." She rubbed her temples. "It's like she's ten different people—and I don't know which one is the real her."

"Maybe she has multiple personalities."

Veta crinkled her nose, giving me a defeated look. "Even if she does? I'd still want her."

I laughed. "They say love is blind." My eyes drifted to Sean. He was talking to a couple of guys, making wide hand gestures.

"I'm not one to get starstruck, either," Veta continued. "It's not about who she is. I don't know if it's her voice or her presence—there's just something about her that makes me feel . . ."

"Like you're home," I muttered.

"Kind of. She feels familiar—like I've known her for centuries."

Sean caught my eye and smiled. For a second, everything but his face went out of focus. We were the only two people in the room. And then he looked away.

"You know what I mean?" Veta asked.

I tucked a lock of hair behind my ear and nodded. "Do you believe in past lives?"

"I do." She nudged me. "I think me and you were sisters in a former life."

"Really?"

"Yeah—you don't feel it?"

I grinned. "You're kind of like an older sister to everyone."

Zia broke away from the crowd and headed toward the kitchen. Veta's eyes trailed her.

"Go talk to her," I said.

"You think I should?"

I gave her a shove. "Yes—go."

A squeal came from her throat. "Wish me luck!"

"I'll be around in case you crash and burn."

"Gee, thanks." She hopped down the last two stairs and shoved her way through the crowd.

"Excuse us," a guy's voice said behind me.

I scooted over as Felix and Samantha hobbled their way past me. Both of them had messy hair and glazed eyes. They waved and said hello before joining the party.

Now would have been a really good time to bail, but something kept me sitting there. Who was I kidding? More like *someone*. Which was stupid, since he'd pretty much ignored me all night.

I closed my eyes and downed the rest of my soda.

"Hey—that better not be SoCo," a familiar voice said. Sean. Maybe he'd read my mind.

He plopped down next to me and took a swig of his Corona.

I nodded at his bottle. "That doesn't look like root beer."

He smiled. "Hey, I know when to stop. Unlike some people."

I gave him a playful punch in the arm. "Bite me."

His shoulder touched mine. "Don't tempt me."

My eyes focused on his soft lips. They were redder than usual and a little damp. Talk about tempting. I looked down at my empty cup. "It's about time you came over and said hi."

"Sorry. There are a couple of people here I haven't seen in ages, so—"

I put my hand up. "You don't need to explain yourself. It's just . . . I'm—" Being my blabbermouth self.

"It's hard for you; I get it," he said. "You don't know anyone."

"Yeah." That wasn't it. I wanted to go somewhere with him—alone. Be in our own little world, like Felix and Samantha. But we weren't Felix and Samantha. "You don't have to sit with me—or whatever. I'm okay observing the chaos."

He put his hand on the small of my back. "What if I want to?"

A flutter of excitement hit my stomach. "Then that's . . . fine." I looked up at him, the music fading around me. It seemed like he was inching closer.

"Hey," a girl said.

I turned to face Amy, of all people. She stood in front of us, her fingers tapping against the railing.

"What are you doing here?" Sean asked, shifting away from me.

I folded my arms and contemplated bolting.

Amy grabbed his Corona and took a swig. Then she burped. Classy. "Ajay invited us. It'd be kind of lame to turn him down, don't you think?" She held his beer out to him, smiling.

He waved her off. "Keep it. Teddy here too?"

Amy's grin faded. "Yeah. You should return his calls. He misses you."

"How's that your concern?" The tension in Sean's voice was enough to make me hold my breath. He wasn't over her. Not even close.

She shrugged, her eyes flicking to me for a second. "It's not, I guess."

"What do you want, Amy?" he asked.

"You've got some of my stuff. And . . ." She looked down at her feet, pursing her lips. "I was hoping we could talk for a minute."

"What stuff?" Sean asked. "I'll go grab it."

She cocked her head. "Why are you being like this? I thought we were cool."

His fingers drummed against his knees. "I don't feel much like talking."

"Just for a minute—that's all I'm asking." Her voice was soft, almost sweet. The girl knew what she was doing.

He sighed and looked over at me. I knew he wanted to go. No matter how much he tried to hide it.

"What, you need her permission?" Amy asked.

"Shut up," he replied.

"Go ahead," I told him. "I'm fine."

His hand brushed against my shoulder as he stood. "I'll be back in a minute."

Amy gave me a cold smile. "You can time us if you want."

I flipped her off.

Her knee bumped my shoulder as she moved past me. I watched them climb the stairs and disappear into the loft, my throat tight. I didn't know what I expected him to do. Tell her to go scratch, maybe? Did I even have the right to expect that?

Then again, he said he'd only be a minute. So I waited five. And then five more. Then two more. A lot could happen in twelve minutes.

After seventeen minutes, I realized sitting here and waiting like a puppy dog wouldn't change a damn thing. It didn't matter what his excuse was. The fact that he was still in there with her and not out here with me said enough.

I headed into the crowd, weaving my way toward the front door. But I didn't get very far before Teddy blocked my path.

He pushed his long black hair out of his face. "Jasmine?"

What did *he* want? "Yeah?"

"How's it going? I'm Te—"

"I know who you are." You're the guy who hops in bed with his best friend's girl.

"Listen, um . . ." He leaned toward my ear, talking louder. "I wanted to say sorry for how the guys and Amy treated you at the show. They can be dicks."

"I'm not the one you owe an apology to," I said.

"I th–thought," he stammered, "someone should, um . . ."

I felt this surge of adrenaline running through me—not anger as much as clarity. "He's upstairs with Amy. Seems kind of unfair, doesn't it? You both screwed him over, but she—*she* still gets to be with him." Okay, maybe it was anger. "Excuse me." I moved past him. The ocean was calling my name.

Unfortunately, someone grabbed my elbow just as I reached for the door handle. "Look, Teddy, I need—" I stopped when my eyes met Nile Morel's.

His lips stretched into a crooked smile. "Who's Teddy?"

"Um . . ." My back pressed against the door. "The drummer for Newton's Whore."

"Oh yeah. We saw them tonight—they rocked."

Rocked? No, they were supposed to suck. "Great."

He drank me in with his gray eyes, a slow scan from my face to my clasped hands. "You got a minute?"

"Uh, sure."

"Sweet." He placed a hand on either side of my head and brought his face closer to mine. His black henley smelled like cigarettes and laundry detergent. My heart started to race. "I'm working on a side project—it's this downtempo deal," he said in a softer voice.

"Like Massive Attack?"

"Similar." His grin broadened. "Anyway, I really like your style—that whole atmospheric thing you do."

Holy crap. "Thanks."

"It's just what I'm looking for." He glanced over his shoulder and moved a little closer. "Would you be interested in collaborating on some tracks with me?"

My eyes were probably bugging out of my head. "You want me to play guitar? For you?" *Pinch me, I'm dreaming.*

"For my side project, yeah. It's not a band or anything. Yet."

"I'd love to." Did my voice have to sound so high?

He stared at me expectantly for a few seconds. Did he not hear me?

"I'd love to. Really," I said.

His lips curled up in another lazy smile. "You going to give me your number or not?"

"Oh," I said, patting my pockets for my phone. Wait, what the hell was I doing?

He pulled a cell out of his pocket and handed it over. "Dial it in."

"Right, okay." I glanced up and caught Sean's eye. He was coming downstairs with Amy, smoothing his ruffled hair. The excitement I felt turned back into nausea.

"Nile," a female voice said behind him. "Need to talk to you." Zia. She spoke. And she was glaring at us. Not good.

I plugged in my number and handed Nile's phone back to him, avoiding Zia's stare. Were they together?

Nile brought his mouth to my ear. "You free this week?"

"Yeah—I mean, I can be." I scanned the room for Sean, but I didn't see him or Amy. Maybe they sneaked out the back door. "Depends on the day."

"Cool. I'll call you tomorrow." Some of his hair fell into my face as he spoke. It smelled like expensive, musky shampoo.

"Nile," Zia said again.

"Later," he whispered.

Once Nile walked off, I could see Sean making his way toward me. I flung the door open and escaped outside. My feet carried me across the damp lawn, but I had no idea where I was going. For a drive, maybe. Or a walk along the cliffs. Anything to get myself together before he saw me.

"Jasmine, wait up," Sean called.

Obviously I didn't make a decision fast enough. He caught up to me and put his hand on my shoulder.

I jerked away, heading for my car. "Don't."

"Could you stop for a minute?" His voice sounded breathy. "Please?"

I leaned against the passenger door of my Jetta. It felt cold and hard against my back, but I didn't care. "My definition of a minute— or yours?"

His eyes combed my face, like he wanted to say a million things but didn't know where to start. He ran his hands through his hair again. Too bad that couldn't smooth away what was written all over his expression. "She broke down in my room. I—I've never seen her like that."

"Can you honestly tell me you're over her?"

His lips parted, but he hesitated.

It felt like there was something caught in my throat. I couldn't even breathe. "That's what I thought."

"I didn't say anything."

"Exactly."

"She was crying—I couldn't just throw her out."

"'Course not." Somehow I couldn't imagine Amy crying—at least, not real tears.

He shoved his hands into his pockets, shifting his weight. "I still care about her. That part doesn't just go away."

"Is that why you hooked up with her? To show her how much you *care*?" I hated how my voice shook. I hated how much *I* cared.

He shut his eyes. "Jasmine . . . that's not—"

"Don't deny it."

"We started to, but I—"

I held my hand up. "So that's a yes."

He leaned against the hood and exhaled, keeping his head down. "I'm sorry."

Was it that easy for him to be with her again? "It's not like we have anything real. We just mess around, right?"

"You know it's more than that," he said softly.

Dad always told me to look for answers in actions, not words.

I faced him. "No, actually, I don't." He couldn't even lift his head, much less look me in the eye. "After what she did to you—I thought . . . I thought you were stronger than this."

A burst of air escaped his lips. "You talk like this is easy. Like you have a clue what it's like to . . ."

"To what? Be in love?"

He focused on a car moving down the street. "Yeah."

"She cheated on you with your *best friend*—and you call that love?" I shook my head. "You're an idiot."

He finally faced me, his jaw tensing. "Look, I fucked up—I admit that. But I did stop."

"Oh, congratulations! You want a medal?" My fists clenched. Part of me wanted to hurt him, make him feel like I did inside.

"I'm sorry I can't be like you. Okay, Ice Queen? I'm sorry I feel something."

"What the hell are you talking about?"

He leaned toward me, his face inches from mine. "When was the last time you let yourself feel much of *anything*, Jasmine?"

I sucked in my breath, pulling back. My eyes burned and my lips felt melded together. But I couldn't run. I didn't want to give him the satisfaction. "Look how far it's gotten you. You're a mess."

He inched closer. "So are you."

The front door opened and a chorus of voices echoed across the yard. Ajay, Nile, and Zia came out, discussing the mating behavior of banana slugs.

"They, like, chew each other's dicks off," Ajay said. The others made faces and groaned.

"Dude, why do you even know that?" Nile asked.

Sean sighed and moved away from me. We both waved and said bye. Ajay and Zia waved back but thankfully kept walking.

Nile grinned at me. "Talk to you tomorrow," he said before catching up with the others.

"Tomorrow?" Sean asked, his voice wary.

"He wants me to collaborate on a side project with him. So he's going to call, I guess."

Sean tipped his head back. "That's a classic musician's pickup line."

"He said he really liked my style. It's what he's been looking for."

"And you bought that?"

"Why would Nile have to *lie*? The guy has groupies coming out of his ears."

"Because you're a challenge," he said.

"I'm a good guitar player—why can't it be about that?"

He shrugged. "The way he was leaning all over you should be a clue it's not."

"It was noisy in there." The idea that Nile could want me, like *that*, was ridiculous. I wasn't the kind of girl regular guys noticed, much less rock-star types.

"Think what you want. But guys have pulled that shit with Amy a few times."

"Gee, that's shocking."

His brow crinkled. "Meaning?"

"She practically asks for it. She's a sl—" I stopped myself. Despite my anger toward Amy, that was fifty different kinds of wrong. "I—I didn't mean that."

Sean moved in front of me. "You sure?"

I closed my eyes and let out a breath. "All I'm saying is, I'm not Amy. You can't compare me with her."

"It happened to Veta once too. Did she *ask* for it?"

"What? No!"

His eyes narrowed. "Why do you think you're so above everyone else?"

"I don't!"

"You've got this sense of entitlement—because you're the holier-than-thou Jasmine Kiss. You never make mistakes, right?"

"That's complete bullshit." I held back the urge to shove him, my hands shaking. He thought he knew me, but he didn't. Not even close. "I'm sorry for what I said. But don't try and ease your guilt by turning this all on me."

"Why should I feel guilty? We don't have anything real, right?" His voice matched his words. Cold.

I thought of a million horrible things I could say, but why bother? His mind was made up. "I was really starting to like you. I was starting to think that you . . . that we could . . ."

He folded his arms. "Could what?"

I looked away, my nails digging into my palms. "Be friends."

"Friends . . ."

"But it'll never happen." I pushed past him and headed into the house, swallowing the lump in my throat. I was done. So done.

Chapter 18

Nile called just after three. Luckily, the shop was dead—Tina was dealing with another visit from Regina Price and her online dating troubles, and Veta was reading a magazine on the couch.

Veta looked up at me, grinning. "Jason?"

I shook my head and answered. "Hi . . ."

"What's up?" Nile asked. His voice sounded deep and strange on the phone. I couldn't believe he was actually calling. Part of me figured he'd forget or change his mind.

Veta cocked her head and mouthed "Who?" I turned away, leaning against the front counter. I hadn't told her about Nile *or* Sean yet. "Not much—I'm at work."

"Oh. You need me to call back?"

"It's fine." Gee, I was a great conversationalist.

"I was thinking—maybe we could do this tonight. My friend bailed on me, so I'll just be hanging around."

Tonight? Oh man. I was hoping for Tuesday or Friday since I had those days off work. "Uh, well, we have band practice . . ."

"Okay?" He sounded almost insulted.

"But maybe I could check out early." I looked over my shoulder at Veta. She raised a wary eyebrow in response. "Like, what time were you thinking?"

"That depends if you need a ride or not—I live over the hill in San Jose."

"We're going to do it at your place?" For some reason, I'd pictured a studio—maybe the one Luna's Temptation rehearsed in.

"Oh, this is getting good," Veta said.

"Yeah." Nile laughed. "Where'd you think?"

"I, um, didn't know." I lowered my voice. "Anyway, I have a car."

"Great—well, I'm usually up pretty late. Give me a call after practice and I'll give you directions."

"Sounds good. Do I need to bring an amp or anything?"

"Nah," he said. "It's covered."

We said our good-byes and hung up.

When I turned around, Veta was curled over the counter, her elbows resting on the glass. "Explain . . ."

"Nile Morel wants me to play guitar for a side project he's working on."

Veta's mouth dropped open. "No way."

"Way." I felt like I should've been more excited. But my thoughts kept going back to Sean.

"And you didn't tell me about this immediately because . . . ?"

I crinkled my nose. "I wasn't sure he'd call."

She smirked. "Does he know you're only seventeen?"

"What difference does it make?"

"You should tell him. Just in case he has other ideas."

I rolled my eyes. "You sound like Sean."

She straightened and shrugged. "Hey, my brother has the psychic gene—even more than me. He just doesn't want to admit it."

"Whatever—he doesn't know everything."

Veta gave me her intense squint. "You two had a fight, didn't you?"

"He told you."

"Give me a little credit, will ya? You've been moping around all day and your energy went all oogy when you said his name."

I laughed. "Oogy? Do you use terms like that when you give readings?"

She folded her arms. "Of course. So what happened?"

I told her everything, including what I said about Amy—which made her wince. "And the thing is, I tossed and turned all night, trying to hate him. But I can't. I've never felt like this."

Her expression softened. "Oh, babe . . ."

"I'm pathetic, right?"

She sighed. "You know what kills me? In a different situation, you and Sean would be great together. Seriously, I'd be thrilled to see him date a girl like you."

"Really?"

She scrunched up her face. "You should've seen some of the girls he crushed on before Amy."

"What were they like?"

"Amy."

I looked down at my clasped hands. Why didn't that surprise me?

Tina and Regina Price walked out from behind one of the dividers. Regina was digging through her large pink bag and babbling about a guy named Thomas. Tina kept nodding and moving her along.

"All I've got are small bills—wouldn't you know it?" Regina asked. "I had to break my twenty today, because the diner raised their price on the Sunrise Special. After *two years*, mind you. Can you believe that?"

"That's just fine, Regina. Don't stress." Tina cast us a look that said "Help me."

Veta covered her smile, her eyes flicking to me.

"All right, well . . ." Regina slowly placed the bills in Tina's hand, counting each one aloud. Then they hugged and Regina made her way out, still rifling through her bag.

Tina let out a long sigh after the door shut. "I need a meditation just to prepare for her visits." She walked over and handed me Regina's money. "So, what are you ladies talking about?"

Veta grinned and flicked her long red hair over her shoulder. "Sean and Jasmine's torrid affair, of course."

"Veta," I hissed, putting the money in the register.

"What?" She gave me innocent eyes. "Mom already knows."

I covered my face. "Oh . . . my God." Did she have to tell Tina *everything*?

Tina put a hand on my shoulder, chuckling. "Don't worry. I like you a lot better than Amy."

"Great." I gave her a tight smile. This was so awkward.

"He hooked up with Amy last night," Veta said, like she was talking about anyone.

I wondered if Sean had any idea his mother and sister discussed his sex life. Maybe that was why he moved out.

Tina's mouth dropped and she said something in Spanish. It didn't sound good. She shook her head at me. "Obviously I need to talk to him. Again."

"Please, don't," I said. "I mean, he said they stopped. Or didn't finish—or whatever."

"Ew, Jasmine." Veta held her hand up. "TMI."

Was she serious? "Um, sorry." I faced Tina. "So—you hate Amy?"

Tina exhaled. "I don't. But she's got major issues to work out. And she won't be good to anyone until she does. And Sean—he takes on too much, you know? That boy can be like a sponge."

"Yeah, I can see that," I said, looking down.

Tina patted me on the back, giving me a sympathetic smile. "What can I say? Boys, men—sometimes they need a Mack truck to give them a clue."

"Tell me about it," I muttered.

Practice was long. Way too long. And Sean refused even to look at me. I tried to add life to my playing by reminding myself that I'd be at Nile Morel's place soon, taking advantage of a huge opportunity. I mean, the guy had loads of fans. What if he put our tracks up? People all over the world would hear me—maybe even know my name.

"Can someone tell me why we suck tonight?" Bryn asked. We'd just finished "Encryption," the bane of my existence, apparently. "Jasmine, you're playing like your dog died. And Sean, you're all over the place. What the fuck, man?"

"Sorry," I said. "I'm a little distracted."

"Me too," Sean muttered, keeping his head down.

Bryn threw his hands in the air. "We've got less than a week, guys! Now isn't the time to go all emo."

"Jasmine has good reason," Veta said, turning to face us. "She's going to Nile Morel's tonight."

Bryn stuck a drumstick behind his ear, giving Veta a perplexed look. "That's . . . interesting."

Sean's head perked up, and his eyes met mine.

"I'm just doing some guitar work for him," I said, avoiding his stare.

"Whoa!" Felix said, grinning at me. "That's so cool. Congratulations."

"Thanks."

"Well, shit," Bryn said. "What are you still doing here? It's after eight."

"I didn't want to miss practice?"

"Get out of here," he said. "And talk us up. A lot. Just don't run off and start a new band with him or anything."

I rolled my eyes, lifting my guitar strap over my head. "Yeah, right." I guess I should've taken it as a compliment that Bryn worried—even jokingly.

"See if you can get any info out of him about the tour," Felix said, his eyes excited. "Like who else they're considering."

"Please don't do that," Bryn said.

I packed my purple guitar in its case. "I won't."

"Have a blast," Sean said, his voice low and tense.

I faced him, taking in the hard look in his eyes. "Thanks. I will." As I walked out the door, part of me wondered if he'd come after me—tell me not to go or something lame. But this wasn't a sappy Hollywood movie. And Sean had way too much pride to be that guy.

Driving Highway 17 felt like a video game, with its sharp turns and endless walls of trees. The orange glow of Bay Area lights shone in the distance after I drove over the Summit and crossed the Santa Clara county line. It was weird to be on this side of the line again and not prepare to merge onto 85 and go north toward Dad's.

I got off at the Hamilton Avenue exit and headed toward Bascom. Fortunately, I was pretty familiar with the area. Nile said he lived right near Streetlight Records, a music store Jason and I haunted all through high school.

Nile's duplex looked nice enough—well kept but dated, like most of the places around here. He probably paid $1500 a month in rent easy—unless he owned it. Music throbbed behind his brown door, a thick, industrial beat and screechy synthesizers. I was afraid to interrupt something. Hell, I was afraid even to be standing here. But this was my chance—to get my guitar playing out there. To learn something from a successful musician. There was so much I wanted to ask Nile. If I wasn't careful, I'd probably pick his brain for hours.

I took a deep breath and slammed my knuckles into the door.

Nile answered, towel-drying his wet hair. Where was his shirt? "You made it." He grinned, opening his door wide and moving aside. "I was afraid you'd get lost and call while I was in the shower."

"Nope." I shoved my hands into my pockets and stepped inside. A sweet-smelling incense overwhelmed the faded stench of cigarettes, and a guy with a giant blond 'fro was camped out on the couch. He appeared to be playing video games. "Did your friend decide to show up after all?" I asked.

"Nah," Nile said. "That's Marty, our professional couch surfer. He can fix any instrument known to man."

Marty nodded at me. " 'Sup, baby girl?"

"Hi." I tried to smile, but my heart hammered. Something about Marty creeped me out.

Nile moved in front of me and extended his arm toward an open door. "Step into my office. I'm going to locate a shirt."

"Okay." I let out a nervous laugh and walked past him. He shut the door behind me.

The room had a velvety red couch, a long desk with two wide-screen monitors, two keyboards, and a variety of recording gear—the kind I could only dream about owning. A Fender bass and a black Gibson hung on the wall. God, I was really here—in Nile Morel's studio. Pinching myself didn't make it disappear.

I plopped onto the couch, setting my guitar case in front of me. The walls were lined with posters, concert stubs, and signed pictures of topless women. One read *lick me. xoxo morrigan*. Gross.

Fast food bags, mainly from Taco Bell, covered the floor around the desk, and there was a giant green stain in the middle of the brown carpet. A couple of open prescription bottles lay near an overflowing trash can, along with what appeared to be a stuffed unicorn. Interesting.

I waited for at least fifteen minutes, listening to the muffled sounds out in the living room. It was mostly Marty groaning or cussing. Sometimes there'd be a loud thump. I never got people who took video games *that* seriously.

Another five minutes went by. Did he forget I was in here? I checked my phone. 9:32. I really didn't want to drive home any later than midnight. Highway 17 was brutal enough when I was fully awake. But it was okay. It gave me time to calm myself and think of questions to ask.

Finally, the door opened and Nile breezed in wearing a black thermal shirt and vinyl pants. His long brown hair had been swept back in a ponytail, and it looked almost like he was wearing foundation. But maybe it was the yellowish lighting in here.

He plopped onto his computer chair, rubbing his temples like he had a headache. "Man, my ex is the biggest bitch."

That seemed to be going around lately. I folded my arms. "Oh, I'm . . . sorry?"

He leaned forward, lighting a cigarette. Indoor smoke always made my throat tickle, but what could I do? Ask him not to smoke in his own room?

"Get this." He blew out a trail of smoke and tossed his lighter onto his desk. "I cosigned on a car loan for her 'cause her credit blows. She suckered me into it."

I nodded, hoping confusion didn't show on my face. I didn't know much about loans or the real world, but how did one get *suckered* into signing a loan document?

"Well, guess who calls me last week?" he continued. "Her fuckin' creditor going, hey, we haven't received payment since March."

"Uh-oh," I said. Why was he telling me this?

"She just now calls me back—after a week of me trying to get ahold of her. I'm, like, what the hell is going on? And she says, '*I replied to your e-mail.*'" His voice went up an octave. "And I said, 'What reply? I didn't get it.' She goes, '*I just sent it five minutes ago. Go check it.*'" He took a deep drag. "So, I said, 'No, we're gonna talk about this now. You need to get this shit paid. They're trashing my credit.' And she goes, '*Well, I'm trying to sell the car.*'" He threw his hands in the air. "What the fuck?"

"That sucks," I said, tapping my foot.

"I said, 'You owe more than the car is worth, moron.' And she hangs up on me. Nice, huh?" He spins around and clicks on his mouse, waking his computer up. "Let me check this so-called e-mail real quick."

I glanced at my cell clock again. 9:47. "Okay."

When he opened an e-mail that resembled a novel, I groaned inside. A wave of smoke hit me in the face, making me cough. I pinched my nose and held my breath for a second so I didn't make a scene.

"Can you believe this shit?" Nile jabbed his cigarette into a blue ashtray. "She says, 'You're a lying, cheating loser who lives in his own filth. You don't even buy toilet paper unless someone reminds you. And you're lecturing me about responsibility?'"

"Um . . ." Why was he reading this out loud? I'd be completely humiliated if someone wrote that about me.

"Ohhh." He lit another cigarette. "What a bi—"

"Maybe we should get started. I'd rather not be driving home at two a.m. My night vision kind of sucks."

Nile spun his chair around. "You can crash here."

And where would I sleep—with creepy Marty in the living room or the Taco Bell wrappers in here? "Can't. I have work in the morning."

"Oh, well, that's a bummer." He studied me for a second before resting his head back on the chair. "I'm done with hot chicks. They want everything for nothing, you know? They're lazy as hell in bed too."

I leaned forward, hugging myself. Obviously I wasn't a *hot* chick. But I wasn't a counselor either. "So, um—"

"I want to date a real girl. A girl who can take care of herself. That's sexy," he continued.

"Well . . ." I motioned to his walls. "You've got plenty of adoring fans. I'm sure there's a great girl out there for you."

He laughed, putting out his second cigarette. "Are you kidding? Most of our fans are dumb, psychotic, or fat—usually all three."

I thought about Jason's boyfriend and his goth friends—how one of them framed a CD Nile had signed. Another talked about what a nice guy he was, that he always made himself accessible and responded to fan e-mails. Sure, she kept calling him her "future husband," but that was beside the point. These people adored him, believed in him—paid his bills.

"You're looking at me like you think I'm a jerk," he said, squinting at me.

I knew I should probably bite my tongue—for C-Side's sake. But I couldn't. "Well, I know some of your fans—I'm one of them. We're sane—for the most part. Not dumb. And being fat doesn't make someone a bad person."

"Dude, I wasn't talking about *you*—and I'm sure your friends are cool. But you've been to our shows, right? Have you seen some of those people?"

Of course there were rabid fans at every show. But they didn't make up the majority.

"I've seen girls—who claimed to be best friends—give each other bloody noses over who got to get on the bus first," he continued. "I've been proposed to, ring and all, at least five times. Married chicks tell me they're single on a regular basis. Guys have asked me to kiss their girlfriends so they'd have a shot at getting laid that night."

My stomach was beginning to turn. "That's . . . insane."

"Exactly!" He tossed his lighter back and forth between his hands. "If you go on tour with us this summer? You'll see. It'll wake you right the fuck up."

"But aren't those extreme situations? There are a lot of people who just love your music. It heals them or speaks to them in some way. Doesn't meeting them make it all worth it?"

He grinned, shaking his head. "I was like you before my first tour, all pumped and starry-eyed. But I learned one thing real quick: People are dumb. Dumb as rocks."

Or maybe you're just a jaded ass, I wanted to say. I'd heard the stories about musicians who let it all go to their heads. But I always pictured those people to be pop stars with vacant smiles or mainstream bands who played stadiums for a hundred bucks a pop. Sure, Luna's Temptation was signed to a huge electronica label and they'd shared the stage with the biggest industrial acts around, but they weren't of NIN fame—at least not yet. It seemed a little early for a Jupiter-sized ego.

"We really should get to work," I said, trying my best not to sound rude. Normally, I'd tell a guy like him to stick it, but then I'd be out of a band.

"All work and no play, huh?" He pursed his lips. "I can dig that. Go ahead and play something, then."

"Oh—okay." I scrambled to open my case. "What am I playing through?"

He motioned to an amp modeler, a way to record without an amp. I preferred real amps, because I loved the raw sound and the vibration beneath my feet. But this would do.

I leaned over him to hook my guitar up, since he didn't offer to help. His breath hit my arm and it felt like he was smiling.

"A girl who knows her way around equipment. That's refreshing," he said.

"Glad you think so." Okay, maybe that sounded too snarky. "I mean, thanks." I lifted my guitar strap over my head.

He clasped his hands behind his head. "So, what are you going to play for me?"

"Aren't you going to put on one of your tracks?"

"I thought maybe you'd want to share something of your own." His foot tapped mine.

I backed away. "That's okay. I don't have anything ready."

His eyebrows rose. "Not much of a songwriter, huh?"

"I am, actually."

"But you don't have a completed song?"

If he wanted me to come prepared with a demo, he should've said so. "I thought I'd be adding to your tracks."

"Fair enough." He faced his computer and opened up Pro Tools, recording software I could never afford. "I'm going for a Morcheeba feel on this one, kind of sultry and bluesy. You heard of them?"

I sucked in my breath with excitement. That I could do, no problem. "Yeah—love 'em."

The song kicked off with a lazy beat, reminiscent of a million trip-hop songs. A simple but catchy synth bass blended in. I tapped my fingers against the fret board, hearing a wah guitar effect fading in and out. "You got a wah setting on this?" I asked, scrolling through the presets on his modeler.

"Try the A bank."

I found a setting that was serviceable, but not even close to a pedal. And then I dove in, adding bits of color. Nothing too overwhelming. "You're going to have vocals in this, right?"

"Yeah—I was actually thinking of your singer."

"Veta? She'd be stoked, I bet."

"Sweet." He lit yet another cigarette. I was surprised this dude could still breathe. "She models for Ink Angel, right?"

"What's that?"

He exhaled a cloud of smoke. "An alternative modeling site— hot chicks with tats and piercings. Pinup-style stuff."

"I don't think so." I added a few more notes to the basic lick I was playing.

"I thought Ajay said it was her. Is it true she's only into chicks?" he asked.

"Yep." Was he listening to this at all? I closed my eyes, focusing on the song. My foot tapped to the beat and I let my fingers explore, not knowing what would come next.

"Oh, wait. I know who it was," he said. "That chick in Newton's Whore. What's her name?"

I hit a sour note. "Amy."

He typed something. "Amy what?"

"Castellano, I think." I opened my eyes to see his browser opened to InkAngel.com. Girls with tattoos, dyed hair, and a lot of skin decorated the page. Was he seriously this rude?

He pulled up a page that showed a girl with intense eyes and a mess of dark hair. Amy stood with a bass, her head tipped back. And worst of all—she had nothing on but a bra, underwear, and thigh-highs. "Damn, baby," Nile said in a husky voice. "Maybe I should ask her to sing."

Growling chicks with vocoders and downtempo music did *not* go together. It would be like Rob Zombie singing a Portishead song.

I jerked my guitar off my shoulders and sat back on the couch. Any hope I'd had for tonight had vanished. Now I just felt sick.

"Hey." Nile turned back around. "Why'd you stop?"

"You seem a little preoccupied." I laid my guitar back in its case.

He rubbed his eyes, standing up. "Sorry, Jasmine. It's been a long day."

I slammed my guitar case shut. "It's fine. Another time. Whatever."

He sat next to me, his arm pressing against mine. "Don't be mad."

I gave him my best tight smile. "I'm not."

"We can hang out. Talk music—if you want." His fingers ran up and down my thigh, making my entire body tense.

I scooted away. "I should go."

His lips stretched into a playful smile. "Oh, come on. Really?" It was amazing how beautiful people could turn ugly when you got to know them. Nile's chiseled features morphed into pointy shapes, making him look like the wicked witch in *The Wizard of Oz*.

"Yes, really."

He sighed—like, actually *sighed*. "Can I get a kiss good-bye at least?"

"Um, no."

"See?" He cupped my face. "You *are* mad." His fingers smelled like Marlboros and spicy cologne.

I removed his hands and stood up, grabbing my guitar case. "See you around."

"Aw, Jasmine, lighten up. I'm just—"

I yanked the door shut behind me, muffling his voice, and got the hell out of there. It wasn't until I got in the car that I let myself breathe. Long, shaky breaths that made me feel like puking. I hated Nile for being—what he was. I hated him for proving Sean right. But most of all, I hated myself for falling for it.

I just wanted this chance so bad. This chance to prove that I was worth something as a guitarist. But maybe I wasn't worth anything, if I needed someone else to validate me—the least-talented member of Luna's Temptation, no less. All he did was look pretty and bang on a keyboard. Zia and Ajay wrote and produced the songs—they were the driving force of the band. Their revolving door of bassists and guitarists couldn't even be brought into the equation. And the way Nile talked about his fans, the things he said about touring—his eyes were so dead. It was like he left his soul on a stage in Kansas somewhere.

My hands slammed into the steering wheel. Was this what I gave everything up for? To be laughed at and ridiculed, treated like I was nothing? It wasn't like I expected rainbows and sunshine—or for anything to be even remotely easy. But I didn't expect to feel like this, doubting the one stable thing I'd ever had in my life. If I didn't have music, what was left?

I forced myself to look in the rearview mirror. At my damp cheeks and heaving chest. Red-rimmed eyes. Trembling lips. Desperation. Fear. Lots of fear. I didn't recognize myself—who was this pathetic person?

I thought about my dad, what he'd do if I came home right now. Probably what he always did when I finally gave in: smile, nod, and make another phone call. But what if I walked in just like this? Would he have a clue what to say?

I thought about my mom, but I didn't see her curled up in a cell somewhere. I saw her putting on red lipstick, her eyes bright and alive. I saw who I thought she was when I was little, the woman she could've been—if she really wanted to be. If she'd had the strength to make different choices.

My hands grasped my seat, squeezing tight. And I just sat there, parked outside Nile's duplex, bawling like a fool. I didn't care who saw me. I had to get it out, because right now everything was a blur. And I had no idea where I was going.

When my eyes had cleared enough to drive, I just barreled forward, not thinking about a destination. It didn't hit me until I saw the SANTA CRUZ COUNTY LINE sign. I wasn't ready to give up yet. I still had fight left in me, even if it meant sucking up my pride—giving Sean the satisfaction of being right. He might've been right about Nile, but he underestimated me. And maybe that was my fault. It wasn't like I ever let him close enough to see the real me. He didn't know that I was terrified he didn't like me as much as I liked him. That, deep inside, all I wanted was to find somewhere I fit.

At the West Cliff house, all three guys were in the living room watching TV. Bryn and Sean took up the ends of the yellow couch, while Felix was reclined in the chair, his bunny slippers bouncing.

Bryn hit MUTE and all three of them stared at me—Felix and Bryn anxiously, Sean more skeptical, like he saw something in my face.

"How'd it go?" Bryn asked with a hopeful grin.

I looked down at my hands, wondering how he'd respond to the truth. If he'd blame me. "It didn't." My gaze moved to Sean. "You were right."

Sean's expression softened, but I couldn't tell if it was pity or relief.

"Right about what?" Bryn asked.

I told them—everything. Even the part about Amy being on Ink Angels, which made Sean turn a little red. I waited for someone to yell or call me an idiot. For Sean to say "I told you so." But they all gaped at me in silence.

Finally, Bryn's fist slammed into the couch. "What a dick!"

"Me or him?"

Bryn crinkled his brow. "Him, obviously. Why would I call you a dick?"

I shoved my hands into my pockets. "I don't know—I thought you might get pissed at me."

"Why?" he asked. "You handled yourself pretty damn well. I would've kicked him in the balls or gone off—you know, if I was a chick or something."

I let a breath out. "I would've, too—if it didn't affect you guys."

Felix shook his head. "What a perv. Isn't he, like, old?"

"Twenty-five or something," Bryn muttered. "Maybe I should talk to Ajay."

"Do you really think he'd care?" I asked.

Bryn shrugged. "Probably not, but still—Nile had no right to treat you like that."

I was surprised to hear those words coming from Bryn, the guy who didn't seem to have a soft bone in his body. "Well, thanks. I appreciate that."

Sean stared down at his hands, his hair falling over his eyes. I wished I knew what he was thinking—if he was thinking anything at all.

"Group hug?" Felix asked.

Bryn shotgunned a pillow at him. "Hug this."

I rolled my eyes, feeling this odd mix of sadness and comfort. Mostly, I was exhausted. I could probably sleep for days. "Good night, guys."

"'Night," they called as I went up the stairs.

I didn't quite get to my door when I heard footsteps coming up behind me. I didn't have to turn around to know who it was. I could just sense Sean now, his quiet tension. "Yeah?" I asked, keeping my back to him.

"I'm sorry. For everything." His voice was soft, almost a whisper.

I faced him. His eyes searched mine, like he was almost afraid of what I'd say. "Me too."

We stood there for a minute, him drumming his hand against his leg, me hugging myself. Both of us safe in our bubbles. Maybe this was how we should've kept things.

"Good night," I said finally.

He brushed his hair out of his face, his lips parting. " 'Night," he whispered.

I went into my room before either of us was tempted to say more.

Chapter 19

I stayed remarkably calm the day of the big show. Right until Bryn showed up with the van. Watching him hop out and scramble to the studio made my heart pump faster and my fingers go cold.

I closed my eyes and took deep breaths, focusing on the sound of the ocean—a calming technique Veta taught me. I would *not* psych myself out. Not again.

We'd practiced every song on the set list at least a hundred times this week, and I'd been nailing each one. Even without Sean taking my mind elsewhere. We hadn't said more than five words to each other since the night I went to Nile's. Yes, I'd actually counted. *Hey. What's up? Not much.* But there was no shortage of lingering stares and awkward silences.

After we finished loading the van, Veta and Felix whisked me off to the bathroom to get ready. I'd agreed to a compromise again, but one that suited me better. This ended up being my ripped jeans paired with a black velvet corset top Veta brought over. I actually kind of liked it. The laces down the front narrowed me in the right places, and it made my boobs look kind of, well, okay.

"I was afraid you'd look like you walked out of a bad '80s movie," Veta said, combing out my hair. "But I may have to steal this look."

Our other agreement was that I'd wear my hair down instead of up. No biggie. As long as it wasn't in those ridiculous ringlets again.

"Seriously," Felix said, eyeing me up and down. "You actually have kind of a nice body, Jasmine."

"Felix!" Veta shot a rubber band at him.

He covered his mouth, laughing. "What I meant was, you're always hiding under, like, clothes."

"That's the idea," I said. "Not all of us enjoy walking around in little towels all day."

He pouted. "I don't."

"Yes, you do," Veta and I said in unison.

His eyes widened at both of us. "Not all day!"

Veta fluffed my hair and inspected her work. "There ya go, *mamacita*."

"Thanks."

"Now shoo." She waved me out. "I need to fix Felix's makeup."

"What's wrong with it?" he whined.

I walked out, chuckling. Bryn and Sean were shooting pool—well, Sean was. Bryn watched with his arms folded. Both had their stage garb on—Bryn in a tight-fitting shirt that showed off his physique and Sean with his fedora and button-down shirt.

"You finally done?" Bryn asked me.

"She needs to fix Felix's makeup."

Bryn rolled his eyes. "Oh, good God."

Sean made a shot but didn't pocket it. He glanced up at me, scanning my top. I folded my arms over it out of habit.

"Hey," he said, standing up.

"Hi."

He stood the cue up and motioned toward me. "You look . . . um . . ."

"Wipe the drool off your chin, will ya?" Bryn bent over to make his shot.

"You look really nice," Sean continued.

"*You look really nice,*" Bryn imitated in a high voice. "What are you—her grandmother?"

Sean shook his head, a smile twitching at his lips. "Why don't you focus on *not* scratching this time, man?"

I smiled and headed for my balcony, my last chance at solitude before the show started.

Fifteen more minutes, they told us. Every part of my body quivered. We'd just finished setting up, and we were standing in the backstage area, twiddling our thumbs. At least, Veta and I were. Bryn was talking to some girls on the floor, Felix had disappeared with Samantha, and Sean was outside, probably chatting it up with Amy. She'd been hanging around out back since load-in time.

We were playing at this club called Pacific Edge. It was the biggest venue in Santa Cruz—three times the size of the Roach—and the show sold out an hour ago. It took deep concentration to keep my dinner down.

Veta put her hand on my back. "Breathe. Don't forget to breathe."

"Shh, people can hear you."

Zia watched us from the corner, sipping from a water bottle. She had this analytical glint in her eyes, like she was an anthropologist studying our primitive behavior.

I nudged Veta. "I meant to ask—what happened with you and Zia at the party last week?"

"Nothing worth mentioning," she mumbled. "I introduced myself, and she was, like, oh—hi. And then Ajay started talking to me and she disappeared."

"Lame."

"Whatever. I'm over it." She checked her compact mirror, smoothing her lipstick. "You think this color is too dark?"

I shook my head, biting back a smile. "Yeah, you're over it, all right."

She stuck her tongue out at me. "I'm going to change colors. I'll be back."

"We don't have"—she flew out the back door—"much time," I muttered to myself.

I glanced over at Zia, who was still watching me. Great. Now what? I rubbed my hands together, searching for something to busy myself with. But everything was in order. The venue required a sound check from us beforehand, and we were the first band going on, so there wasn't a need to scramble this time.

"Hey, Jasmine," a deep voice said behind me.

I turned to face Nile—something I'd been dreading all night. Veta and I had come up with a list of things I could do if he approached me, but I just stood there with my mouth half-open, like I was waiting to catch a fly.

"How's it going?" he asked.

I folded my arms. "It's going." My mind scrambled to remember the list. It was on a piece of lined yellow paper and written in Veta's supergirlie handwriting—circular letters and loopy *y*'s.

He scratched his pointy nose. "Listen, I hope there are no hard feelings about last weekend. I just wasn't feeling it, you know?"

"Not feeling what?"

His gray eyes combed my face. "Your guitar work."

"I played for, like, a minute."

"Yeah, well . . . To be honest, I'm kind of leery that you haven't finished any songs of your own. And I expected a little more enthusiasm."

A laugh escaped my lips. It had to. This was so absurd. "Are you kidding?"

He squinted at me. "Jasmine, you didn't show up until after nine. And then you walked out an hour later."

"And nothing says enthusiasm like spending the night. Got it."

He shrugged. "Whatever. I thought I'd let you know." With that, he stuck a cigarette between his lips and headed out the back door.

I glared after him, wondering if Nile was the exception or the rule. Sean would probably say the rule—a depressing thought.

Bryn appeared from the stage area, his eyes darting between Zia and me. "Where is everyone?"

"Not here," I said.

He scowled but lowered his voice. "Can you be more specific?"

"Veta is fixing her lipstick. And the guys are outside, I think."

He rolled his eyes and leaned toward my ear. "Do me a favor and stay put."

I nodded—where else would I go? It wasn't like I knew anyone else here, and not going outside lessened my chances of having to deal with Amy. Or, worse yet, seeing her and Sean together. The thought *still* made me boil a little inside.

After Bryn disappeared outside to round up the troops, Zia approached me. Well, not really approached. More like, suddenly appeared.

"Hi," I said, jumping a little.

Her ruby-red lips stretched upward, and her almost-alien blue eyes bored into mine. The bleached hair pulled into a high ponytail only added to her otherworldly look. "Can I give you some unsolicited advice?" Her voice was high—almost childlike. Not at all what she sounded like onstage.

"Sure . . . okay."

Her small hands gripped both my shoulders. I sucked in my breath.

"This business will devour you like an afternoon snack," she said. "If you're not ready for the fight of your life . . . run." She touched my cheek, making me tense. "Run like hell."

Whatever I said back was unintelligible. Probably "yeah" or "thanks" or "okay." This girl couldn't possibly know anything about me—except that I'd been duped by Nile. And that was probably what she was referring to. But I'd been in the fight of my life since I walked out my dad's door.

Sean and Bryn returned just then. "Where's Felix? He was right behind us," Bryn said, his eyes doing that nervous, buggy thing.

"Still kissing Samantha?" Sean guessed.

Zia backed away and headed for the exit, her black, Victorian-style skirt trailing after her. A cool wind blew in as she left, giving me goose bumps. She reminded me of the Oracle—or something not quite human.

"Am I the only one who cares that we're going on in five minutes?" Bryn asked, running his fingers through his dreads and pacing.

Sean gave me a small smile, but his fedora hid his eyes. "Hey."

"Hi." How long were we going to do this?

"I'll be back. Again," Bryn growled. He pointed at both of us. "Don't even think about going anywhere."

"Were you just talking to Zia?" Sean asked.

"Yep," I said.

He didn't push for more—which was smart. I wasn't going to share.

"How are you holding up?" he asked in a soft voice. "Okay?"

I may have had plenty of idiotic moments since moving here, but I wasn't going to break. I knew that much. "Pretty good, actually."

He shifted his weight, nodding. "I only asked because you've got the whole deer-in-headlights thing going on again."

"I'm about to perform for a thousand people, Sean." I laughed. "But at least my shoes fit this time."

"Good—glad to hear it." He took his fedora off and swept his hair back. "*I'm* scared shitless."

"Please. You're the king of calm."

He looked up at me, a playful glint in his eyes. "I'm also unbeatable at poker."

"Yeah?" I let a smile escape. "You've never met my dad."

Bryn burst through the door with Felix *and* Veta in tow. Impressive. But he didn't look terribly happy.

"It shouldn't be like this every fucking time, Veta," he said. "Do I look like your mother?"

She stood next to me and grinned. "No, but you act like her sometimes."

Sean and Felix snorted a laugh.

Bryn threw his hands in the air. "Someone has to take the initiative."

"I know." Veta batted her eyelashes. "And you're good at it. That's why you're the best person for the job."

"Yeah?" Bryn walked toward her, his eyes dark. "Well, I'm sick of it."

"Relax. We're all here—with two minutes to spare," Veta said. "As always."

"Yeah, thanks to me." He turned toward the stage, folding his arms. "As usual."

I had to admit—I felt for Bryn. It couldn't be easy, always being the responsible one and then taking crap for it. "I appreciate you, Bryn," I said. "Even if we butt heads."

He gave me a nod over his shoulder. "Thanks."

Veta laced her fingers through mine. "You ready?"

I took a deep breath and let it out slowly. "As ready as I'll ever be."

"Just close your eyes and know I got your back," she whispered. "We all do—even Bryn."

I shut my eyes, tightening my grip on her hand. Her fingers were warm and callused, like mine. My mind tried to picture everyone out on that floor. I could see Amy and Dave, their cruel smiles and whispers. My heart pounded with anger this time—not fear. I'd already given them too much power.

There was a whole crowd out there, waiting to hear our story—whether they knew it or not. Most of them were probably grabbing drinks at the bar or chatting loudly, hoping we didn't suck. Because at least then their wait for Luna's Temptation would be bearable. But opening bands didn't earn respect by being just bearable. We needed to be unforgettable—perhaps even give Luna's Temptation a run for their money.

Sure, I had pretty high expectations for someone who'd graced the stage only once before—and blown it. But I had nowhere to go but up. Why not aim as high as possible? And if I screwed up this time, at least I could say I went down fighting—not standing there like a deer in headlights, as Sean would say. I owed the band that much. I owed myself that much.

"We're on," Veta squealed.

A hand touched my shoulder. I knew it was Sean. "Good luck," he whispered.

"You too." I opened my eyes and put one foot in front of the other.

The stage seemed to go on for miles in the dim red light. I could see silhouettes and hear a chorus of voices below. Some people were crammed up front, but most were walking around or huddled near the bar. They weren't going to make this easy.

We were opening with "Encryption" again, and Felix didn't waste any time starting up his underwater drum loop. His rumbling bass synth bounced off the walls and vibrated the floor, but most of the crowd kept their backs to us. I tapped my foot, my fingers preparing for the verse arpeggio.

"What's up?" Veta called out. She got a couple of hoots in response, but not much else. "We're C-Side—some of you may have heard of us." A few more people hollered. "This first—"

"Just shut up and play already!" a guy shouted. Laughter followed and someone else did a wolf whistle.

Veta's shoulders tensed. I expected one of her smart-ass comments, but nothing came. I wanted to hug her.

"This first song is called 'Encryption,'" she said finally, standing taller.

Bryn added in his hard-edged beat; it seemed to have even more punch tonight. And Sean mirrored Felix's synth bass, his upper body moving in rhythm. I closed my eyes, hoping for the best. My arpeggio flowed out of my monitor, taking me back to the balcony— where the ocean was my only audience.

"Lost in pictures." Veta's smooth voice glided over the waves, like snippets of sunlight. "Writhing with conviction. You walk among the phantoms you breed. Your lips catch my breath, but your talk is cheap."

It was as if I were hearing Veta's lyrics for the first time. My entire body reacted, sending chills down my bare shoulders and arms.

I joined in with the four power chords of the chorus—heavily distorted, even strums. My head tilted back and my right foot stomped in time. Red, blue, and green lights flickered around us, following our sound, our movements. But they still made me dizzy.

Veta lurched at the mic, her long legs in a wide stance. "You rise above it all. Press my back against the wall . . ."

My lips moved along with hers as I whispered every word, my mind giving each one personal meaning. I may not have written the song, but I could add my story to it. Everyone out there could. That was what made music so powerful.

During the solo, my fingers flew up and down the fret board. Every note was breathing through me, luring me to venture past my limits. Veta followed my rhythm, dancing around me in a circle. She leaned into me as our melodies entangled and repelled each other at the same time.

The vocal break wasn't supposed to be this long, but the guys kept up well. Bryn lightened the beat, and Sean changed up his bass line, reducing it to a couple of notes.

I dared a glance into the swelling crowd. People were dancing and moshing. Others closed their eyes and reached for the sky. Every inch of my body tingled.

I probably could've played like this for days. But I finished up with a high vibrato C and threw myself back into the chorus, my hair flying around my face.

Veta returned to her mic. "You rise above it all. Press my back against the wall. You spew promises you can't keep. But I can't hear a thing. No, no, I can't hear a thing." She jumped up and down with her guitar. "But your sweet . . . your sweet . . . encryption!"

Bryn ended the song with a crash, and a wave of claps and appreciative yells followed. Veta shot me a glance over her shoulder and gave me the thumbs-up. I wiped the sweat off my neck and forehead, trying to catch my breath. One thing was for sure—if I wanted to perform like this all the time, workouts were in order.

The floor was now at least twice as packed as it was before. We'd definitely gotten their attention. Now we just had to keep it.

Felix cued up the start of "Acceleration," a high-pitched synth (or *mosquito tone*—according to Bryn). Felix was adorable tonight with his blue pigtails, skinny green tie, and white shirt. One hand danced in the air while the other slid across the keyboard.

Sean hammered the bass—tight, quick notes crammed into 130 bpm. He looked incredibly sexy, with one boot on his monitor and his eyes shut in concentration. But I had to stop seeing him like that. As good as touching him felt, I missed his friendship most. In some ways, he understood me better than anyone I'd ever known.

I stomped on what I called my "crusty distortion" effect and followed him with two power chords. The growl of my amp and the heat of the lights made me feel like I was on a desert road somewhere, just like the song. I imagined Sean's car—because it was a cool car. He was going fast, letting the wind rip through his hair. No smoky air or crowds. Just me and him, watching the sunset ahead, not even needing to talk.

Veta chugged hard on her blue guitar, her hips roving from side to side. "Tight curves, raw moves. Rough you up, bend the rules. I never play nice, 'cause I made up the game."

I pressed my EBow to the D string and let two high notes sing behind her vocals. A spotlight shone on the crowd. Arms and fists jabbed the air and mouths were open wide as if they were singing along. I got up the nerve to scan the various faces up front. It didn't take me long to find Amy's big hair, Teddy's long face, and Dave's eye glitter. Teddy was grinning, but Amy and Dave looked like their parents had dragged them to Neil Young Unplugged. Amy folded her arms, her eyes glued to Sean. Would it kill her to show him some support?

I closed my eyes again and pushed myself harder, finishing "Acceleration" with an impromptu lick that spiced up the song even more. The crowd reaction wasn't as loud as it was for

"Encryption," but it would suffice. At least they weren't booing or calling me Blondie.

"How's everyone doing tonight?" Veta called out. A couple of people hollered a response while others whistled.

"What's your phone number?" a guy yelled.

Veta grinned. "I'll never tell." She nodded behind her. "But our drummer is terminally single and listed."

This got a bunch of girls screaming. For Bryn's sake, and all of us who lived in his house, I hoped she was joking.

"I want your CD!" a girl called out. The thought that we were actually gaining fans, right this very minute, blew my mind.

"You can download our EP at C-Side.com now," Veta said. "But our new album, *Encrypted Lullabies*, will be available from our online store August second. Remember that date, people!"

We dove into "Puppet Girl" next. It slowed the audience some, but their eyes looked wide and interested. And by the end, some of them were singing along.

Each song we did put me deeper into my zone. My fingers were slick, making me miss a note here and there, but it didn't matter. I didn't want to hide from these people—I wanted to be heard, for once, in all my raw glory.

We'd decided to save "Back-Seat Love Affair" for last again. And considering I was all about risk tonight, this song would probably take me over the edge. But the thing about the edge was, it wasn't so scary anymore. I knew what would happen when I hit the ground. What I needed to figure out was how to jump off and stay afloat.

The intro beat—a thick kick drum—started, and for a second I wondered what would happen if I dropped my pick or screwed up this lick again. I could freeze, yes. But I could also start playing with my fingers. Or turn the screwup into a new idea.

I dove into my intro guitar part, my pick gliding between the strings in an odd rhythm. The melody echoed out to the crowd, promising something bigger. Something more. That's when Veta and I cranked our distortion and joined Bryn in an explosion of sound, driving everyone into a fury.

Felix's synth notes rang out like little alarms, firing up the crowd even more. Then we killed the guitars, leaving Sean and Felix to fill out the verse. Bryn played a simple beat, allowing Veta's vocals to shine.

Veta grabbed the mic and worked the stage, extending her arms toward the crowd. "Come into my little world. Where twilight reigns and kisses taste like novocaine." She returned to her mic stand, arching her back. "And all your plans go to waste." She let the last word ring out before charging into the chorus. "Back-seat love affair. With that leather stare. Hardened ecstasy. You'll never come down."

I joined her up front, letting her brutal vocals take over my movements. My foot stomped and my body rocked back and forth. I jumped up and hit the ground just as we moved into the speedy chords of the next section.

Sean moved in front of me and smiled—as if challenging me to a duel. I took him on, palm muting the frenetic notes of the bridge. He stayed in sync, tilting his chin up and closing his eyes. And then he did something unexpected. His fingers moved up the neck of his fret board and our roles reversed. He played an ascending bass solo that circled around my repetitive notes, taunting me.

I cut bait on shadowing Veta and moved down my fret board, playing in harmony with Sean. Veta grinned and backed away from the mic. Felix compensated by adding in a low, billowing synth. Bryn switched to a quieter but more incessant beat—as if he knew just where we wanted to go.

Sean played faster and I slowed down, letting each note blend together into a river of noise. As the sound faded, my fingers sped up and Sean scaled back, following and defying me at the same time.

A random blur of images swam through my head: my dad's doubtful stare when I told him my plans, Jason's cherubic grin, the horse wallpaper still plastered to the walls of my old room. I'd fought Dad for an hour to get it when I was seven—he wanted some generic kind with yellow flowers. And then I saw the last few weeks—everyone I'd met, good and bad. How they all inspired me in one way or another. Everything from terror to ecstasy spilled out of my fingertips and bled into the strings. I took the tight turns as they came and didn't flinch.

It all ended with the scream of feedback and me on my knees—I didn't even know how I got there. I cut the volume and stood, my chest heaving and my hands shaking. The roar of the audience followed—whistles, squeals, shouts, and the dizzying effect of hundreds of hands clapping at once. I was covered in sweat and half my makeup was running down my face, but I didn't give a damn. I couldn't even describe how I felt, other than to say nothing—*nothing*—could have prepared me for this moment.

Sean wrapped his arms around my waist. He tucked a lock of hair behind my ear, and I closed my eyes as his breath caressed my neck. "You blew me away," he said.

I knew something was up when Bryn corralled us into the studio during his after-party. He deflected at least five girls on the way there.

"Hurry up and spill," Veta said after we all piled in. "Zia was actually talking—*to me*. Mostly about how much Jasmine rocked." She bumped her shoulder into mine, grinning. "But I'll take it."

"Shut up and I will!" Bryn said.

"Fine—jeez. I—"

"Veta," Bryn growled through his teeth.

"Shhhh," Felix joined in.

Sean and I exchanged a smirk.

Bryn clapped his hands together like an excited child. "So, I just got done talking to Ajay."

Veta's eyes widened. "And?"

My heart started to thud—it had to be good news, right?

"We got the gig," Bryn announced, his lips stretching into a huge grin. "We're fucking going on tour!"

Felix jumped up and down, covering his mouth. "Will we get our own bus?"

Bryn rolled his eyes. "No, Felix."

Veta threw her arms around me and squealed into my ear. Good thing I was mostly deaf from the show. "Ah, easy," I said, patting her back. Not that I wasn't completely stoked about the tour. I was. As long as I could avoid Nile as much as possible. Plus, tonight still hadn't hit me yet. I was walking around in a daze, the kind with tinnitus.

"Okay, so—Jasmine," Bryn said. "We need to record your guitar parts right away—like, this week."

"No problem," I said, pulling away from Veta.

"And we've got a shitload of things to do—so much that I can't even think of it all." Bryn rubbed his temples. "But for now, let's just party."

Veta gave him a salute. "Yes, sir."

We headed out, weaving our way through people standing in the backyard. Some of them said hello and gave us approving nods. I didn't really want to go inside, though. A few of the locals were starting to warm up to me, but most still seemed wary. Like I had to prove myself a little longer before they would give me more than a polite smile.

I broke away from the others and headed across the street, toward the ocean. The moonlit sea churned and hissed, drawing me to that benchlike rock. I settled in and listened to the calls of sea lions and the grinding industrial beat filtering from the house. It was oddly comforting.

I'd just closed my eyes when I heard footsteps climbing the rocks behind me. Sean. I sighed, pretending to be annoyed. But part of me hoped he'd end up out here. A tiny, tiny part.

"You're on my rock again," he said.

"Yep—wanted some alone time."

"That's too bad." He plopped something heavy on the rock next to me. "I brought your acoustic out, hoping I could cash in on your promise."

I glanced over my shoulder. Sean had his hands shoved into the pockets of his black cords. He was eyeing the ground, as if he expected me to tell him to get lost.

I moved over and patted the space next to me. "Sit."

He slid in a little too close. I had the urge to lean into him and move away at the same time.

"So, hey," he said.

I rolled my eyes, a smile stretching across my face. "Hi."

We sat in silence for a few moments. The stars were out in droves tonight, casting a halo around Sean's profile. Even the barbell through his eyebrow was lit up like a Christmas light.

"What?" he asked.

"I've missed you." There. I said it.

"I've missed you too." He looked down at his hands again. "I finished that sketch . . ."

"Yeah? Can't wait to see it."

"You will—after I paint it."

My eyebrows rose. "You paint too?"

He grinned. "Yeah, a little."

I shook my head. "What can't Sean Ramirez do?"

"A lot of things."

"Like?"

A smile twitched at his lips. "Oh, I don't know—spellbind an entire audience with a solo and make it look effortless."

"Oh, please. Don't fish for compliments. You know you're good."

He nudged me. "Not like you."

Heat crawled up my neck, and I laced my fingers together. Taking compliments still wasn't my forte. "So, how's Amy?" And neither was changing the subject, apparently.

He exhaled a laugh. "Um . . ."

"Sorry—it just kind of came out."

"It's okay." He touched my knee. "She's good, I guess. We haven't talked much since I told her there wasn't a chance in hell we were getting back together."

"Oh, when did you—"

"Last weekend—the night you went to Nile's."

"Ah." My mind struggled for something to say. "Sorry it didn't work out."

"I'm not." He looked out toward the water. "I called Teddy yesterday. Let him have it. He told me he's had a thing for Amy since high school."

"Wow."

"Yeah," he said softly.

"I don't know the guy, but from what I've seen, he really does seem to feel bad."

"That's what he says. But it's kind of hard to trust someone after that."

I nodded. "I know."

He looked over at me. "Have you talked to your dad?"

"He called a couple of days ago. Same old stuff." I deepened my voice. *"Have you changed your mind yet? It's not too late."*

Sean chuckled.

"But he's agreed to let me get my bed and other stuff—if I can find a way to get it down here."

"No problem. We'll take the van." He bumped his shoulder into mine. "Maybe check out some bands at Whiskey Hill while we're there."

"Har, har."

His fingers ran through a lock of my hair. "Couldn't resist."

"You never can." I sucked on my lower lip. "I wish we could go back. Not that I regret what we did. It was . . ." I let a smile slip. "Kinda nice."

"Kinda?" He wrinkled his nose. "Ouch."

"You know what I mean."

"Yeah, I do."

I wrapped my arms around my knees. "What you said—about me not letting myself feel anything . . ."

"I'm sorry about that."

"You were right, though—to a point. But that night with you—I felt every second of it."

"I did too," he said.

"I'm tired of being this girl. I want something real."

He touched my cheek. "You deserve something real."

I faced him, swallowing the lump in my throat. "But you can't give that to me right now. You know that."

His thumb traced my cheekbone. "I want to."

"You need time."

He dropped his hand. "I wish I didn't."

A large wave smashed against the rocks, sending spray across my cheeks. I closed my eyes. "It'll happen—if it's meant to."

"I hope so."

I batted my eyelashes at him. "Just be ready to treat me like a princess."

His lips curled up. "No problem. It's not like that would be a far stretch of the imagination."

I shoved him, shaking my head. "Jerk."

His eyes lingered on mine for a few seconds before he spoke again. "In the meantime, you owe me."

"Owe you?"

He popped the latches of my guitar case and handed me my acoustic. "A song."

I set the guitar on my lap, brushing my fingers across the strings. "I can, but I'm warning you that I'm not—"

"Jasmine?" He smirked. "Don't make me shut you up."

"Just remember, you asked for it." I smiled and began to play a song about a girl who risked everything to find her way home, off-key vocals and all.